Ambrose Conway

RESOLUTION
An Eighties Grown-up?

KINGS HART BOOKS

First published in 2011 by
Kings Hart Books
An imprint of Publishers UK Ltd
6 Langdale Court, Market Square,
Witney, Oxfordshire, OX28 6FG
www.kingshart.co.uk

Copyright © David Hughes 2011

The author has asserted his right to be identified as the author of this work.

All the characters in this book are fictitious, and any resemblance
to actual persons, living or dead, is purely coincidental.

Cover design: Kelly Twiggs of
www.commercialcampaigns.co.uk/

ISBN: 978-1906154-16-5

A CIP catalogue record for this book is available
from the British Library.

This book is dedicated to:

The Conway and Hughes families of Rhyl, Colin Shearing and Liz Plant of
Kings Hart Books for keeping the faith, Emily, Goodricke College and York
University and the friends made there, Davy Major, Ann Lawrence, Marco
Roginski, Andrew Pickering, Alison Broomfield, Theresa Archibald, Colin
Chadfield, Elaine Readman, Adam Myers, Rose Gardiner, Barrie Sherwin,
friends I grew up with in Rhyl, Brian Jones, John Courtman, Gail Metcalfe,
Carol Edwards, Keith Jones, David Close, Susie Turpin, Sue Gibby, Maz
Parkes, Gill Weale, Linda Evans, Paula Jones, Sian Jones, the staff and pupils
of Rhyl schools, Ysgol Emmanuel and Rhyl High School,
Blessed Edward Jones RC High School, Tir Morfa School, Christ Church CP,
Bryn Hedydd CP, Ysgol Llewelyn CP, Ysgol Mair CP, Swavesey Village
College, Hartford High School and Ald. Derbyshire School, Bulwell,
Nottingham and Reso residents past, present and future.

About the Author

Ambrose Conway is the pen name of David Hughes. He is a former secondary school teacher and educational consultant who has a particular passion for developing positive reading habits among teenage boys who are so often lost to fiction. He has taught in rural, suburban and inner-city schools and has successfully tested out many of the ideas for *The Reso* on his unsuspecting students.

He was fortunate to grow up in the old Welsh storytelling tradition and recalls the ancient tales of *The Mabinogi* read in school as well as the stories of hardship, poverty and joy recounted by his parents. Access to educational opportunity has been a decisive influence in his life and the inspiration for his books.

He is a regular contributor to the educational press with articles on e-learning, raising achievement, metacognition and inclusive learning among his credits. He has spoken at regional, national and international conferences on similar themes. In 2009 Ambrose was made a Fellow of the Royal Society for the Arts (FRSA) following a period on secondment to the RSA Academy in Tipton in the West Midlands. He is also a contributing author to Literature Wales (formerly the Welsh Academy).

Married, with two grown up children, the contrast between his children's upbringing and his own prompted the writing of *The Reso* trilogy as he found himself constantly comparing the quality of his own experiences of childhood with that of his own sons.

He divides his time between schools, military and industrial archaeology, infrequent flying, keeping on top of the garden, reminiscing about the past and worrying about the future.

For interactive resources on *The Reso* trilogy –
The Reso, Beyond the Reso and *Resolution* please visit:
www.the-reso.co.uk
(please note this site is not controlled or owned by Publishers UK Ltd and as such no responsibility is accepted for the website content)

That's just the way it is,
Some things will never change…
But don't you believe them.

Bruce Hornsby and the Range
1985

RESOLUTION

CONTENTS

Chapter One
FRESHER

So this was it, University life. I'd made it. Apparently I was now a Fresher. Fresher was not a term with which I had previously been familiar. It had a distinctly American feel to it. It seemed to be plastered all over the Goodricke notice boards now though. Exhortations to attend a formidable range of events and social gatherings arranged to meet and greet the new First Years, 'the Freshers'. It had been placed over the 'official notice boards' with their dark blue letterheads with *University of York* embossed on them in that classily distinctive flowing font. Eric the porter would no doubt be having an official conversation with the member of the Junior Common Room who had made so bold with his, or her, fly-posting.

At that moment a thin, reed-like boy in flared black jeans, worn baseball boots, red polo neck jumper and plain black glasses burst past me carrying Fresher Ball posters, a pair of scissors and a box of drawing pins. I resisted the temptation to shout after him, "Don't you know not to run when you are carrying scissors!" in the manner of my primary school teachers.

The Fresher Ball posters were also in the correct place on the 'Ents' noticeboard, obscuring the Captain Beefheart poster donated by some musically progressive student and next to the elaborate floral poster for that Friday's upcoming concert at Central Hall, the spaceship like edifice which rose out of the lake opposite Goodricke College.

The concert featured Steeleye Span, the folk/electric combo who had recently been in the charts with *Gaudete*, a song that had the style of a Gregorian chant. It seemed a long way from the only chart band that had deigned to make a stopover in Rhyl in recent years, The Sweet. I'd deliberately avoided going to see The Sweet, as, along with bands like the Rubettes, Mud and the Bay City Rollers, they encompassed all I hated in popular music and could be linked directly to the nadir of bad taste in music, Middle of the Road's 1971 minor hit, *Chirpy, Chirpy, Cheep, Cheep*.

I must have had toothache at the time because I can't recall its pointless tune and lyrics without a feeling of deep and hollow neuralgia. It was the summer of standing in the High Street at the front of a shop selling rock in the shape of false teeth, and cheap plastic crap imported in horrendous bulk from Hong Kong for tourists to amuse their friends and family with on their return home.

What did these presents say about their purchasers and the people who would receive them as valued friends and family?

"I've been on holiday to the Welsh seaside, was wandering aimlessly along the High Street when I came across a massive set of false teeth fashioned out of reconstituted coloured sugar and thought immediately of you. Without contemplating the irony of the tooth decay eating such a confection would promote, I bought them for you anyway, such is the esteem in which I hold our friendship."

And every day *Chirpy, Chirpy, Cheep, Cheep!* would be played incessantly through the odious patter of Tony Blackburn on "wonderful" Radio One. It was the one time that I didn't mind him jabbering through the introduction and end of the record; that, truly, was how much I despised Middle of the Road. Five weeks it spent at Number One, five long, miserable weeks. Again and again it was played until, on the Thursday of the fourth week of the holidays, I waited until being paid my week's wages (having learned from previous experience to take the pay before walking away) and threw down the blue nylon jacket with the Barney's insignia on the breast and buggered off home without a word of explanation.

"You walk away from my shop and you won't work in this town again!" shouted Barney after me. I couldn't think of a time when I was less perturbed.

It was a blessed relief to be away from that tune and that job. I enjoyed a leisurely rest of the holiday and was ecstatic when Marc Bolan replaced the record at number one with *Get It On!*

Pity, I thought, not for the first time, not to have been a decade older, when The Beatles, and a whole string of the Merseybeat bands had included Rhyl in the places they could play and get back to Liverpool in their battered Austin and Morris vans in time for work in the morning.

Yes I thought, I'd follow the instruction to beat a path to the University shop and purchase a ticket for Steeleye Span. Fleetingly, I wondered if I could afford the £1.50 for the ticket and then remembered the thought of the night before, which by an incredible feat of synchronicity, Pol Pot was having at about the same time, 'Today was day one of a completely new start.'

So how was my new life going to pan out…

The Fresher reception was to be held in a room numbered G101. In wandering around the gloom of the campus to get my bearings, I'd worked out this code. It was hardly rocket science, but I'd grown up in schools where the room was always associated with a particular teacher. This was a first floor room in Goodricke College and I made my way up the stairs opposite the porter's lodge to find it. One thing I had not got used to yet was the peculiar sprung floors in the college. Being of CLASP design, all the superstructure of the building hung of an internal steel structure and this meant that the floors all had a distinctive spring to them, exacerbated by the thick lino used to cushion the effect. This meant that negotiating your way along any corridor in the college felt like walking across a trampoline and the staircases vibrated as excessively as you ascended them. This was very much an acquired taste.

There was no mistaking G101 judging by the buzz of earnest conversation and the shining faces of the reception committee drawn up outside to meet and greet. I didn't feel particularly confident in such situations but fell back for a few seconds on something I'd read in the summer to strengthen my resolve.

I finally knew I was coming to university at York when a thick envelope arrived about a week after the A level results came out. In it was the confirmation letter, a sheet about Goodricke, the college to which I'd been assigned, and a chunky reading list running to several pages from the Faculty of Social Sciences.

I perused the reading list with studious intent, then read the total of books included on it. I would have to read at a rate of more than a book a day to complete the reading list before starting at college. Not wishing to fall at the first hurdle, I'd resolved to keep to this frantic reading schedule. The resolve lasted less than an hour.

I decided to trim the list to what seemed the more interesting books, but on that basis I'd probably not touch any of the Statistics and Economics tomes, so I deliberately ringed one from each of those sections. By far the most interesting books appeared to be in the Sociology section and one in particular caught my eye, Erving Goffman's *The Presentation of Self in Everyday Life*. It seemed an enticing title, and appearing next to *The Naked Ape* by Desmond Morris, who I knew from his zoology programmes on the television. Desmond's was the only tome on the list that I had read, so I thought I'd give Goffman a go.

The next day I was at Rhyl Library, beneath the clock tower of the Town Hall. As luck would have it, it was undergoing another episode of underpinning caused by the general concern that the clock tower was leaning and would eventually topple forwards, demolishing either the Midland Bank, the police station or the little pub between them. As was becoming habitual, I had to negotiate a hastily erected structure of dusty scaffolding to enter this repository of free learning in Rhyl.

I was becoming something of a celebrity reader at the library. The librarians heartily approved of my reading in support of my A level English studies in the previous year when I'd gobbled up Vladimir Nabukov, Anton Chekov and Alexandr Solzhenitsyn. In fact, having hoovered up most of Nabokov, the head librarian suggested to me that I might like to sample the delights of *Lolita* and reached underneath the counter for a pristine copy. That saved me having to request it like a teenager asking for contraceptives in the chemists. I think they considered that I was a cut above the usual requests for westerns and romances by Barbara Cartland and could appreciate *Lolita* at a cerebral level, which I'm ashamed to say, I didn't.

I handed my reading list over. The Head Librarian caressed the embossed University of York letterhead with reverence, in much the way that I had, before consulting the pages of recommended reading. She was now a long way from the day her reading list for university had arrived, but realised that this represented a significant rite of passage.

Her eyebrows knitted in frustration as she realised that she would be unable to supply most of the list, even after having consulted her micro-fiche machine to pull on the additional resources in the newly created Clwyd archive. She was personally mortified not to be able to service the list but she booked Erving Goffman's tome for me as she was familiar with it and thought reading it would repay the investment. I went to pay the charge for ordering a book from the central catalogue, but she brushed my hand aside magnanimously; any child of Rhyl requiring such books for university would most certainly not be charged on her watch.

Indeed it did repay the investment. Good old Goffman's 1959 tome *The Presentation of Self in Everyday Life* was to have a lasting impact on me. In it he suggested that in our daily life and conversations we were not actually ourselves, but played characters in a series of dramas or social interactions. That explained how we could be so different with our friends than with our teachers or parents. In each case there was a play going on, and we had to keep in appropriate character, use the right language and gestures. Socially awkward situations were caused when someone did not stick within the script for the setting or did not know the conventions.

Having this information, and knowing that everyone was operating within a script was tremendously liberating for me. It meant that I could rationalise myself out of being shy, particularly in social situations. It was with this knowledge that I entered G101 and accepted the offered red wine and vol-au-vent.

The room was half full of tight knots of people, clinging like *Titanic* shipwreck survivors to the member of the JCR allocated to "break the ice". They all seemed to be talking or listening too intently. In each knot, or liferaft, the universal starter question was "Which A levels did you do?" For the present, it was the only common ground, but in this room could be people who would become lifelong friends. Or maybe not.

There was a bewildering array of names to remember. I habitually remembered the importance of listening and capturing the name of the person I was talking to, seconds after they had told me and I had not taken it in. There were a couple of awkward situations when someone new joined our circle and people took turns to introduce the group, which by now was swelling to fives and sixes as more freshers abandoned their lonely rooms to sample the deep, freezing water of the inaugural social gathering.

I excused myself, feigning a full bladder the first time I was in the awkward position of introducing everyone in the group, and realised that I could not pull this trick twice (I could see Erving tut-tutting at my social *faux-pas*).

I was now desperately trying to remember everyone's name, but a couple more had joined the group in my absence. Gareth Edward's statement about it being incredibly difficult for the human mind to hold onto a random list which is more than seven items long was beginning to torment me. This was one of a multitude of profound, profane and miscellaneous information Gareth had shared with me at the back of our English A level class. We'd pooled our understanding of the afterlife and the existence of God; Gareth was rational and sceptical, whereas I was more open-minded, as well as the lyrics for Billy Connolly's *Wellyboot* song and the stars of the Russian ice hockey squad for the Munich Olympics. From the back of the room we had contemplated heinous sexual deviancy with the girls in our English group. Had Susie, Linda and Sue known our mental ramblings, we would have been in deep, deep trouble. At a guess, I'd have ventured that our metaphysical fantasies, inspired by our reading of John Donne, would have been deeply unwelcome...but you never knew with those three. I developed a great faith in Gareth's observations, taking them as gospel and, as the group now expanded to eleven I was in a state of panic, knowing that when the next person joined, it was my turn to do the introductions.

This second time around I pulled a masterstroke. Remembering no more than three names of the nine in my group I deliberately introduced the boys with girl's names and vice versa. I got to my last remembered name and introduced a lad who turned out to be Tom, an earnest Scottish lad with a beard and glasses, as Sarah. I stopped and thought for a second and declared, "No hang on, that can't be right, Sarah didn't have a Scottish accent. Come to think of it I'm not sure she had a beard either – not sure about that last point though!"

Luckily everyone burst out laughing and Sarah, a petite girl with exceedingly dark hair and a floral dress, who was standing next to me, elbowed me in the ribs in mock outrage. Pushing my luck a little, I added, "Steady on Arthur, no need to get violent!" which brought a second bout of laughter. At which point I announced that I was off to join another group as it was getting too aggressive in this one and disengaged in what I thought was an act of some aplomb.

They'd all laughed, but were they really amused, or was it just social awkwardness? According to Goffman, it didn't matter, I'd laid a laughter card and they had all responded to it appropriately.

I returned to the table where the drinks and vol-au-vents had been laid out. It looked considerably less neat than when I had come in. I helped myself to a second wine and drew breath. The vol-au-vents had been reduced to shards of pastry, for which I was relieved. I'd always considered them a little suspect.

My mum had mastered the art of the vol-au-vent using the special Be-Ro pastry mix and she wisely stayed within the prescribed limits in terms of fillings. You had either mushroom and onion or sausage meat and onion at my mum's New Year's Eve family gatherings. However, I'd once attended a family christening for which there were outside caterers and had mopped up a vol-au-vent with gusto only to find on first bite that it was a disgusting mush of what was described as 'smoked salmon mousse'!

"I'm surprised you ate that David!" said my mum enthusiastically seeing me gagging on smoked fish, with too many onlookers to spit it out, and too far to walk with a full mouth to reach the toilets without someone trying to engage me in conversation.

"I didn't think you liked smoked salmon."

And she laughed her usual laugh until her eyes filled up with tears and she couldn't speak any more.

"Sorry about the vol au vents," said a southern voice next to me, "didn't arrive until late this afternoon and haven't eaten – did a bit of a hoover job really. I'm Adam."

I turned to face Adam and found a long-haired, burst jeans, unkempt sort of guy who had either had a bad day or had gone to some lengths to cultivate this unkempt look. He proffered a puff pastry stained hand, like a man with some leprous condition, wiping his mouth with the other hand.

"If you tell me which A levels you did, I'm going to punch you," he declared and I found myself warming to him.

"I think I've managed to gather all the misfits together in the group over there, come and join in. Not sure if you are eccentric enough to be honest, tell them you are Albanian or something."

He set off back to the group giggling in the corner and seemingly taking the piss out of everyone else. I felt compelled to follow.

"This is Zoltan from Tirane in Albania."

The greeting was warm and I fell into feigning what I hoped was an approximation of a Slav accent (technically were Albanians a Slavic people? I wasn't sure but I reckoned, neither was anyone else.)

"I Zoltannnn errrr, verrrrry pleased meet you, verrrrry pleased come to York to make study."

I pronounced York "Yolk" to heighten the effect. Adam winked at me in admiration of my effort.

"So Zoltan, tell us which A levels you did in Albania?" asked a long-haired lad in an Army greatcoat and a thick Northern Irish accent. I wasn't sure what was thicker, the greatcoat or the accent, but he was laughing infectiously now and I knew he was on to me.

"Hay leevels? I know not hay leevels?" I stumbled.

"Wise up!" came the reply, "you've been rumbled."

Everyone was now laughing, the lad with the curly black hair who looked really intense but had a laugh like a machine gun; the girl with the long *Dr Who* type scarf, multicoloured leggings and bright red shoes, the Irish lad and Adam.

"Fair play! Adam didn't do me any favours – an Albanian called Zoltan from Tirane, I ask you!" and I was able to join the laughter.

The evening improved greatly from this point. I was in the company of an Italian Pole from Leicestershire called Marco, Davy, a Belfast boy with a seemingly encyclopaedic knowledge of popular music, a female, football playing winger called Rose from Rossendale and a hungry home counties sartorially challenged wit called Adam. Unlikely as it seemed, I felt I'd found a lifeboat.

Chapter Two
VICTUALS

One of the hardest things to get used to when first arriving at university is the new regime for eating. Nothing defines a family more clearly than what and how they eat. The strange thing is that, because we only know our family intimately, we assume everyone's eating pattern is the same as us.

My diet and eating patterns at home had been the only conservative thing about our family: dinner was between 12 and 1, tea between 5 and 6, except on Sundays when dinner could be comfortably pushed back as late as 1.30 p.m. This could be stretched at Christmas when lunch might be served up to, but no later than, 2 p.m. That would allow for the eating and a quick tidy before the Queen's Speech.

Amongst my new found friends at university none of this held true. Some referred to the midday meal as luncheon, whilst High Tea was the only tea time they recognised. They acknowledged both dinner and supper, the latter being a crafty bite, later in the evening which was a new one on me. Unfortunately when I was privileged to be asked off campus to the flat of some second years for supper, I made the mistake of thinking they meant a round of late evening toast and scavenged a bag of chips on the way over, to be confronted, greasy lipped, by a full boeuf bourguignon.

Clearly, at university, none of my meal times held true. For the first few days I contented myself with food from Goodricke canteen which was plentiful and reasonably priced and included salad all year round. Eating at the canteen meant conforming to canteen hours which were 12.15 until 2 at lunch time and 5.30 until 7 for an evening meal. Usually, this was fine, but occasionally it conflicted with social or sporting arrangements.

Luckily, beyond the canteen there was always the fall back of the Gorilla Grill which consisted of the sandwich bar converted for the purveyance of cheese toasties. It was amazing what some sliced white bread, left over from the day, a catering pack of cheddar cheese, some industrial scale toasters and a few energetic volunteer student caterers could achieve. Few of us who were housed in Goodricke had any fear of later life brittle bones syndrome, or any other protein deficient malady, given the sheer volume of cheese toasties we consumed at the unbeatable price of 10 new pennies.

The Gorilla Grill was the social hub of Goodricke evenings. If you were at a loose end there would always be mates there to have a chat and a bite with.

I would have been quite happy to confine my dining arrangements to the canteen and the Gorilla Grill for they adequately covered all my culinary and nutritional needs. Other counsels prevailed however. Along each corridor of the L-shaped Goodricke C Block was a basic kitchen. And in each kitchen was a melodic plastic water heater which sang as it boiled, cupboards, a small oven with two electric hobs and a circular white formica table with five plastic chairs.

Most people were content to simply make tea and coffee in the kitchen and loaf around chatting and whiling away the wee hours. I think it was Adam who suggested that we should form a dining club with each of us taking it in turns to cook a meal for the five lads in the syndicate. It seemed a reasonable idea on the surface and, foolishly I went along with it.

So it was that on a late Friday afternoon in October, with our lectures and tutorials over, the Goodricke Epicurians braved the Arctic winds and made our way over Badger Hill to Hillards supermarket just off the Hull Road. Five of us had made the journey. I was unsure of the motives of each person.

For my part, I wanted to make sure that Adam, for it was he who was leading the charge with an infectious enthusiasm, khaki army greatcoat flapping in the wind hair flowing, did not stray onto the wider shores of exotic cuisine. I'd made sure that my nut allergy had been entered into the buying equation and, I hoped, that whilst each of us were capable of taking a joke too far, Adam would desist from cooking any form of nuts for fear of sending me into anaphylactic shock, although you never knew with Adam. He had never seen a case of anaphylactic shock before and he might feel that it would be a useful adjunct to his biology studies to witness one first hand.

When I say anaphylactic shock, I might be over-egging it slightly. I simply hated nuts, the smell, the taste, the texture and there was no brief way to explain this total antipathy adequately, so anaphylactic shock became my shorthand expression, leaving no-one in any doubt that nuts were a taboo eating subject.

"Hazel nuts. Can you eat hazel nuts?" asked Adam unhelpfully.

Hoping to silence him, I replied with brusque finality, "Adam, I can't eat any nuts at all. Of any variety."

"Macadamia?" he ventured, warming to a theme with which to torment me, and proceeded to ask me individually about any and every variety of nut that I might be able to stomach.

"Adam," I stated with authority and irritation, "the thing about all the nut varieties you have mentioned, and no doubt wish to continue to mention until you can think of no more nut varieties is that they all sit within a very large Venn diagram. The title of that Venn diagram would be Varieties of Nuts. I cannot eat any of the varieties of nut that sit within that Venn diagram. It is therefore redundant to ask me about any other nut varieties as they are covered inclusively by the aforementioned Venn diagram, Varieties of Nut!"

There was a moment of awkward silence.

I was quite pleased to have embroidered mention of a Venn diagram into my riposte. It was the first, and probably the last time, that the Statistics course I was bound to attend as part of the Social Sciences degree was to be of use to me.

"Pine nuts – can you eat pine nuts?" continued Adam, undeterred.

"No," I said through clenched teeth with an air of resignation, "I cannot eat pine nuts."

Marco laughed his distinctive woodpecker laugh and the others joined in the inquisition.

I had to hand it to Adam and my new found amigos, they certainly knew their nuts.

Having harvested the common or garden varieties, cashews, pistachios, monkey, almonds, chestnuts, pecans, pistachios again and walnuts, Adam set off on a tour of the wilder shores of nut varieties. Roasted sunflower seeds in or out of oil, the Mujejji nut, found only on the western shores of Lake Victoria which fertilises by being passed through the digestive system of an elephant. We called his bluff on that one but he insisted he was right and bade us look it up in the University's JB Morrell Library.

"That's the big building on the top of Badger Hill, Davy, looks like a book warehouse, but if you ask the nice ladies in there they let you read the books for free."

That was a rather sly aside at Davy who had made a virtue of avoiding the library in this, his first month of university.

I did look it up the following week and, although he got the name wrong, there was such a nut fertilised in the improbable way he had outlined!

As we stepped out of the biting wind and into the warm muzak of Hillards he delivered "Indian Betel nut?"

We split up to shop, each with certain ingredients in mind. I had been designated to source some nice bread to accompany the meal. As Adam had only given us one ingredient each to source, we still did not know what his final dish comprised.

We each foraged the shelves for our allotted ingredients. As we passed a gap in the aisles I heard Adam call out, "Hickory nut?" and he was gone again into the tinned fruit and dessert aisle.

Anyone hearing Adam with his long hair, Army greatcoat and glasses askew shouting "Hickory nut!" to no-one in particular, might have reasonably surmised that he was mentally deranged. The glorious thing was that Adam didn't care.

Having selected a brown unsliced malted loaf my team shopping was complete. The mention of malted and loaf had, like Pavlov's dog got me thinking about what was to become a staple of my university diet and I quickly sought a pack of Soreen malt loaf out. I'd met up with Davy now and he was busily nibbling loose mushrooms from the vegetable display.

"I don't think you are meant to be sampling the mushrooms," I said helpfully and loud enough that the under manager peering down the aisle at Davy might be allayed from the idea that this was some sort of cunning shoplifting ploy whereby produce was transported out of the shop internally.

"Sure you can – this is what we all do in Belfast – try before you buy!"

In a statement lifted incongruously from Dorothy's adventures, I was tempted to reply "But you are not in Belfast now!"

Luckily, the under manager was distracted by a blur in khaki passing the top of the aisle pointing heroically and shouting "Meat!"

We found Marco with Andy eying the tomatoes, or rather the tomato purees. Tomato puree was new to me and I initially thought this was a new way to dispense tomato sauce like toothpaste. I made the mistake of venturing this thought, and Marco, being half Italian, bristled with indignation, and went on to explain how significant was the tomato base of meals. I picked up the cheapest tube and he snatched it from my hand indignantly. Marco had always struck me as being easy going up to this point, but clearly food was something on which he felt passionate. The sharp intake of breath as he replaced the tube and substituted it for one which seemed inordinately expensive took me by surprise.

With flashing eyes and an intensity that burned, he declared, "Never, ever, compromise on the tomatoes."

I decided, there and then, to adopt this as my creed whenever I was in a tight situation.

We gathered at the checkouts trying to find the one with the shortest queue whilst we waited for Adam to arrive with his purchases. The plan was to divide the bill by 5 and all chip in our portion. I had to remember to pay for the malt loaf separately as it was my intention to keep this in my room and hack at it with the steak knife my mum had thoughtfully secreted in my suitcase whenever I was hungry or nostalgic for home. I'd discovered the steak knife whilst decanting my underpants into the wardrobe. My mum had wrapped it a paper kitchen towel but it had fallen from my boxer shorts and I, not knowing what it was had grabbed it before it hit the floor, cutting myself in the process. I could imagine the dialogue in the A and E department. "Yes nurse, I did cut myself putting my underpants away." No doubt the disbelief would be tangible and I could hear my mum's laugh in the background.

Adam finally arrived brandishing his purchases and declaring, like Chamberlain, "I have spoken with Herr Holdroyd, the little man at the delicatessen, and I hold in my hand a purchase that promises meat in our time!"

"What meat is it?" we asked.

"Ham," replied Adam, enthusiastically.

All seemed happy.

"What kind of ham?" asked Andy, slightly perplexed at the limp plastic bag containing the ham.

"Boiled ham," replied Adam as the till assistant announced the total for our purchases.

"Six pounds forty eight pence please."

I quickly tallied up the food items, and even given Marco's expensive tomato puree toothpaste purchase, I calculated that Adam had spent over four pounds on the boiled ham. He had spent on one item my entire weekly budget for food. I was about to query this, but the mood in the late Friday afternoon shoppers queuing behind us was turning ugly.

"Students!" muttered one out loud, accurately capturing the disdain of the impatient mob.

We quickly worked out the five way split of the bill. Unfortunately, as none of us was majoring in maths, we reached different amounts and compromised on Marco's figure, he being a scientist. I tore one pound twenty from my wallet and passed it to Adam, a couple of my fellows struggled with those little pursey things and busily counted out their contribution in ten, five, two and one penny pieces. The till assistant looked away in embarrassment, she clearly did not want to be held responsible for the delay in the queue, and placed responsibility for it squarely on our shoulders.

"So Adam," asked Andy as the purchases were bundled in the plastic bag and we moved away from an irate queue of shoppers behind us, "just how much boiled ham did you buy?"

"A pound," he replied matter of factly.

"A pound!" we all guffawed.

I don't know what the other's point of reference was, but for me, I knew that even when we were having all the family round for the first salad of the summer on Easter Monday, we never required more than a quarter of a pound of boiled ham. You could furnish a full funeral wake with no more than half a pound of boiled ham! It could be that, given the profligate use of our funds, this pound of ham might well service Adam's funeral wake. So we say goodbye to our dearly departed brother Adam, who was taken from us so suddenly, whilst taking liberties with a limited student food budget.

The meal turned out to be peas, mushroom and tomato sauce strewn with copious layers of boiled ham and served with a tasty malted nut loaf.

"I thought you said couldn't eat nuts?" said Adam in a desperate attempt to spark up conversation in the brooding kitchen.

"I've made an exception," I replied, "as I'm already in fiscal shock over the cost of a pound of boiled ham!"

I think I adequately caught the mood of the room.

"Difficult to eat boiled ham through gritted teeth..." added Davy who had seen this week's second hand record purchase sacrificed to the ham.

We never cooked together again.

But we did cook, mainly to impress girls. Each of us developed a signature dish which demonstrated our culinary virtuosity.

Andy went for nutty chicken, despite the anaphylactic shock risk. He worked systematically from a written recipe his mum had secreted in his suitcase as he left home for the first time.

I went for Gammon and Pineapple on the basis that it was simple, yet passingly exotic, a foundation of sizzling ham with hoops of sweet pineapple which had winged its way direct from the Hawaiian Islands – what more could a girl ask for. It's the small details which matter in the art of culinary seduction. To secure the affections of my diner this ensemble was served with an accompaniment of fresh white and brown rolls drizzled with Lurpak, (no point ruining the boat for a ha'porth of slightly salted butter) followed by a malt loaf hillock served with a two litre bottle of Lutomer Riesling (only the best, and in sufficient volume, for any girlfriend of mine – no cheap Don Cortez for me!). It really did feel like I'd arrived and could hold my own with any culinary rival with this menu.

Luckily, one way or another, I was seldom challenged to have to come up with a second dish.

In the lovely Karen's case, meal one came to a grinding halt when she arrived late. The grill was already sizzling with the finest cuts of gammon seasoned with peppercorns that I'd borrowed from Sandra when Karen announced that she was a vegetarian. I quickly rallied from this set back, and commiserated with her vegetarian tendencies as if they were an illness. I was happy to accommodate her culinary quirkiness and she enjoyed an exquisite first dish of 'pineapple totale' which consisted of a dish of pineapple in a jus of pineapple juice. Vegetarian heaven I thought to myself. I was slightly miffed not to have the pineapple juice available to serve as an aperitif but one has to make sacrifices to please the lady of the moment.

I'd not met a vegetarian before and hadn't factored such wilfully, pernickety eating habits into my schedule.

As we downed the last of the Riesling, I heard Karen's stomach rumbling and couldn't help the uncharitable thought that if she was going to be so picky in her eating habits, that was the price she would just have to pay. There had been a bit of a tricky moment when we had had a slight altercation about whether malt loaf constituted a dessert, but I had fended this off by playing my Celtic card and saying that it was the closest thing I could find in York to the Welsh delicacy of Bara Brith. She was unconvinced by this explanation so I became misty eyed and spoke with passion about the Land of My Fathers and Eisteddfodau and she quickly came round.

I could hardly believe my transformation into a culinary giant in such a short space of time. I was hoping that my mastery of the first date dining experience would filter, like good coffee, across the campus and that the most beautiful of girls would be leaving messages in my pigeon hole begging to be included in my dining rota. Unfortunately this did not happen, which I put down to the fact that the girls who had experienced my cooking wished to keep it a secret all to themselves. This they clearly did to good effect, as I didn't receive a single offer of affection in return for my gammon and pineapple.

If my mates from Rhyl could see me now, washing up done, the heady smell of singed bacon hanging romantically in the air, snuggled on a sofa with a hot date, half a litre of Riesling and a few After Eight mints left, they would not have recognised me!

Davy, still harbouring resentment over the lost vinyl purchases, went increasingly vegetarian with concoctions involving soup and mushrooms, well a tin of mushroom soup with additional mushrooms added really.

Marco was able to concoct any range of pasta and tomato based dishes. He once made the mistake of throwing a strand of spaghetti against the wall to test that it was cooked, only to view Adam throwing the whole pan against the wall to ensure that they were all cooked consistently.

As for Adam, he went the way the mood took him, as a biology student, he was certainly experimental in his approach to cooking, being guided as much by colour as taste in the construction of his meals. Many often had a second chance to explore the hues and textures of his meals, at their convenience, later in the evening.

Few girls hung around for a second dining date, which was probably as well really as we had exhausted our repertoires in a single meal, unless of course they liked beans, or cheese on toast… and we could buy that for them for ten pence a round at the Gorilla Grill. Who said there was no such thing as a cheap date?

Late nights at the Gorilla Grill were usually preceded by long evenings in Goodricke bar where the drinks were inordinately cheap and the view across the lake to the spaceship of Central Hall was unsurpassed. Many nights were passed in the bar, under the broken resolve of only coming in for a swift half. Unfortunately the siren song of Maria Muldaur's *Midnight at the Oasis* held us there in thrall until closing time. She was a smashing looking and sounding girl Maria, if the picture on the jukebox, adjacent to record J2 was to be believed. I often wondered if she'd have been seduced by a menu offering of Gammon and Pineapple and Malt Loaf. She definitely looked the type.

Despite the cheap beer, we were still on a budget. We found an exceptional way to enhance the effect of a pint of shandy which we would always put into action on a Friday afternoon.

Most terms, our hectic timetable of lectures, seminars and tutorials was blank on Wednesday afternoon for sport, and Friday afternoon because most of the lecturers were keen to relax into the weekend, a sentiment with which most of us students had no objection to. We always signed up for the five-a-side football league on a Friday and this became a highlight of the week. If it was free, we'd then book a session in the sauna for cleansing and recreational purposes.

Carefully timed, we could be in the Goodricke bar for last orders and, being thirstier from football and sauna induced dehydration, we tended to go for shandy rather than straight beer. The effect of the carbonated lemonade and beer on dehydrated cells was remarkable and immediate. You were pleasantly drunk before you'd finished the pint and Fridays tended to blur somewhat. I have isolated and random memories of being piled three high in the back of a mini van delivering a dishevelled, incoherent, but suited Davy to York station for a first journey to the home of his girlfriend's parents; of locking Andy in the sauna and turning the temperature gauge up to maximum by way of an experiment about human endurance which went well beyond the ethical practices of the British Medical Association, and wading through the lake looking for Excalibur.

Whatever transpired on those Friday afternoons, an early evening toasted cheese sandwich with Branston pickle at the Gorilla Grill was the universal antidote and set me up for the thrills of the weekend.

Chapter Three
HOMEWARD

As with all my friends who could get home and back from university over the weekend, I took my opportunity to head for home in the third or fourth week of the first term of university. In common with all the lads, my rucksack was full of dirty washing.

As returning warriors might have carried home their wounded and broken bodies, so we, weary from the experience of reading lists and late night coffee, dragged our depleted frames home with kit bags of dirty washing and Railcards showing us fresh faced and unblemished.

The rigmarole of returning home was always the same. If the timetable permitted, an early number 5 bus took us from Badger Hill straight to the imposing entrance to York Station. I had time for a quick saunter up and down the platforms with a steaming polystyrene cup of BR tea, a perusal of the passing Deltic locomotives on the Newcastle or Anglo-Scottish expresses and the wonderful aromatic smell of fresh chocolate as a diesel shunter scurried half a dozen freight wagons through the busy station from the Rowntree factory to the marshalling yard at Dringhouses to feed the sweet teeth of the nation.

The station announcement would herald the imminent arrival of the Liverpool train and a dirty, corporate blue, Sulzer engined locomotive of class 45 or class 46 would splutter past with its rake of blue and grey Mark 1 and 2 coaches, coming to an asthmatic stop. Having originated at Newcastle, there would be a heady mix of Scouse and Geordie accents on the train, especially if there was a football match scheduled for the Saturday.

The compartment carriages that had symbolised the mystique of rail travel when I had been a young train spotter had been largely replaced on all but 'extra' or holiday 'special' trains with open coaches, where privacy was sacrificed for economy. Gone too was the plush moquette upholstery in faded and dusty maroons and greys which enveloped your bottom cheeks and cushioned against even the most rough track conditions. Amply padded armrests could be pulled down from the seat back to generously define your personal area and provide a level of luxury usually confined to a London Gentleman's club.

Gone were the BR lamps which provided extra light for reading at the flick of the metal switch. Gone too was the substantial control which opened the heating valve and brought the steam, generated by the diesel engine, hissing and snaking around pipes located at the floor against the window wall and through radiators under the seat, creating an upholstered tropical oasis. Unless of course the heating system was unavailable, in which case the window was misted with condensation and your complaints about the cold shared with fellow passengers hung in the air long after you had expressed them.

Of all the things that had gone with the old compartment carriages, the most nostalgic for me was the tantalising clunk of the glass and wood door as you closed it behind you, defining, for the length of the journey, this space as your own. The effect was further enhanced by pulling down the leatherette blinds on the corridor side to deter potential travel companions. A combination of dispersed luggage and a mock consumptive cough could deter all but the most determined passengers on all but the most crowded trains.

In the lower sixth form, on a school trip to the Royal Institution lectures, I'd once spent three hours cocooned in a compartment carriage with the divine Victoria and two other couples from school. Racing back through the night in a darkened compartment, cuddling and kissing, the heady delights of Willesden, Watford Junction, Bletchley, Rugby, Nuneaton and Stafford were just a blur thrown behind us. I'd not wanted that journey to end. Ever. But it did and we were evicted from our compartment by arrival at our home town. I never more wanted to live in Holyhead or Penzance or Kyle of Lochalsh or Fishguard, anywhere further from London, to eke out those precious hours.

I'd hoped Victoria had felt the same. I had a sneaking suspicion that she might not though. We had had the prospect of four hours left free and unsupervised in London before we were due to attend the lecture. The capital was our oyster. We could sample the heady delights of Soho, Covent Garden or Camden Market, Carnaby Street, Oxford Street or Harrods. Our friends, bold on the train, but less so when the sheer size of the Euston concourse enveloped them, had stuck together, planning on safety in numbers. Having visited London before, I was not intimidated by the station or the complications of the tube map.

I'd conspiratorially whisked her away and refused to tell her our destination. The tube journey raised and dashed her expectations. Joining the Northern Line at Euston we had headed south into the metropolis, through anonymous Goodge Street to Tottenham Court Road, where all our friends alighted to begin the drag down Oxford Street. I'd squeezed her hand saying

"Not yet!" and raised tantalising expectations. She'd obviously been impressed by my knowledge of the capital from the vast experience of my two previous visits.

The tube train lurched forward to Leicester Square and I could see the excitement in her eyes, she looked to me for her cue to leap up and out into the autumn air of cosmopolitan Leicester Square, but I sat impassively. Charing Cross and the Embankment came and went without disturbing me and I could see her following the line of the stations above the seats for any hint of our destination, which was now south of the river.

I suppose, on reflection, the seeds of the end might have been sown on that day.

I thought I'd prepared a feast of delights for her, something she'd never forget. I was right on the latter point, less so on the former.

We eventually emerged onto a broad, tree-lined boulevard. The weak sun dappled through the horse chestnut trees and all the buildings seemed light grey as our eyes adjusted to the slanting sunlight.

"Not far now!" I reassured her squeezing her delicate hand. She squeezed back with a palpable lack of certainty or enthusiasm.

We turned a corner and with a large and theatrical intake of breath I proclaimed that we had reached our destination. The building in front of us was ornate, Victorian and massive, it stood in its own grounds and the adjacent parkland stretched into the distance, if not quite as far as the eye could see, at least as far as the multi-storey town houses in the middle distance allowed. Unfortunately for Victoria, the building in question was the Imperial War Museum.

The next three hours were spent with the poor girl ear-beaten by me explaining the significance of the Dreadnought on naval rivalry. I expounded on the advent of the aircraft carrier rendering the Battleship dead as a projector of sea power, illustrated rather nattily by both scale models, which could be illuminated by buttons, of the Battle of Taranto, and references to an actual Fairey Swordfish suspended from the ceiling. She didn't relish the telling fact that the Japanese used Taranto as the model for their attack on Pearl Harbour a year later.

The development of the tank and its tactical use in both World Wars, included detailed synopses of the merits of the Panzer 3 and Panzer 4, didn't light her fire either and the least said about the genesis of the aeroplane as a fighting weapon from canvas-covered biplane to aluminium jet, stopping at all variants of the Rolls Royce Merlin aero engine and its genesis into the Gryphon, the better.

Boring is a word we usually apply to others. Engaging and knowledgeable might be the epithet we apply to ourselves. In this circumstance I should have had no hesitation in applying it to myself. I don't know what came over me having such an imperturbable idea that for a teenage girl on a once in blue moon unsupervised visit to London, the Imperial War Museum would be her destination of choice.

As I prattled on, all our friends would be collecting their Harrods bags with nothing more substantial than a packet of mints in them, shimmying down undreamt of shops in Oxford Street or sampling the delights of the seedier sides of Soho and doing all the other things that hormone fuelled provincial teenagers do when visiting the capital. But that was a lifetime ago, well two years ago to be precise.

With an ominous jolt the train lurched forward from York's premier platform, escaping heating steam emanating from the underside of the carriages promising a chill journey. I sank in my seat and stared listlessly out of the window as we passed under Holgate Bridge and accelerated past Dringhouses Yard with dirty blue diesel shunters impatiently shuffling the Rowntree and Terry's chocolate filled vans and wagons for onward dispatch. Black coated men leaned on shunting poles and waited to join the gathered assemblages with metal links, much as their father's and grandfather's generations had done.

We rumbled over the high speed junction, where the London line departed to the left, and headed out into open country until the syncopated rhythms of the junction points of Church Fenton sounded under out feet. I caught myself thinking what I always thought when taking a train journey… "I wish I could be travelling twenty years earlier" when steam was king and I'd be passing a bewildering display of exotic Eastern Region engines, Streaks and A3s, Robinson's and Dub Dees, none so humble as not to enthral me.

Overgrown spurs with cow parsley and willow saplings would be restored to their prime and abandoned cuttings and earthworks would echo once again to rumbling mineral wagons and panting engines. But it's not to be, and we are on the outskirts of Leeds now, passing the lines of Chieftain tanks at the Royal Ordnance Factory, before I can blink.

Leeds Station was to become a regular stop off point in the coming years as we headed to the University or the Poly to see the bands that had bypassed York for the larger city venues. The rebuilt station, with its concrete and glass, oozed modernity and even had a resident graffiti artist who would use a marker pen to make observations on the billboards including adding to the bill of the Leeds City Variety Hall a speciality act called Physio The Rapist which caught my attention and kept me amused for a spell in the early hours of a freezing cold Sunday morning, having missed the last train home following a Thin Lizzy concert. Few places are as cold as a railway station in the early hours of a winter's morning, especially one made of glass and concrete, particularly if it is Leeds City.

A sizeable portion of my grant went on Thin Lizzy in Leeds in my university years. For Davy this was always a pilgrimage and he converted us to the cause without much trouble. We took to arriving early at the venue – so early at times that we gate crashed the sound checks and had our own personal performance of Lizzy's finest.

So much were Thin Lizzy associated with the train to Leeds that when I was heading for home on the train *The Boys Are Back in Town!* was always playing in my head in anticipation of the mayhem and revelry that would greet my return to my home town.

It only slowly dawned on me after several returns home that there was no-one eagerly anticipating my return, no party of revellers waiting in expectation on Platform 2 of the station, no Dine and Grill where we would meet up to fight and carouse, nothing and no-one at all really. The boy might well be "back in town" but, in truth, no-one gave a monkey's.

All my friends had either been scattered in the educational diaspora of the A levels or were still in the town and had carved out their social arrangements very nicely thank you, and did not require a "college boy" turning up at the last moment to put a crimp on them. Not having had a telephone at home had meant that I did not even have an address book of friends to fall back on.

So I travelled in great expectation, across the Pennines, through gloomy tunnels and past abandoned track, warehouses, and mills surrounded by cobbles. 'For Sale' boards touted unwanted and unloved properties in a ribbon of dereliction along the railway line where once there had been furious industry. Through Dewsbury, Huddersfield and Stalybridge and lesser communities like Mirfield and Morley and the amusingly titled Diggle until Manchester Victoria was reached.

A range of old and crooked platforms faced east from Manchester Victoria, but only one of them was completely dedicated to heading westwards, platform 11. Platform 11 was famous in the inner railway circle of the anorak as it was, at the time, the longest railway platform in the UK, indeed in the world. Furthermore, until it closed in the1960s, the platform spanned uninterrupted, two railway stations, Victoria and Exchange. But Exchange was merely a Victorian shell of a building now which was, in a poignant sign of the times, slowly metamorphosing from a station to a car park with the platforms being joined by infilling of the tracks to accommodate more and more shoppers and commuters.

We'd descend the bank from the abandoned cattle dock at Miles Platting where live animals, just over a decade before, would arrive by train from Ireland and Wales to enjoy brief acquaintance with Manchester before making their debut as Mancunian Sunday lunch.

A screeching application of brakes would announce our arrival at platform 11. I'd open the carriage window to turn the brass handle of the door to hear the heavily accented announcer explain, with obvious disdain, that this was "the 1.41 departure for Liverpool Lime Street". The accent was so thick you could slice it like salami and each slice would have "Mancunian 'til I die" cast through it. On a previous visit to Liverpool Lime Street I'd heard an announcement equally dismissive of Manchester. The announcer could hardly bring themselves to admit there was a station somewhere between Warrington and Stalybridge.

Shutting the window to preserve what heat had been generated in the carriage, I sauntered across the pitted and rain-sheened flagstones to the buffet. The buffet always seemed to be full of chain smokers, like some hospital waiting room before 'visiting' had begun. The middle aged lady behind the counter with the chesty cough certainly had nicotine stained fingers and matching ginger highlights in her hair and I settled for a cup of tea and a pack of three Jaffa Cakes which, I calculated, had not been standing in this atmosphere for too long.

Despite being 'cooked food' hungry, the sausage rolls and pasties, even the chips, had no appeal in this fuggy room and I hastily beat a retreat onto the cold and damp platform.

Platform 11 at Manchester Victoria was always cold or damp, or both, no matter what the season. I sat, somewhat forlornly on the wind tunnel that was the platform and watched the rain slant down across the tracks and the far platforms with their promised destinations of Bacup, Oldham and Rochdale. Station officials shuffled around with the collars of their coats pulled up and gathered in gaggles for a quick chat before dispersing into the myriad doors and nooks and crannies.

The only thing that habitually captured my attention at Victoria Station was the tiled map extolling the full extent of the erstwhile Lancashire and Yorkshire Railway. Faded and cracked, it adorned a wall just outside the buffet and bore testimony to better days. It mirrored the one at York station which explored long forgotten lines spilling eastwards from the City and into the North Yorkshire Moors.

A series of corporate blue Diesel Multiple Units headed eastwards in a spluttering of ominous blue-tinged exhaust smoke which signalled neglect and need of overhaul. The seconds on the clock receded slowly to the estimated arrival of my rattling connection to North Wales.

I was in luck today, either doused by the rain, or from the wind blowing in a different direction, I was not assaulted by the fumes of the Victorian brewery opposite. The powerful malodorous, sickly, mildewy-decomposition smell caught in the throat and, for me, will always be associated with Manchester Victoria. Beyond the brewery, obscured by decorative red and engineering brick blue buildings that spoke of Manchester's former prosperity, stood Strangeways Prison a notorious point of incarceration. The area around Victoria did not seem to have much holiday potential, unless your vacation desire was to inhabit a gritty northern landscape, and indeed the *Coronation Street* set itself was not very far away as the carrion crow flies.

Eventually, my connection arrived, rattling and trembling like a Parkinson's sufferer and impatient to be away from the platform. The DMU was crowded and I considered myself lucky to find a seat next to a window amongst the grey, winter coat and glove wearing fellow travellers.

We swung right after the station and proceeded through Eccles and Patricroft where once almost a dozen parallel running and shunting lines had been reduced to two. We were away now across Chat Moss and the scrubland on which the original Liverpool to Manchester railway had been built. The rumour was that the railway had been built over a layer of sheep skins to prevent the moss consuming the rails. Certainly as I tried to get some sleep by resting my head on the vibrating window there was a strange bucking motion as if we were at sea and most definitely moving across water.

My gathering slumbers were curtailed by the squeal of the protesting wheels as they negotiated the sharp left turn at Earlestown. We accelerated south onto the West Coast Main Line to Warrington Bank Quay, which sat squat and forlornly between a towering chemical works and the empty marshalling yards. Nobody ever seemed to get on or off at Warrington. Perhaps passengers were intimidated by the chemical backdrop or the electric passenger engines that approached silently and unnoticed before sucking the air off the platforms and distributing litter from platform to track and vice versa in their haste to reach Glasgow or London. Warrington was a momentary provincial distraction for them, as it was for me.

After a cursory stop we were away again, crossing the Manchester Ship Canal and branching left to head on a path parallel to the River Mersey. It was always incongruous watching an ocean going ship negotiate the Cheshire countryside with its cargo from the far and exotic Orient, a resting crewman from who knows where, leaning on the ship's rail near an opened bulkhead door. The swing bridge we glimpsed momentarily from the train was troubled less and less by freighters now as the standard container ship began to dominate world shipping and the good burghers of Manchester and Salford would need to find alternative uses for their increasingly derelict docks.

In the gloom of a late autumn afternoon the ICI works and the oil refineries performed their fiery alchemy, pumping steam and dubious yellowy emissions and flaring hydrocarbons into the atmosphere. Despite the 1973 Arab–Israeli dispute, the three-day week and homework by candlelight, everyone now assumed that the glitch was over and we could go on consuming petrochemicals and calling it progress to our heart's content. The more we consumed, the richer we were and the happier we'd become with our rampant materialism, most assumed in blissful ignorance of the limited nature of the resource on which they had become dependent.

Frodsham and Helsby were passed and I noted our speed compared unfavourably with that of the traffic on the dual carriageway below. In this gloom, the shape of a face appeared in the sandstone cliffs to our left and as quickly melded back into the hillside. Until now it became too difficult to perceive anything but the largest shapes in the monochrome dullness.

Habitually, we would be stopped by an adverse signal in a cutting outside Chester to await the arrival or departure of a London bound train and the resetting of points and signals. This was always a source of frustration sitting a few hundred yards from the platform with no other train in sight. Seconds turned to minutes and these extended inexorably to ten minutes before the semaphore signal was raised in a slow and deliberate manner and our diminutive diesel lurched forward shivering with vibration, impatient to disgorge its loads of passengers at the platform. We'd slalom through the points and past the signal box which controlled the movement of trains at the east end of the station, before drawing to a halt at Chester.

I loved Chester station. I remember visiting once early in the 1960s to see our former neighbour Hefyn, who was incarcerated in the local infirmary with an abscess on the spine. It sounded medievally gruesome, and the sight of Hefyn in great pain, lying motionless on his side and heavily bandaged around his middle had my imagination running riot. Having arrived in the mid-afternoon with my mum and brother, it was a dark early evening before we made our way back to the station. We had an hour to wait for our connection home to Rhyl and whilst my mum and John waited quietly in the station cafeteria, I gathered up my orange squash drink, that had been decanted from the machine with a large stirring arm on the counter, and my three pack of custard creams, and wandered up and down the platforms in search of steam engines.

I was not disappointed. In the bay platforms at the south end of the station a Jinty, 47350 was assembling parcels vans for onward dispatch, complete with shouting porters moving newspaper laden trolleys and shouting jokes and obscenities to each other between gasps of their cigarettes. The first generation DMUs in sombre dark green livery and cream "speed whiskers" shivered in the Manchester bays, waiting forlornly for passengers and clear signals.

The real treat lay in the north end bay. For sitting in the centre road was an unrebuilt Patriot locomotive gently snoozing. Unfortunately there seemed to be no crew on board – they were either in the cafeteria with my mum and brother or in some secluded mess room gathered to swap stories and butties.

The engine was magnificent, simmering in the yellow moonlight of the sodium lamps. Smoke idled from the chimney and steam sweated from the cylinders in total silence. She had an almost Victorian splendour about her angular shape, but I was disappointed to find that on the splasher which should have held her nameplate, no name could be seen. She was one of the anonymous engines, not named after seaside resorts, regiments or notable railwaymen. Beneath the grime, grease and soot she might have been green liveried, but she had assumed the grey pallor of engines towards the end of steam with only rust and the senile dribble of white water residue from her safety valves relieving her careworn livery.

I stood for the best part of half an hour admiring her, as you might an elephant on safari. She quietly consumed coal unperturbed by her onlooker. I bit the top of my custard creams and licked the solidified cream so as to make the biscuits and the moment last longer. I knew, as a seven year old, that such moments were to be savoured and that soon such a slumbering giant would be gone, to be a thing of memory.

I was therefore unsurprised when a jaunty fireman and his elderly and more measured driver emerged from the shadows and made their way over the platform edge and to the locomotive on the middle road. Both wore the tired denim overalls of their trade, with a black jacket and shiny cap with enamelled British Railways badge.

Enthusiastic for the off, the fireman immediately took off his jacket, despite the coolness of the night, and set about feeding the fire with several rounds of coal. In a matter of minutes the cocks and drains which had been idly dribbling water began to hiss and there came a roaring sound from the chimney as the steam pressure rose. A quick blast of the whistle indicated to the signalman in his warm cabin across the platforms that they were ready to move off and, unknown to the uninformed observer a ground signal was pulled off to allow the beast to proceed. With a sharp blast of concentrated steam the engine overcame the initial inertia and fed sufficient steam to her sinews to allow over one hundred tons of metal, coal and water to move off. Several small exhalations of steam allowed the beast to build a smooth and silky momentum away into the darkness at the end of the platforms, leaving only thin wreathes of steam in the space she had occupied. So preoccupied had I been with the grazing Patriot that I almost missed the passage of the maroon behemoth, *City of Coventry*, and her express passenger train moving non-stop through Chester behind me, carrying important people to Holyhead to join the Irish Ferry.

That was more than a decade ago and the nameless Patriot class engine, the rails it had stood on, and *City of Coventry* had long been consigned to the cutter's torch. Yet Chester station remained largely unchanged with even the ancient lower quadrant signals at the south end of the station reminders of more exuberant times.

A late afternoon DMU from Manchester on a Friday afternoon meant being inundated with shoppers and students heading back home across the North Wales coast. The shoppers with their *Owen Owen and Brown's* bags, were full of talk of bargains, and outrageous prices for a cup of coffee and a scone. They wore brightly coloured check or classic hound tooth woollen coats, no doubt bearing fashionable labels which would be unknown to me. The older of the shopping women also wore scarves of rich colours and hats.

The students resembled a slick of denim and cord wrangler jackets and outrageous T shirts with slogans. They clumped together in silence or in animated conversation about the upcoming social joys of the weekend. Only their satchels threatened to spoil the revels, with their incessant demands for attention from homework and assignments with impending deadlines. Such trifles had haunted me through two years of A levels and were no less insistent now in my first year at university.

We were all forced to involuntarily *cwtch* up on the limited seating, and even then the disgruntled were left standing until their stop, or until travellers vacated at the stops at a reopened Shotton, Flint or Prestatyn station.

I was forced up against a steamy, sweating window with vague views of the Dee Estuary flashing by once we had curved westwards out of Chester, pierced the city walls at the same point as the canal and vibrated over the Dee Bridge adjacent to the Roodee horse racing track. It had been here, almost thirty years before, that my dad had habitually found himself working on the Signal and Telegraph cabling whenever there was a race day, thanks to a canny foreman with an eye for the gee gees. This section of cabling must have been the best maintained on British Railways and the S and T gang were frequent enough punters to have their own bookie's runner assigned exclusively to them as they watched from a grandstand view, high above the galloping horses.

The cooling towers at Connah's Quay quickly passed with their condensed water vapour blotting out what remained of a watery sun. At Flint, the market traders were rapidly transferring what remained of their wares into battered light blue Ford Transits, whilst piling the cardboard rubbish, cabbage leaves and burst tomatoes into a neat pile for the attention of the bin men's lorries. Stalls were being quickly dismantled and coloured awnings folded for the next market day. They all seemed oblivious to the passing of our train, for there was no trade or banter to be had with us.

The semaphore signals gave us a clear path past Mostyn, with its overlarge and ornate station building built on the insistence of the local squires, the eponymous Mostyn family. Across the tracks was the fluorescent yellow glow of sulphur, deposited amongst the ballast in the sidings like chunks of fool's gold by carelessly loaded hopper wagons from discharging coastal vessels plying their trade from the Baltic to this insignificant port.

Some miles further along the Dee estuary rows of Merry Go Round coal hopper wagons gathered at Point of Ayr Colliery, awaiting loading and the complicated shunting manoeuvre to send them back eastwards to power stations to play their part in lighting the nation's houses and streets.

My old mate Martin now worked on the technical side at the colliery, having followed his father into the coal mining industry, which, at this stage, was still promising a job for life. I was concerned about Martin's choice of profession for two reasons. Firstly I knew drawing coal from Point of Ayr was particularly hazardous as the seams of black gold stretched out underwater into Liverpool Bay and there was little room for error or complacency if the miners were to work safely and without hazard. Secondly, smashing a guy as Martin was, his technical competence was called into question insofar as he used to pop round to my house to copy my physics homework. Having failed to correctly calculate either the refractive index of glass, the ampage passing though a circuit, the acceleration of a falling body or the volume of a gas, he was quite prepared to jog round to the house of a fellow student once described by our esteemed teacher as "a fool, present only to provide light amusement to those of greater scientific potential when they had successfully concluded their experiments." Martin either saw in my scientific ineptitude some potential that escaped our teacher, or he was truly desperate. I believed the latter.

That someone who had once seen me as a source of expertise on physics was now making scientific calculations on which the lives of men depended was truly appalling.

Phil Lynnott and the band joined us at Prestatyn, and although I could not see them, I could hear *The Boys are Back in Town* insistently pounding in my head. For a few brief minutes I became excited again at the prospect of being home and the tumultuous welcome that awaited me from my friends.

A shuffle through the points just before the Vale Road bridge and I was home. Phil and the boys were obviously heading for a gig in Llandudno, or home on the Irish ferry, as the music stopped the second I alighted the train and shut the carriage door.

A horizontal rain propelled by a north wind hit home once the driver had engaged gear and ground along platform two in the direction of Abergele. Out of force of habit, I usually waited for the train to pass under the H bridge and curve around the bend adjacent the Marine Lake. This also gave time for all the passengers to clear, but today the rain had me heading for the stairs immediately. In the hundreds of times I'd crossed this substantial footbridge, someone, and a decade before it would have been me, would have rattled the heavy metal chain that was stretched between the wooden posts on the overbridge. This would always echo across the bridge with a distinctive sound. Sure enough a small lad with a harassed mum did it today and I smiled to myself in the timeless camaraderie of the child inside.

Harry Hughes was on duty at the ticket collection point today, a job he performed when not acting out a similar role as a doorman at the Labour Club.

"Now then, young man, home from the brain work? And carrying a black baby I see. Will we see you in the Club over the weekend or are you too grand for us now?"

The black baby was a reference to the dirty washing he'd correctly guessed I'd be carrying home for my mum to deal with properly. Harry had picked this expression up from his naval service in the war.

"Are you still willing to let intellectuals into the Club, Harry?" I replied, anxious to give as good as I got and leave my options open.

"Intellectuals!" he laughed, "I knew you before you had long pants, me lad!"

We both laughed and left it at that which would mean that he would be pleased if I turned up at the club, but not surprised if I didn't, which suited me fine.

My dad was waiting in the maroon Ford Escort, with the whip aerial (which was wasted on him but which would have suited me down to the ground), when I strode out against the wind that was blowing directly off the sea and down Queen Street and Bodfor Street into my face. His inclination would have been to arrive early and wait chatting with Harry, his old childhood friend, but he would be nervous of predatory traffic wardens on the station concourse and so stayed with the car for a cigarette and a quick read of the Daily Mirror.

He leapt out on seeing me and unlatched the boot for me to deposit my dirty washing. We said "Hiya" to each other but didn't shake hands or share any other greeting. That was the way we were and it was too late to change habits now. He asked, as he always did, if I'd had a good journey and I had said I had. He then gave me a brief update on what had happened since I'd last been home as he manoeuvred into the traffic and headed past the cabs and buses into Bodfor Street.

Me coming home on the train seemed small beer compared to my dad's departures and arrivals between 1939 and 1946, when my denim jeans would have seemed out of place in a sea of khaki. I didn't quite seem so heroic somehow, telling tales of lectures missed, drinks drunk and football matches played. Phil Lynott and the boys would definitely consider me too tame to hang around with their gang. My head now was empty as were my spirits and I felt hungry and cold.

Having eaten heartily and caught up on the *hanes* with my mum, I decided to replenish my spirits by venturing out to the Bistro that night. The spray from a high tide was creating a fine mist at the entrance to one of the top night spots on the north Wales coast. Some of the early arrivals had managed to grab a table in the downstairs windows, tables of girls looking to get first dibs on any of the fit guys that arrived, tables of lads with similar intent, vis a vis the girls, and a couple of tables of young lovers drinking Mateus Rose with a previously emptied bottle performing the role of a candleholder for what passed as a romantic assignation in my home town. I sauntered in, in as much as you could saunter in wearing a damp fishtail parka with rabbit skin hood surround. I nodded to some of the recognised faces in the melee.

There was a considerable air of excitement in the hostelry this evening and I correctly guessed that the coach that had been laid up outside had a central role in it. I spied my old mate Martin moving in my direction, looking his usual stylish self. He wore high waist beige trousers and an open shirt revealing a medallion. He was also in his dancing shoes which meant only one thing…a Wigan Casino All Nighter.

I'd hoped to have a catch up with him but all I managed was a, "Right, Martin."

"Right, Dave."

He breezed past with a clipboard containing the names of the 53 people and 12 reserves who had booked a ticket on the coach to this week's Northern Soul All-Nighter event at Wigan Casino.

Northern Soul had all but passed me by, but there were serious adherents across the north Wales coast and coaches travelled weekly to attend the casino. Martin's bell bottoms and expensive shirt summed up the standard uniform for lads who would spend the night in ritualistic dancing. This resembled a whirling martial art in format, with drops and kicks punctuating by dodging and weaving, boxer style. My cousin Tim shot past to join the coach with nothing more than a furtive wink followed by a dozen other lads off the estate. It didn't pay to get in the way of lads on their way to the casino. Many now passing me by were wearing denim jackets with badges from previous All Nighters worn on breast and sleeve like campaign honours, which, in truth, they were.

An equal sized group of girls were in tow dressed similarly, mostly with short cropped hair, their platform shoes and boots skidding on the sodden marble floor outside the Bistro in their charge to the back of the bus where the lager and cider were stored.

The Bistro suddenly felt empty and I made my way uninterrupted up the stairs to the top bar.

I was aware of blue flashing lights outside as I turned up the stairs. I didn't think this was part of the usual light display at the venue and this was confirmed as the Maclaren brothers, bottles in hand, passed me by heading downwards with more than a little haste.

"All right lads," I said, as it paid to keep onside with the Maclarens.

"All right," they replied, their attention clearly elsewhere.

They had that wild look in their eyes like cattle in a stampede, and it was apparent that neither of them had their foot on the brakes of their conscience or their common sense. It was clearly a normal Friday night for them.

I looked back down the stairs in time to see the Maclarens leaping headlong down the last of the stairs and into a posse of police officers that had massed at the bottom. Some old hand coppers were ready with truncheons drawn, but a couple of raw recruits had a look of abject horror in their eyes as they were taken unawares by a pair of flying Maclarens.

I continued upstairs, not wanting my evening to be ruined by having to write a witness statement in the local police station.

I settled in the corner of the bar and nursed a pint of lager. I made eye contact with a few people I knew from school but everyone seemed pretty preoccupied. I wasn't sure who I expected to be here to brighten up my night, but whoever it was, they weren't in. Actually I knew precisely who I hoped was there, and she wasn't and had moved on, so I was toying with cutting my losses on this night when I was grabbed by the shoulder.

This was ominous, it could be the law wanting a statement about an incident they believed I'd just witnessed downstairs or the start of a fight that I wasn't looking for. I braced for either an official request or the first blow from an unknown assailant to land.

To my surprise it was neither. A large hunched-shouldered lad with a gap-toothed smile and long lank hair confronted me.

"David, you old bugger, where the hell have you been, haven't seen you since you moved off the estate!"

"Glyn?" I muttered, unsure if this mountain of a lad was the same one that I used to play on the estate with and who taught me to spit with attitude and keep my nerve when playing split the kipper with his fold away pen knife. He smiled again and I knew it was.

"What are you up to now?" I asked, not believing how the years had passed. I think this, at the age of nineteen was the first time I used the term "doesn't time fly?" which becomes the anthem of grown ups.

"Well, I'm sitting over there with my little brother and Dewi looking over here, and I said, is that David from the estate over there at the bar, and John says, it can't be, because he's too mutt ugly and he has the look of a bloody student about him! So I came over to check you out and it is you and you are mutt ugly and if you are a student, I'm going to give your arse a good kicking!"

Glyn was always colourful in his speech but his florid complexion and unsteadiness suggested he was clearly well on his way into a heavy drinking session. He confirmed this, saying that they had been laid off by the hospital building maintenance department where they worked as brickies that very day, and they had started at lunchtime laying into their redundancy payments.

In one of the plush dark red upholstered booths, the table was laden with empty pint and short glasses. A figure I last saw when he was ten, and who I presumed was Glyn's younger brother John, beckoned me over. John, teeth shining in the atmospheric gloom of the plush upholstered booth, was even less coherent than his older brother. His eyes were bleary and red and his voice sounded like a transatlantic telephone call, disconnected and incoherent. Not that I'd ever received a transatlantic telephone call.

"Right!" said Glyn, "Seeing as you are a miserable tax dodging student, the drinks are on us tonight. Sit yourself down!"

They made space for me in the middle of the booth from where I was clearly trapped from making any escape.

"What you havin'?" enquired Glyn.

"Lager and lime please."

They giggled like school girls at my choice and Glyn nodded sagely to the others.

There followed a large number of pints, which from the first, tasted off if they were lager, and strange if they were bitter, nevertheless it would have been rude not to drink them and the whisky chaser that accompanied them.

The conversation went around the houses of long forgotten events from our childhood, of dens built and hedgehogs captured, of fights started and stopped and games of cricket which lasted for several weeks over the summer holidays. The raid on our rival's bonfire on the cob on the 4th of November was recalled as were skirmishes on the tip and the abandoned bin lorry where we could sit in the cab and turn the steering wheel as we watched the evening trains passing on the mainline. Abandoned things seemed to be something of a theme as we remembered climbing through the slats of the abandoned cottage across the donkey field behind our gardens in Gwynfryn Avenue. We would sit there for hours talking in the summer, imagining ourselves on the summit of Everest.

We'd build machine gun nests in the bushes, complete with stones and half bricks, ready to repulse an onslaught of fanatical Japanese soldiers.

We'd construct trip wires which we deployed across all the routes across the donkey field which sounded on attached baked bean cans when activated. One dusky evening we ensnared a passer by and were about to launch a salvo of stones and half bricks when we realised it was one of the MacGuinness clan.

Unfortunately John had already released a half brick which had the correct angle but insufficient velocity to do much damage. It landed harmlessly on the mud path and rolled to the Macguiness' feet.

The Macguinness looked directly towards our bush outpost and declared "Glyn and your brother – you're dead! So is anyone else in there."

I took a second to weigh up the situation. I hadn't been positively identified. The Macguinnesses, if they could be persuaded to forego a game of football for long enough, were big enough, and mob-handed enough, to issue us with a severe regulation beating. I'd gathered enough evidence. I broke the cover of the bush and legged it towards the gap in the hawthorn hedge from where I could skip over the Roose's hedge and enter my back garden. In my haste, I didn't follow the zig-zag of the path around the tussocks of grass, but blundered directly on through the sheep droppings, nettles and brambles until the fence was reached.

I'd abandoned Glyn and John to their fate and perhaps this night in the Bistro was to be their revenge. I was now a captive on the comfy curved booth seat, trapped left and right with salvoes of drinks coming my way in booming pint glasses and staccato shorts. My only release was to the toilet after the sixth round, an incredible journey in itself as the Bistro management had installed a Waltzer in the toilets which spun me round violently and the spirals on the bar floor appeared to be spinning and fluorescing. I saw John at the bar ordering the next round and heard him call for another round of pints of Barley Wine and Southern Comfort chasers. Things looked ominous.

I finally made my escape two rounds later. I have no recollection of tackling the stairs but remember vividly leaving the warm fug of the Bistro for a howling gale and copious amounts of sea water which seemed to be being thrown by the bucket load directly into my face. The black and white tiles below me seemed like a chessboard and my feet, when I lifted them, moved diagonally, like a bishop, to my intended direction of travel.

I'd had too much to drink before and had felt a tad unsteady, I'd talked too much and too loudly and had then become morose, but this was different. I had absolute clarity in my head but my body was busy doing its own thing and I was mindful that even the most rudimentary things like balancing were taking an inordinate amount of effort. No sooner had I had this thought, than my legs went from under me by combination of a windy squall and a complete lack of control.

"This is going to hurt." I remember thinking as I fell. I was wrong again, for the impact, when it came was feather soft. I took a second to compose myself amidst the black and white tiled squares. I was aware of vomit to my right and the last bite of a hot dog beyond that.

I don't know how I got up and found home that night.

I was oblivious to the rain and wind, no sensory information was reaching my brain at all. The voice inside my head was calling out instructions to my body parts, but my body, like a skittish runaway horse was very much doing its own thing, despite the calm words of encouragement.

I can clearly remember leaning on the sandstone of the Vale Road Bridge thinking I'd never make it home without being picked up by the police. I wondered if my old Nemesis from the Reso, Sergeant Walker, had had the good sense to retire by now. I imagined looking over my shoulder and seeing his craggy visage glaring at me from the open window of his old Morris Minor panda car, a hint of smug satisfaction playing around the spittle in the corner of his mouth. At last, a conviction for him, 'Drunk and Disorderly' or even better 'Drunk and Incapable!'. The horror, the shame of it!

But make it home I did, in a slow and hideous process which involved the comic walk of the drunk, convinced he was stepping on treacherous ice. I crossed the road rather deliberately on the zebra crossing opposite the chip shop having made both Tufty the Squirrel and the Green Cross Code Man more than happy with my road crossing vigilance. Perhaps looking both ways fourteen times was rather excessive, but as the voice that sounded uncannily like Eric Morecambe in my head declared, "You can't be too careful these days, sunshine!"

At the telephone box on the corner of Prince Edward Avenue I had an overwhelming desire to phone Victoria one more time and tell her how I still loved her. If only I could remember her number, Eric chipped in one more time with his famous "You've got all the right numbers sunshine, I'll give you that, but not necessarily in the right order!"

It was God Know's What time now and I decided against it, besides, I didn't have my Binatone Cassette player with me so I couldn't play her *Nights in White Satin* one last time. I was reasonably confident that in my present state I couldn't remember the words of the song anyway. However, I was excessively confident though that I could, at this moment, sing with perfect pitch – something that had eluded me at every point of my life to this date. I took some solace in that in the course of the next twenty minutes as I attempted to open our front door with a penknife, my college room key, a bottle opener and finally the house key.

In all this time two people in my head were giving me instructions about the best way to get the door open. To the casual observer on the Avenue, and thankfully there were none, all that could be heard was me repeating the word "Shuuuuuuuush!" incessantly.

I opened the door to find my mum standing the other side of it with a very large bucket, a pint glass of water and some kitchen towels. She had had a good twenty minutes to prepare these she explained, although she hadn't seen fit to help me get the door open. She was smiling at the uniqueness of the situation.

I attempted to sleep in the fairground ride which was my bedroom with lights and music and endlessly rotating walls and ceilings. I made an oath to forsake alcohol for ever as I didn't want a replay of this night - ever.

This was an oath I kept for eight months until the notorious Summer Ball Rum and Blackcurrant fiasco at University.

Chapter Four
TAXI

The need to live frugally at University meant that I was rather choosy about when and how I spent my money on socialising. There was a growing fad for heading into town for a group meal at weekends in one of the continental or Asiatic eateries. Not having had a large city convenient in North Wales, unless you count Chester which, at thirty miles away was hardly convenient, this was the opposite of what I was used to – heading out to some country pub where the food was characterised mostly by baskets containing chicken and chips. To be honest, I'd found that eating food out of a basket was pushing the envelope of the acceptable really, so continental and oriental food was always going to give me a problem.

I was caught on the horns of a dilemma when people gathered in our communal kitchen in groups of twenty and suggested a night in town, prefaced by a meal. Inevitably the choice would resolve down to Italian, Chinese or Indian. All these cuisines tended to illicit my stock response that I didn't like Italian or Chinese or Indian. I'd learnt early on not to come out with "I don't like foreign food!" which sounded too much like some "little Englander", but the truth of the matter was that I'd never ventured far beyond meat and two veg. Really. My parents had done a good job on developing a stubborn nationalistic streak in my food preferences which was now in danger of showing me up. Memories of my dad's disgust at being served steak and chips with salad and mayonnaise in Belgium some years before came flooding back. I saw once again my mum's face contorted in disgust when my old pal Brian had brought a silver foil dish full of fluorescent red sweet and sour chicken into our house from the King Wah Chinese Restaurant.

"I don't want to be around when he 'Wah's' from eating that stuff!" my dad had added unhelpfully. So you could say that my family had form in terms of their conservative dietary proclivities. Clearly my suspicion of foreign foods was genetic.

Having forsaken a trip to Biba's Italian Pizzeria a fortnight before, which had apparently turned into a riotous evening, I was thumbs in for a visit to the Manzil Indian Restaurant this Saturday, despite my qualms about the foreign menu choices.

Having a group of almost twenty students arrive at a restaurant on time was akin to herding cats. The process was not helped by the fact that we had dog-legged into York by a rather circuitous and beer sodden route. We had initially gathered outside Heslington Hall to catch the number 5 bus, but someone had suggested a swift one at the Derry, so this became our first port of call. From here we had spilled out onto a cold Heslington evening and had collectively decided to walk into town.

At Bleachfield we had taken the back entry round past the Retreat and the Nursing Home to "Reclaim the Night!". A number of students had been assaulted down this alleyway and the Student Union had resolved, by suspending, in an unprecedented way, Standing Orders 7 and 11, to resolve to "reclaim the night" by having large numbers of students marching up and down this God forsaken passageway in a show of solidarity. A related motion by the Surreal Action Faction to have all the walkers dress as Mickey Mouse to juxtapose the posture of International Capitalism and night time violence against the individual was defeated. Such was the student politics of the day. Any view, no matter how ridiculous could be held so long as it was held sincerely and expressed with due note of the constitutional niceties.

We walked down this dim and dingy passageway in this spirit now, past the graffiti that some politically astute student had daubed "Non Pasaran!" with appropriate quotation marks, and then crossed out the Non in red paint, which dripped like revolutionaries' blood. I liked the sentiments of this graffito and the nod to the International Brigade in the Spanish Civil War, but I'd have been bloody livid if some bloody student had daubed my wall with paint.

Entering the long haul down Heslington Road and past Fairfax House, a dispute broke out about whether we should head to the Rose and Crown or the Shire Horses next. In the spirit of compromise, and without the suspension of Standing Orders 7 and 11, we decided to visit both. However a supplementary motion that we should deviate and visit the Wellington, which, excellent pub that it was, was in precisely the opposite direction to our destination, was shouted down.

We took a circuitous route once we entered the City Walls. Davy delighted in finding new and alarming routes through the City and the route we now followed was one of his. Despite my good geographical sense, even I was confused from the constant twisting and turning down narrowing alleyways. My last point of reference had been the Stabber's Arms, so named after a notorious violent incident a few months before. After that I was lost. It felt like we were entering some narrowing alimentary canal and I hoped the Manzil Restaurant and not some blind alley would be at the end of this headlong excursion. I felt the intake of beer up to this point was not helping either.

If our group had been spotted by any locals, we would have passed as a "typical group of students". There was a mass of denim among the attire of the lads and lasses. Army and Air Force greatcoats predominated amongst the lads whilst the girls sported bell bottom jeans and platform soled footwear. A couple of the girls had gone rather rustic with floral patterned dresses, but overall Mr Levi Strauss could anticipate healthy profits on the basis of our fashion choices.

Of course, as students, we were talking too loudly and trying too hard not to sound banal. We were like a pack of ground starlings boisterously heading towards food and, due to Davy's insistence, seemingly wheeling madly close to, but never quite at, our chosen feeding station.

We finally emerged onto the lower part of Goodramgate and I was able to get my bearings from the Minster, shrouded in floodlights to my right, and the Cross Keys directly opposite me. It was in the Cross Keys that you could while away many an hour playing on the bar billiards table with its worn mushrooms which negated your score if you knocked them over. I had hoped to be playing there later this very evening but we were running late as it was, and there would be little time to eat and return there before closing time.

The walk had been a long one and people had worked up a thirst, so despite being late for the meal already, we popped into the Angler's Arms for a swift one, sending Sandra, and her beloved Jeff, on to placate the restaurant manager and assure him of our imminent arrival.

At the best of times the Angler's looked crowded if there were more than three people in. Our host of hungry students, combined with a busy Saturday night crowd meant that the bar was heaving with little room to turn around. There wasn't space to reach out to remove our coats so we sizzled within them aided by the real fire blazing in the grate. For me in my dark blue cord jacket, that wasn't so bad, but for the girls in their dubious Kaftans or Coney Skin fur coats and Adam and Davy in their Army Greatcoats, this was more of a sufferance. It had been so cold and damp outside that the collective heat of our bodies in such a confined space had led us to develop our own weather system. Steam rose off us as we all talked and no-one listened. I swear at one point it started to rain above us in the pub, such had been the localised evaporation and the subsequent condensation.

We drank quickly and hurried along the wet stone pavement up to the Manzil, no more than fifty yards away. As we were guided solicitously by the waiters to our seats, Sandra and Jeff sat quietly. Sandra made a studied attempt at consulting her watch to signify we were later than required for "a swift half" to be bought and consumed. She was equally studiously ignored as we took our places.

The Manzil, upstairs in Goodramgate, was all you would apparently expect from an Indian restaurant, all plush red flock wallpaper with oriental pictures of gaudily painted Hindu deities. The tablecloths were thick and starched and the owner wore a waistcoat which matched the flock wallpaper.

The wooden stairs had reverberated to the beat of twenty pairs of student feet and loud talking and laughter as we ascended. I could imagine the ruined romantic assignations caused by our arrival amongst the couples sitting together holding hands in the body of the room.

The manager greeted us with a wide grin and turned to bark orders in what I assumed was an Indian dialect to the four waiters who were milling round the room delivering dishes to tables. They winced as they received their next set of orders from the boss. All twenty of us were shepherded to a series of tables joined together next to the window that looked out on the street and glowed green due to the combined efforts of hidden lighting and a strategically placed tropical fish tank.

Complimentary poppadoms duly arrived together with the menus. I tasted a shard of my poppadom cautiously, trying to develop an expectation of the taste based on its look and texture. Quavers the aerated potato crisps was my expectation. I was not that far out and I decided I could add poppadoms to my list of acceptable foreign foods I could now eat.

"Enjoying your poppadom nut crisp?" enquired Adam, unhelpfully returning to an earlier theme. This gave me pause for thought as to its nut content.

My friends seemed keen to dip their crisps in an assortment of potions and sauces that had now been delivered to the table. I recognised the finely chopped onions, tomato and cucumber but could not work out the logic of having salad with crisps. The other three concoctions in the rotatable silver server were more ambiguous. In one, small cubes of cucumber stood suspended in what looked like yoghurt. A second contained a rich orange brown gloop, the consistency of runny marmalade but much darker. The final container was brimful of a similar coloured substance with what looked like citrus fruit suspended in it.

"Do you like lime pickle?" asked Alison rather seductively, I thought. "I love it."

"Yes, I do."

She dunked a medium-sized piece of poppadom in the pickle and offered it to me. I hoped my look was one of nonchalance as I bit down on the morsel for my inner feeling was utter revulsion. She had included a piece of lime in the pickle and the sensation of the pickle hitting my tongue was nothing less than sensational. Immediately the tip of my tongue felt burned, then anaesthetised then burnt again.

"Jesus Christ!" was probably not the epithet to scream out at this point so I stifled the urge and screamed into my head.

"Lovely, isn't it!" declared the elegant Alison looking directly at me.

"Uummmm," I replied, hiding my disgust in sounds of fake oral satisfaction, my vocal chords having gone into spasm. I was hoping beyond hope that she didn't offer me a second helping.

The noise of chatter now had subsided into studied reading of the menu. Friends were discussing their favourite curry dishes and accompaniments. There was talk of shared Naans and chapattis, of what I thought was 'writer' and Bombay aloo, all of which went over my head. I desperately searched the curry page for something acceptable. Someone mentioned that Korma was a mild curry so I thought I might plump for that until I read the small print description that outlined lentils and coconut. The begum bahar, balti and biryani all fell by the wayside as containing nuts. Other dishes were described as having 'special spices' which could have been shorthand for any concoction really. I found it really suspicious that whilst some dishes were described as Prawn, Chicken or Lamb, others were simply described as having 'meat' which was a tad vague for my taste.

The options were reduced now to a Jalfrezi which contained my old staples of egg, onion and tomatoes with the dubious addition of spices (which were neither described as special or exotic – in truth I hoped they would simply be salt and pepper) as well as the more suspicious fresh chillies, or the Madras which even the restaurant warned was 'hot'. As no such warning had appeared on the lime pickle currently raging in my mouth, I assumed that these curries must be thermonuclear in their effect.

I didn't consider eating out to be a competitive sport, but clearly Marco and Davy did. They scanned the menu and dared each other to plump for the Ceylon curry which came with an advisory notice in the menu as *Very Hot!!!* Three exclamation marks constituted a health warning as clear as the graphic 'Danger of Death by Electrocution' notices on electricity sub-stations.

Only the foolhardy and mentally insane would venture beyond that point of warning. Davy asked for a large jug of water as a side order, clearly having some inkling of what he was taking on.

The waiter was proceeding down the table now taking orders and reading them back, and, in Davy and Marco's case, ensuring that the restaurant had been indemnified from their reckless menu choices. In desperation I turned the page to be confronted with yet more curries and side dishes such as Bengen Paneer Bharjee, which could have been anything really, and a bewildering array of rice options from boiled to fried with innumerable eggs, fungi and vegetables added.

In my desperation, I scanned the smaller print at the bottom of the page and found my salvation, a section entitled Traditional English Dishes. Amongst the omelettes and Sunday roast options was a Porterhouse steak. This was possibly the most expensive item on the menu, and I clearly wouldn't be seeing much change from a five pound note, but it would be worth it for the 14oz steak, chips, peas, onion rings and tomato. I heaved a huge size of relief.

When I ordered, quietly so I thought no one would hear, only for the waiter to repeat my order very loudly, there was a gasp of disbelief from the party. "You've ordered steak and chips in an Indian restaurant?"

"Yes," I said, bluffing furiously, "I'm a free spirit me, don't always go with the flow." And I looked Alison fully in the face and winked, hoping that she would find me unconventional and interesting and would keep playing footsie under the table.

The heady conversation subsided as the food arrived. All the curries looked the same to me except for the slightly different hues and side dishes. There seemed to be an inordinate trying of each others dishes which was too sociable to my taste. I liked to eat what I ordered, otherwise I would have chosen something else. It was other people's misfortune if they now found that they preferred my choice of meal to their own.

Nobody was interested in sampling my food, despite my generously offering a chip to each of the assembled diners. Neither were they interested in sampling Davy and Marco's curry Vesuvius. Neither lad was speaking now, each eating with a stoic look about their eye and one hand on the glass tumbler to wash down each furnace-like mouthful. Beads of sweat were running down their brows and Marco was perspiring from his ears, which was something I'd never seen and hoped never to experience.

"Too hot for you Davy?" asked Andy mischievously with a look of mock concern.

"Wee buns, wee buns!" replied Davy. The expression was pure Ulster but his thick accent had been eradicated like a blowlamp blisters paint. He tried to order some more water but was forced to rely on hand gestures as his vocal chords had incinerated.

The steak was scrumptious and I cleared my plate savouring the well-cooked familiar flavours.

There was talk of dessert, which quickly dissipated, much to my relief. The pictures of the desserts on the supplementary menu were Technicolor in pastel range and overly complicated, with nuts featuring prominently. The only thing that appealed to me, and no doubt Davy and Marco, was the hollowed out orange with sorbet in it, but the moment had passed. Like gentleman's club members and despite no-one yet having reached the age of twenty one, everyone was now ordering coffee and liquors.

I settled for a large rum and a Cona coffee with cream floated on top. This was a regular party drink at Christmas and New Year in our house and my mum had even purchased some Irish Velvet glasses, which were ordinary glasses with a green shamrock imprinted on them. I was thankful that there was no Egg Flip or Advocaat on the menu or, had I been at home, someone would have ordered a Snowball. This evening all seemed so much more sophisticated.

I did a quick calculation of how much I'd spent and realised that my food budget would have to be drastically revised downwards this week. I'd done a calculation at the beginning of term of all my major expenses, and then divided them by the weeks in the term. That way I knew exactly what my food bill could be on a daily basis to keep the figures on track. Of the £740 of my grant, I'd aimed to keep a huge contingency of £200, "just in case". I thought it best to be prudent because I knew there would be no fallback cash from parents should I overspend. But tonight, what the Hell – drink and be merry, for tomorrow you may be in overdraft!

Some of the girls ordered drinks I'd never heard of before. Francesca, becoming increasingly raucous, regaled us with tails of cocktails in the south of France with daddy's banking chums and how one of daddy's chums, in a London cocktail bar had consulted the cocktail list and said to the young waitress, "I'll have a long slow screw against the wall...and possibly a drink afterwards."

Francesca brayed with laughter and reminded me of all the things I didn't like about her. Some laughed embarrassed. "What a hoot!" she honked when her paroxysm subsided, by which time the conversation had thankfully moved on.

The Cona coffee machines duly arrived on their hotplates with the small paraffin heaters beneath. I was fascinated by them and was pleased to be asked to be "mum" and serve the coffee for the group around me. The ensuing coffee was rich and strong, stronger than I favoured really, but carefully running some rum down the spoon and through the rich cream resolved that issue. More coffee was ordered, and more after that as the additional alcohol had people talking animatedly. I had doled out the umpteenth cup of coffee and had replaced the Cona coffee dispenser back on the hotplate, when there was a loud bang and the supposedly heat resistant glass shattered.

Everyone looked at me, some even made a loud "aaahhhhhh!" and pointed as we might have done at primary school. Very quickly the veneer of sophistication, of post-prandial drinks, descended into farce.

"You'll have to pay for that and they are hideously expensive!" said Francesca unhelpfully. I waited for the mass outpouring of sympathy and offers of financial support which were not forthcoming.

Andy blew out the paraffin lamp in an 'after the horse had bolted' gesture and ventured, "Perhaps the manager won't notice if we don't mention it."

I looked at the top of the Cona coffee flask, still suspended above the paraffin heater and the rest of the glass shattered on the table, like a light bulb that had exploded, a growing coffee stain soaking through the crisp white table cloth, and thought this unlikely.

"Look out, the manager's coming!" whispered someone and we all tried to look casual, especially me.

The manager looked at the broken coffee machine and I got in quickly, "The glass just shattered, I'm afraid." I was picturing me being unable to pay the cost of its replacement and the York equivalent of my nemesis, Sergeant Walker, arresting me for wilful damage, drunken disorderliness, going equipped to eat an English meal in an Indian restaurant and reckless use of a napkin.

The manager thought for a moment and then did that Indian way of shaking his head from side to side of which I was uncertain if it meant yes or no and announced, "No matter, no matter, accidents will happen!"

He had clearly calculated that he had secured sufficient profit from our party for the flask not to matter. I was heartily relieved and paid my money to the person doing the nit picking calculation of who had had what and how much everyone owed and headed for the street before the manager had second thoughts.

It was now midnight and, as predicted, my game of bar billiards would have to wait. Someone suggested a nightclub, but as the cost of the evening began to sink in, in the cold air, we decided to phone for five taxis to take us home to college where we could drink any supplies we had on site.

Kieron was back within a couple of minutes from the phone saying five taxis were on their way. Within minutes the first arrived and four people got in. Another few minutes passed and a second cab arrived. Alison, Davy, Andy and I piled in.

"That was quick, the first cab arrived in just a couple of minutes." said Andy, occupying the front seat while I whispered sweet nothings in Alison's ear.

"I'm the first cab! What was on the side of the car?" retorted the taxi driver.

"Ebor Cabs. I think" said Andy, not realising the firestorm he was about to unleash.

"Bastards!" retorted the driver "You ordered Alpha cabs. He's a bloody bandit. I'll have him!" and he spoke loudly into his intercom "Alpha 74 Goodramgate pick up. Bandit. Bandit. Bandit. to York University. Intercepting. Over."

Thoughts of Sunday afternoon war films came to mind and I was about to add that the driver should have included altitude as in "Bandits, Angels fifteen. Over." But the way the driver was gunning his engine as we lurched headlong from the pavement suggested this might not be the time for levity.

The driver kept up a tirade of abuse throughout the journey as we sped like a police interceptor vehicle down wet cobbled streets and swerved round corners with a menacing squeal of tyres.

"He's not insured, this was our shout and we are not allowed to pick up on the street, the job has to be phoned in, so he's not insured. If he crashes there will be all hell to pay and a mountain of paperwork. I'll bloody fix him. This isn't the first time you know, oh no, but it'll bloody be the last if I have anything to do with it."

We, white faced in the back, were rather more concerned with our own safety. It would be little consolation when this taxi was fished out of the river having somersaulted spectacularly off the road at amazing speed, for our parents to be told that we were all dead, but that at least we were insured.

Alison held my hand tightly, which was a bonus. Pity I wasn't going to have the opportunity to get to know her better I thought.

I had no idea where we were now. The driver was intent to cut corners and take back cuts to get to the university in time to intercept the other cab.

Davy had gone beyond white now into that *verde gris* tone and there was the very real prospect of his curry revisiting, as hot as when it went down. Given the lack of support over the Cona incident, I wasn't chipping in towards the fee for cleaning the cab in the unlikely event of us surviving the journey. I tried to concentrate on something else and alighted n the tattoos on the back of the driver's hands of Swallows and anchors. I just knew that had I been able to see his clenched fists, all alabaster white, his knuckles would read HATE and HATE.

Unfortunately, the other cab was still in the car park at Vanbrugh College when we roared in and skidded a number of yards on the wet surface. We looked at the meter and put together the fare, but our driver was long gone, equipped with a starter handle, he was now chasing the reversing taxi of the competing firm, slamming the starter handle on the bonnet. We quickly surveyed the scene, threw the fare on his seat and ran laughing over the bridge to Goodricke, our footsteps echoing across the lake.

All in all it had been a good, if rather quiet, night out.

Chapter Five
HOUSE

The story of anyone's time at University is, in large part, the less than glorious story of the accommodation they find themselves saddled with for the academic year.

A home in Hall was guaranteed for the first year and I was glad of my room in Goodricke C Block. To many it was functional and stark in the extreme with its breeze block construction and magnolia walls, but I considered it a step up from my cold, small room in the back of Prince Edward Avenue.

I was happy with the functional desk with accompanying graffiti, red angle poise light, massive wardrobe and small wash basin. I liked the manila coloured notice board on which I'd organised a whole host of timetables, official notices and a "things to do" list.

I'd filched a couple of posters from student theatre productions to display on my notice board, one a fetching yellow and blue counterpointed poster from the production of *Murder in the Cathedral*.

Thankfully I hadn't attended this production by earnest students playing would-be actors. I was caught out once in a production of the *Mikado* when a fellow student of Canadian origin insisted I attend. It had been dreadful. The only relief was to try and guess who was who under the alabaster white make-up which made the girls rather fetching and the lads appear deathly. The *Murder in the Cathedral* poster had been lifted from the corridor next to the pinball machines in Goodricke simply on the basis of its vivid blue and yellow colours.

Other than that, I had made no effort to personalise the room, unlike all of my friends who had gone to enormous pains to recreate their home bedrooms in their college accommodation. My relationship with this room was temporary and I was happy to preserve its tidy look. Not for me a tennis playing girl, revealingly adjusting her underwear. Nor a frieze of obscure beer mats obtained from hostelries nationwide, advertising Old Peculiar Cobblers or Black Spitfire Sheep. Not even posters of music festivals I'd attended, as in truth, I had not attended any. I had my wish list of bands I'd like to see, but I was happy to see them in concert in a stadium or other "fit for purpose" venue, rather than combine the experience with camping, mud, spaced out hippies and incessant rain. I was a little anal about this and had to fight off a number of "great ideas" to meet up at a music festival at the end of the first year. I was pleased to have been asked and to be included in the group, but I had no intention of going.

I believed the best chaser for a full-on rock concert was a good night's sleep and I was blissfully unaware of how old that made me sound when I said it out loud to the gathered throng in the Goodricke bar one evening. It was generally assumed that I had been joking and playing out a character, as we habitually did. But I wasn't. I could just about tolerate the deprivations of camping from my experience in Mid Wales and the Lake District where the "great outdoorness" of the scenery and wildlife (mosquitoes and midges excepted) just about compensated for the inability to sleep and the freezing temperatures. Being woken at 4 a.m. by cows nibbling your tent lines had its benefits if it meant you got to look awestruck at the primeval sight of the mist shrouded Llyn Bala with not a human being in sight and totally silent, but to share the experience with 100,000 others, with limited toilet facilities, was not my idea of heaven. I would have made a wretched hippie, too keen on my sleep and my personal space.

Apart from the toiletries on the shelf above the sink, the papers on my desk, the few colourful artefacts on my notice board and the text books on the two wooden shelves above the desk, my room was bare and anodyne. That was how I liked it so that there was no mess to tidy. I suppose I was anticipating the "minimalist look" by a good few years.

Had I stepped back to view my room dispassionately and objectively I might have surprised myself about what it said about my personality. It might appear cold and austere, which had not been my intention. I might have come across as humourless and stand-offish. I thought I could hold my own on the first count but shyness with new people, despite Goffman's insights, might support the second charge.

Certainly the anonymity of university, where you turned up with large or small groups of people that you'd never met before at a timetabled slot and place to listen to someone you didn't know hold forth on a subject which, despite the pre-reading list, you knew next to nothing about could be hugely intimidating. But it was also exciting and I was determined to overcome my shyness and make the most of the opportunities now granted to me.

After all, I had worked inordinately hard to be here. Eight months of a hermit-like existence with only colour coded cards and charts and quotes, all cross-referenced, as company had proved, that when I put my mind to it I could be successful academically.

I'd had every incentive to succeed and leave home after the debacle with Victoria had put an end to any abiding reason to stay in my home town and seek employment, such as there was. Despite this, there was a niggling doubt that I didn't really deserve to be here and could, at any point, be exposed as a fraud.

Anyway, I, like just about everyone else, had endured the painful first days of this new life where self-doubt and what an early Sociology lecture had helpfully isolated as a sense of "anomie" had been overcome. Luckily, we had only ventured onto the dangerous ground of Emile Durkheim's extensive treatise on suicide in the fourth week, by which time we were all safely settled in.

The Fresher social had begun the process of gathering a friendship group and other students, who were to be avoided at all costs, had been provisionally identified.

The latter group consisted of those with double-barrelled names, and an excessively right wing outlook, those who talked too loud, those who smoked, those who spent most of their time and money drinking, those with a hastily acquired excessively left-wing bias and a father who was an affluent stockbroker. It extended to people who considered the library their second home, residents of Vanbrugh College, whose catering arrangements were dire, those who knew the procedures for suspending standing orders 7 and 11 at Student Union meetings and girls who started every sentence vacuously with 'Actually…'

Other than those exceptions on my list, I considered myself both open-minded and outward looking in my socialising and imagined myself as a valuable and valued social asset in conversation. On reflection, I think I might have come across as a little dogmatic and quick to judge, but hindsight is such a wonderful capacity.

So much for my resolve to completely reinvent myself at University and be whoever I wanted to be. I'd had some superficial success in reinventing myself by my ability to pick up and mimic accents. I'd convinced Karen from Coleraine that I'd actually grown up down the road from her. She was so amazed to meet a fellow Colerainian (or whatever the term for a native of the parish was) in her college that she had made it too easy for me. She listed people and places I might know and events I may have attended. It was just too easy to say yes and no in an Ulster accent that I'd developed from Davy's Belfast brogue and combined with Karen's more sing-song intonation. She actually sounded like a harp playing, beautiful, melodic and flowing. I merely filled the short intermissions before the breathless Karen launched excitedly into another person or event with a "Didn't she have a brother?", "Wasn't that in the centre of town?" for Karen to be content that I was bona fide and exclaim characteristically "God! We're practically family! Wait 'til I tell my mum about this."

It was too late before I realised my mimicry had led me in too deep and I'd have to disentangle myself from this web of deceit without hurting her feelings. Not learning my lesson, I convinced Dereth, with a sizeable portion of a rural Welsh accent, that my name was really Dafydd and that I hailed from Aberwystwyth and intended leaving York as it was proving too cosmopolitan for my rural palate. She had spent the best part of the evening counselling me with great skill to reconsider and take time to reach a decision. She'd been such a good and attentive listener and was so sincere that I'd committed, in character, to follow her advice. I didn't know at the time that she was a volunteer Samaritan Counsellor. I suppose I only had myself to blame that she always viewed me with suspicion after that.

By Easter of the first year thoughts were turning to accommodation arrangements for the following year. Unlike the first year, when college accommodation was guaranteed, the second year was premised on the idea that most students would want the great adventure of moving into off-site accommodation in York or, transport arrangements permitting, in one of the outlying villages. I did not share this view and reasoned that I had decided to attend a campus university on the basis of the proximity of all the facilities so I could not see the logic of transporting myself away from them and paying a bonus to a private landlord for the privilege of this inconvenience.

I was clearly in a minority among my friends in this view as they were busily forming syndicates to search out flats in the town. I was delighted to find, and genuinely touched, that I was considered an essential ingredient of these groups of four, five and six, looking to set up independently, but I politely refused the offer to join their brave bands.

I reasoned that the more that chose that life of accommodation uncertainty, of erratic plumbing and extortionately priced heating, of lapse security measures and indifferent decorating, of dubious electrical and gas services and intermittent waste removal arrangements, the greater the opportunity for me to secure a room in college.

Despite the determination to secure college accommodation, I was not prepared to go to the lengths of some of my fellow students who, like punters queuing for some January sale, were prepared to camp out overnight outside Sally, the Deputy Accommodation Manager's office in order to secure a particular room. These tended to be the established couples who were anxious to secure a double room to prevent the habitual backache which accompanied the regular attempts at co-habitation on the standard size university beds. The luxury of being able to push two beds together was both practical and romantic.

Sally was a very accommodating lady, which presumably helped her land the job in the first place, and tried to help meet the requests of the couples in a reasonable way. In doing so she was, by popular tradition, in contravention of a specific edict in the grant of land that had established the university. The Quaker chocolate makers and good burghers of York had granted the land with a codicil that no male would remain in the room of a female without having both feet planted firmly on the floor. This was a truly bizarre regulation if it were true, and betrayed a naïve understanding of the full range of sexual acts that it was meant to deter. Still, honour was maintained by its inclusion and, as no effort was made by the college authorities to enforce the impossible by bursting into rooms to find student couples in statue-like poses with both feet on the ground, the rule was effectively ignored.

Unlike the queuers, I was happy with any room from the College stock. I'd have preferred C block to the sprung floors and CLASP architecture of A and B block, and a vista of the lake rather than a view looking into the loose courtyard of the college, but neither of these preferences was immutable. A room in College was a room after all.

I attended morning lectures, went to the bank in Heslington, had some lunch in the College canteen before sauntering up to see Sally in her office, reasoning that the rush would be over by 2 p.m. and I could have a social chat with Sally as well as reserve my accommodation for the following year. Sally was indeed alone when I knocked and entered the room and glanced up to smile at me as I entered. She was not in the frame of mind to engage in social chit chat though, seemingly engaged in the several pages of colour coded room plans in front of her.

"Busy day?" I asked unhelpfully as this was probably the busiest day of her year, when her projections and plans met with the first chunk of cold reality. The second chunk of reality corresponded to the publication of the A level results in August and the flurry of anxious phone calls from prospective students and their parents keen to secure accommodation. .

"Yes, yes indeed," she replied thoughtfully without looking up from her colour coding. She made no enquiry as to what I wanted so I launched into my pitch.

"So, I've come to reserve a room for next year," I added, prompting her.

"You are joking!" she replied in horror, "All the college rooms were allocated by eight thirty this morning, students were queuing all down the corridor and round into the Maths department!"

"No worries," I persevered, "I don't want a double room, just a single, and I'm not fussy, I'll even consider A block!" I continued, flashing what I hoped would be a winning smile.

The winning smile was lost as Sally didn't even look up.

"I've no rooms at all," stated Sally boldly, "what with the increase in student numbers next academic year and the unprecedented demand from final year students, I have no rooms left to allocate at all, in fact I have a deficit of rooms to the number of seven!"

She looked up at my obviously dejected face and didn't realise I was going through a number of damning 'what if's!' in my head which were headlined by the what if I'd stayed up all night outside this office – I'd have secured accommodation by now.

"I'll tell you what I'll do," she continued in a more positive tone.

I was hoping she would take up her fountain pen, cross out the name of a student who was already allocated a room and insert mine instead, whilst winking conspiratorially at me.

She didn't do this though. I cursed her professionalism and sense of fair play which clearly trumped her personal affection for me. She did lift up her fountain pen though, raising my hopes, and then reached for a couple of sheets stapled together under the title 'Reserve List'.

"I'll add you to the Reserve List, although to be honest I'm on to page 2 already and you, as a prospective second year, rank behind third years and freshers in precedence. What I'm saying is that I hold out very little hope of you being allocated a room in college next year and you really should explore other avenues to secure accommodation. I'm afraid my hands are tied."

I pictured Sally tied to her office chair and gagged to prevent her crying out as I lifted her fountain pen and inserted my name over that of a student already allocated one. Clearly this wasn't going to happen, and I hung on her next words which had been prefaced by, "I'll tell you what though…"

These words were marginally supportive.

"I'll write you a recommendation to take to Miss Cosway, the whole university Accommodation Officer. She'll know if there is anything going on the wider properties like Eden and Lawrence Court. I'll warn you now to be on your best behaviour if you want to win her round though."

With an official endorsement from Sally in a College envelope in my hand I hastily beat a path to Miss Cosway's door in Heslington Hall, anxious not to repeat my dilatory approach to accommodation in Goodricke College.

I made my way into the venerable administration building of the university and pondered its role as a Bomber Command operational planning unit in the Second World War. I thought about the melee of clipped accents and scrambled egg decoration on hats, the maps, the serious intent and determination to give "the Hun a bloody nose of the sort he wouldn't forget in a hurry!"

I really should not rely too heavily on the rakings of a thousand British war films digested after lunch on a Sunday afternoon, or rather about two dozen films sampled time and time again until it amounted to thousands. I could see in the front courtyard, a squadron leader wearing an Irwin flying jacket sat in the driving seat of a Jeep, consorting with a Group Captain sitting in the back of a green and black camouflaged Humber Staff car, discussing the target for tonight and stressing how vitally important this one target, whatever it was, U boat pens, the Tirpitz, the Ruhr dams, V1 launch sites, Gestapo headquarters, a Norge Hydro heavy water plant, a prison full of French Resistance fighters, or Berlin itself, was to bringing the war to a premature end. In my mind I'd already cut to some well known British character actors, Sam Kydd, a young and cheeky Michael Medwin, or the likes of Bill Owen as RAF 'erks busy on a local bomber station, Elvington, Church Fenton or Pocklington bombing up Lancaster bombers and exclaiming "Not another bloomin' raid – if I could get my hands on that ruddy Group Captain I'd..." at which point the string of mild expletives were drowned out by the roar of Merlin aero engines.

I made my way up the steps of Heslington Hall in order to play out this fantasy, rather than taking the direct and more prosaic route through the back door.

The entrance to Hes' Hall was almost regal with a fine staircase and beautiful plaster mouldings on the ceiling. I'd had good call to remember such detail as I'd spent forty eight hours in the building waiting for the authorities to accede to our 'legitimate and reasonable' demands in 'the occupation' of the previous term.

I can't, in all honesty, remember what our demands were now, nor can I recall what the action of the authorities had been that provoked them. I knew others, whose opinion I respected, thought this the only course of action forced on us by the University authorities' inflexible and belligerent stance, so I was all for it. I'm proud to say that I took part in the 'occupation' of

Heslington Hall the previous term. Perhaps 'bemused' might fit better than 'proud' in that sentence.

Anyway, I was there when the Hall was occupied, paralysing the administrative function of the University and bringing them back, with their tail between their legs, to the negotiating table for whatever it was that they had done, or failed to do, that had provoked the crisis in the first place.

When I say I took part in them, I should clarify. I arrived thirty six hours after the Bastille of University administration had been stormed, bringing some sandwiches and crisps for a good friend who had been in the first assault. I'd been quizzed by some student union rep. wearing a red armband at the door. He was clearly under the impression that I might be an administration fifth columnist until another union apparatchik had recognised me and beckoned me in, much to the chagrin of the over-officious red-guard.   I thought how emboldened this doorman had been and wondered how he would have got on in the Bistro in Rhyl when the Maclarens arrived on a Friday night anxious for a pint, a pull and a good fight, not necessarily in that order.

The main area of the Hall was full of feverish activity. Banners and placards were being manufactured on an industrial scale, in what I assumed was a modern equivalent of a scene from the Leningrad Soviet in 1917. A union official addressed the worker bees below from the balcony using a loud hailer which I thought was a little superfluous, and not a tad pompous, given the size and acoustics of the room. No doubt this particular official, who harked from the further reaches of the Revolutionary Trotskyist Workers Liberation faction within the Socialist tradition was internally bemoaning the fact that York was too far from the sea to dramatically re-enact the scene of the baby in the pram from the seminal Battleship Potemkin film, down the few steps of Heslington Hall.

It was cartoon socialists like this that really cheesed me off about student politics. It was all pose and no substance, the better off their backgrounds, the more extreme they felt they could be, for there were no implications or consequences that mummy and daddy couldn't extricate them from if they got into trouble. For them socialism was a fairground in which they could amble, trying out the 'dangerous rides'. It was not about the lives of people I'd known on the Reso estate, who lived decently with little material benefits and tried to look after their family and their neighbours with good humour.

There had been a feverish revolutionary fervour in the main Hall but all I could summon up was the observation that if that red poster paint they were using for the placards got into the carpet it would be the devil itself to clean up.

In the rooms that were open, the mood was much calmer. Indeed, when I found Elaine, squatting on an expensive carpet in a wood lined room that backed onto the ornamental gardens with their Henry Moore statues, with my gift of a ham and tomato roll and two packets of cheese and onion crisps, she was busily engaged writing up the notes for her assignment which was due in during the next week. Given that we shared a similar working class background, the opulence of her surrounding was lost on Elaine as she was too busy in her work to notice them.

With admirable foresight and characteristic organisation, she'd brought all her data and a large pencil case containing all her pens, slide rules, protractors, compasses and set squares. Elaine, being a biology student, I'd learnt early not to ask what her experimental work was about. I'd been regaled in the past by biologists outlining in microscopic detail (for indeed this was the level in which they were interested in viewing the world) the experiments they were conducting, from the stomata of tomatoes to the mitochondria of human cells, the reproductive cycle of drosophila (fruit flies since you ask) to the breeding habits of the natterjack toad.

They did have some interesting machinery to work with that was denied to us Humanities students, it had to be admitted. The best was an electron microscope which required you to coat samples in gold before photographing them in god-like detail. A late night visit to the Biology labs felt like being in the nerve centre of a Bond villain, such was the weirdness of the technology. The highlight of such visits had been when Ross had taken a duck's feather from the side of the lake and drenched it in liquid nitrogen so that it shattered like glass in my hand. Cool I had thought, and it was, exceptionally cool indeed.

Elaine was busy compiling scatter graphs of her results and calculating the line of best fit. It looked like scientific embroidery to me. She was glad to see me and devoured the roll and crisps quickly before asking if I could guard her place whilst she slipped back to Goodricke for a shower and a change of clothes. The occupation was formalising into an increasingly strictly "one in, one out" affair so that there was, at every moment, sufficient occupiers to repel the impending onslaught of the reactionary forces of the administrators.

It made for an evocative image, but the administrators were probably at home now, enjoying an additional day's paid holiday in the garden in the spring sunshine, with not a jot of reactionary intent. So I became a chosen man of the occupation and ended up staying on shift through most of the night until the reluctance of the revolutionaries to turn out the lights so that we could get some shut eye (hence my detailed knowledge of the ceiling plasterwork) the cooking of highly spiced lentil soup by the food and nutrition cooperative and the repetitive singing of revolutionary songs drove me out and into my comfortable bed back in Goodricke. Trotsky would indeed have had me down as a fellow traveller.

"Where is your replacement occupier? You can't leave until one replaces you." asked the same Stakanovite Red Guard at the barricaded doorway.

"Piss off," I replied with Maclarenesque clarity and pushed my way out into the clear, early morning air.

Unfortunately, the initial occupation of Heslington Hall had been initiated by the jemmying of the front door by a student who had clearly arrived with a jemmy or crow bar. Somehow the identity of this student had been supplied to the authorities and although the occupation had ended with an amicable settlement of whatever had been the initial cause, there were legal proceedings now in place against the student with the jemmy, who was also threatened with being sent down.

The lad in question was called Larry or something similar and I knew him vaguely. He had an earnest face, with deep set eyes, came from Liverpool and habitually wore a denim jacket. My first though was that coming from Liverpool, he could argue that it was standard practice to carry a jemmy. No self-respecting scouser would leave home without checking that he was carrying his wallet and change, house key and jemmy. On reflection, I thought that this was uncharitable as a joke, given that Larry was facing a criminal conviction and being sent down as the scapegoat for what had been a collective act.

Rumours grew about Larry's plight and matters were intensified when a member of the administrative staff appeared on the lunch time university television channel outlining the determination of the authorities to proceed with a court case to make it crystal clear that the university would not tolerate "breaking and entering" particularly when it was perpetrated with violence using (and I quote here) "a goose-necked wrecking bar" There was bemusement in the canteens at the use of the term and slowly there was a ripple of understanding as the term was translated into the word jemmy or crow bar.

Fiona from Sevenoaks still asked "Whatever is that?" in genuine ignorance of all things artisan. Sid from Harlow New Town advised her "It's what your dad would order from the Harrods catalogue and send your butler to collect in the Roller if he was going out on a twocking spree."

"Oh," replied Fiona, none the wiser but in a way that suggested that the first part of the scenario could well be accurate. "What on earth is twocking?" Sid bit his lip at this point.

The scape-goating of Larry over what came to be known as the "Goose Necked Wrecking Bar incident" was inflammatory and within five minutes, independently of any discussion groups and union meetings, groups were heading to Heslington Hall from every college. By arriving in the early afternoon we could all simply walk into the building without the use of any animal anatomy shaped metal levering tools. Pity the original occupiers didn't have the same foresight I thought.

Sheer weight of numbers forced the closure and evacuation of the building by the administrators and within twenty four hours an amicable solution was reached which left Larry accepting an internal disciplinary charge and the criminal damage charge dropped. The Student Union meanwhile were faced with the bill for almost ten thousand hand bills and posters they had hastily concocted in support of the Heslington One but had been unable to distribute before the issue had been resolved.

So ended the sorry saga of the Heslington One. In my time at University, this was the only incident in which amicable relations between students and the administration were strained and I hoped that the same spirit of reconciliation reigned now as I entered the building for the first time since the occupation with my accommodation request.

"I'd like to see Miss Cosway about an accommodation issue please." I addressed myself to the elder of the two women manning, or womaning (as the radical feminist group insisted) reception.

Without looking up and in a sing song voice that sounded like she was answering the telephone or making an announcement at York railway station, she replied, "I regret to inform you that Miss Cosway is not in the building at the moment as she is on annual leave, returning tomorrow. I can however direct you to the second floor where her secretary can deal with your enquiry. Thank you."

"Can you tell me where on the second floor I'll find her secretary please?"

"You will find Miss Cosway's secretary by alighting the adjacent staircase, making a sharp left turn on the first landing and proceeding to the end of the corridor. Here you need to alight a second flight of stairs. Miss Cosway's secretary will be found half way along the corridor, the third door on the left marked *'Miss Cosway'*, although this is in fact an ante-room to Miss Cosway's office, in which you will find Miss Cosway's secretary who will no doubt be able to deal with your enquiry. Thank you muchly."

"No, thank you. Thank you very much," I replied, with the thought that I was the subject of some in-house joke. This feeling was not dispelled by the fact that both secretaries started giggling when I started to 'alight' the staircase as instructed.

I'd never heard the word 'muchly' before and doubted it was a real word that could be used in sensible conversation. Perhaps they were playing the game we had played solely for our amusement in sixth form in which one person had to come up with an outlandish word and the other had to use it in conversation within that day. My English A level pal, Gareth in Rhyl High School, rather than the Welsh rugby captain, had been a literary genius at this and we had kept ourselves amused for many a long hour at the back of the English class with this game. The fact that we were studying John Donne and the Metaphysical Poets at the time gave the game added impetus.

"We are studying the use of arcane language in modern English as an A level project," ventured Gareth to the Deputy Headteacher having used the word "Forsooth" in a sentence addressed to him. There was nothing the deputy Head could do but mutter "Carry on!" through clenched lips. It was definitely one of those "you had to be there!" moments, but satisfying nonetheless in blatantly taking the piss out of authority figures.

The receptionist's instructions were perfectly accurate and I couldn't help mounting the staircases without the childish thought that the balustrades would be brilliant for sliding down.

Heslington Hall was a sumptuous building with thick pile carpet and reassuringly creaky floorboards. Portraits, old and new, punctuated the wall spaces between the office doors and I couldn't help think that if I were sixty, this would be the kind of working environment in which I'd like to be employed.

I knocked politely on the door to the ante room of Miss Cosway's office and was answered by a curt, "Come!"

I stiffened at the formality of it and harked back to Sally's warning words about Miss Cosway, which no doubt applied to her secretary as well.

The door opened into what I was surprised to find was one of the eaves of the building. It struck me that there was about six foot by ten foot of useful headroom in which I could stand up straight but that I'd have to stoop or lean back like a limbo dancer to make use of fifty percent of the floor space. There were no windows in the room and a harsh row of fluorescent strips provided the available light in the room, one of which was supplying the annoying hum which seemed audible to only me and dogs.

"How can I help you?" asked a Laura Ashley floral dressed lady a few years older than me, but infinitely more grown up. She smiled broadly from behind a neat oak desk and swivelled on her chair to give me her full attention whilst gesturing for me to sit in a blue upholstered chair. She now leaned back in her chair and crossed her legs seductively and the tallest high heels I'd ever seen.

"I'd like to make an appointment to see Miss Cosway tomorrow about an accommodation issue please."

There was a sharp intake of breath and the secretary stated, "You've not met Miss Cosway before have you?"

It was a statement rather than a question really.

"No, no I haven't" I replied meekly.

"It doesn't work like that with Miss Cosway. If you give me the details of your enquiry I'll put them into a format which will encourage her to give it a high priority. She will have me notify you through the internal mail the date and time of your appointment."

"But…"

"Miss Cosway does not do buts. Nor does she do a great many other things which she considers wasteful of time. Outline the problem and I'll inform her as soon as she is in tomorrow morning."

So I outlined the issue, passed over the letter from Sally, and was assured it would be dealt with as soon as possible, a note having been made of the details written in fountain pen by immaculately presented, varnished nails.

I got up to go with a smile and a thank you. To my surprise Miss Cosway's secretary smiled back and proffered her hand for me to shake. The reason for the high heels was now apparent as even with this excessive elevation, she stood no more than five feet four. I tried to shake her dainty hand firmly without damaging it. She looked me up and down slowly and added the thought,

"Wear a tie, a striped tie and a suit for the interview. Miss Cosway does like formality."

I nodded in affirmation, grateful for the insight.

All was the same as I arrived for my interview the next day. Miss Cosway's secretary smiled when I entered the room and gave me the quick once over to ensure I passed muster. Apparently I did, or at least once I had responded to her hand gesture to straighten my tie. Nodding, she gestured to the door to the inner sanctum of Miss Cosway's office and returned to the seat at her desk. .

I knocked twice, trying to be decisive but not too Wagnerian in my approach.

"Come!" sounded a shrill voice from inside the office.

I was confronted by a space which must have been sixty feet long and twelve feet high at its apex but no wider than ten feet. It had cathedral or castle like proportions. At the end of the room behind a sizeable wooden desk sat a figure outlined by the bright sun from the window behind her.

"Forward young man, I have not got all day," added the voice as if talking to a recalcitrant horse. I moved forward across the uneven floor which defied anyone walking sensibly in a straight line.

"Hmm. Not a military man are you?" asked the chatelaine. The grey suit clearly doing its job as a tool of first impression. This seemed a very strange start to a conversation about accommodation but I played along, anxious to pick up any clues which might help me to secure accommodation.

"Not presently, but I'm considering a career in the forces at the end of my degree," I offered, slightly disingenuously. I would have considered a role in the Armed Forces, but only if HM Government had signed a disclaimer stating that they would not expect me to bring physical harm down on another person. I felt it very unlikely that they would accede to this request, nor would they allow my complete career to comprise of flight training and permanent attachment to the Red Arrows. So truthfully, I probably wouldn't be seeking employment in HM Armed Forces.

"I would strongly suggest you follow up such employment young man."

"Yes indeed." I replied with mock enthusiasm, but no firm level of commitment on my part.

"You are looking for university accommodation for next year, despite being a second year?" was her next succinct statement.

"Ubique!" I replied.

"I beg your pardon young man!"

"The badge on your desk – it is the Royal Artillery badge – Ubique everywhere" I ventured, hoping to pick up on her military leanings.

"And how would you know that?"

"My father was a gunner in the Second World War."

"Really, and where did he serve?"

I reeled off the list of my father's training and deployment areas as well as I could remember from conversations over the best part of twenty years.

There were training camps in Sheringham in Norfolk and Walney Island, both of which he described as godforsaken windswept areas.

I looked up to see Miss Cosway had cocked her head slightly and removed her glasses. I took this as a positive sign to blunder on.

I outlined how, as a family, we had toured northern Europe in 1967. My dad was looking to find places at which he had served. We couldn't afford to go as far as Arromanches where he had landed in 1944, a week or two after the initial waves of troops on D-Day, but we chased all over northern France, Holland and Belgium. I explained how my father seemed to have very clear views of a "little square" in most towns he served in, which in northern Europe is nothing like as specific as he might have been! We turned countless corners to be confronted with 'a little square' with a café in it which might or might not have been the square in question. Nothing lost though, as there were thousands of other little squares to choose from.

He did find the point where his unit has set up their 3.7in Anti Aircraft guns to shell the German garrison on Walcheren Island. This was to prevent them disrupting the resupply of Antwerp. He also remembered the unit downing a Dakota which failed to show the colours of the day! He ended the war guarding the Prinz Eugen at Wilhelmshaven. The vessel later met its fate in the Atomic tests at Bikini Atoll having been part of German reparations to the United States. I paused for breath at this point thinking that I had added too much detail and anxious that I could not remember anything else to add without straying into more ephemeral territory such as a girl called Yvette from Ghent, that my father had dallied with and with which he sometimes good naturedly taunted my mum if he wasn't getting his way.

"Young man, it is rare to meet someone of your generation who has a proper respect for the experiences of the generation who fought in the wars."

"For all its terror and deprivations, I'm not sure I'll experience anything in my lifetime which matches what my parents lived through," I answered truthfully.

"Good man," said Miss Cosway.

I seemed to have struck the right chord as she continued, "Right, accommodation. I have nothing at present for second years but you will go to the head of my list should anything come up. With third year students and graduates taking priority over second years I cannot guarantee anything for September though, so you need a contingency plan to tide you over until I contact you. But rest assured that I will support the earliest consideration of your request."

She got up and shook my hand very formally whilst surprising myself by finding that I'd come to attention. I glanced at a photograph on the table, which up until now I'd only seen from the back. It was of an officer in the khaki uniform and black beret of the Royal Artillery and a neat black ribbon covered one corner of the frame. Clearly my story of my dad's exploits had struck a chord for, given her age, the smiling, self conscious soldier was probably a brother or boyfriend who didn't return from the war.

Strangely enough, this wasn't the last time that my dad's wartime exploits in the Royal Artillery were to serve me well.

I had every confidence that Miss Cosway would come up trumps for me, but even her best efforts couldn't find university accommodation for me until the following Christmas so I threw myself on the generosity of my friends for the autumn term of my second year.

In many cases, the generosity of friends did not extend as far as an offer of accommodation for other than a few nights of settee time or temporary space on a mattress, but I was grateful of any night's sleep frankly. I learnt a lot about people from viewing their accommodation from floor level. Under miscellaneous items of furniture, in that term, I found a pair of handcuffs, a cheque book, a scuba flipper, some dirty magazines, a quarter of jelly babies with a tube of KY jelly hidden in it, and assorted pairs of girl's knickers. Not all in the same accommodation I hasten to add and, as the respective owners were at pains to reassure me, there was a perfectly acceptable explanation for why such items were lurking on the floor. Many seemed less keen to share that explanation with me, and, being the grateful guest, I didn't press them.

My lad friends saw my plight as a practical one and simply offered a settee/ mattress full stop. Girls tended to be 'holistic' in the provision they provided. None more so than Dora, who with boyfriend Colin, put me up for a couple of months in what was to become a legendary student flat in Heslington Road.

I'd known Colin and Dora from the first week of the first year. They were in the year above me and you couldn't think of Dora without Colin or vice versa. They seemed to complement each other perfectly. University was made for Colin. He had a rapier like mind and could dissect an idea to infinity. We shared similar tastes in music and he would often surprise me with a compilation cassette of bands like Genesis and, post Genesis, Peter Gabriel.

Colin never did things by halves and he had the best stereo system I had seen to that time. Once he set his mind to something he would read up and become expert in it in a remarkably short time. Colin didn't do mediocrity.

Dora was a whirlwind of happy energy. I hoped Colin realised how lucky he was to have her as a girlfriend, and I think he did.

I spent that summer with them in Heslington Road as I'd reasoned that it would be easier to find work in York than in Rhyl. I was wrong in that assumption, for with a recession kicking in, neither Terry's nor Rowntree's required my services and were in fact laying off casual workers. I was forced to sign on, which had not been part of the plan. It would have been a depressing summer but for Dora and Colin.

Dora included me in everything they did. We visited Scarborough on the train and headed out for picnics in the country. Sometimes we just sat in the living room listening to music from Colin's collection. Whenever I'd been out, Dora always welcomed me with a shout of "David!" almost as if she was genuinely surprised to see me. I think it was part of her half Greek heritage and it certainly brightened up that summer to be included with them, almost as a younger, rather feckless brother. If we had nothing else on in the morning, we'd hurry to the bakers at the end of the road to get the freshest bread baguette and race back to eat it, still warm, with tomato soup. Dora's dad was a grocer in Nottingham and, given her mum's background, she had experienced a whole range of food that was alien to me.

Dora, unlike many of the girls I came across, liked to cook and used exotic ingredients like olive oil. The only olive oil I'd ever come across before was kept in a minute bottle in the medicine drawer at home. It had been used on me only once and was warmed up and poured into my ear, secured by some cotton wool to ward off a particularly painful ear infection. I had no idea it could be used for cooking.

I'd watched Dora deftly pour some into a pan to warm, thinking she must have one monstrously bad earache. She added herbs and seasoning followed by an onion which she diced in a blur of flashing blades. Given the volume of ingredients now in the pan I thought she might have a sore throat, but then she diced some tomato as finely as the onion and added that with a flourish of pepper from the pepper mill! It dawned on me that she was actually cooking, rather than preparing a poultice. She cooked with a precision and a finesse that I'd never seen before. She was clearly enjoying herself rather than simply preparing a meal. That just about summed up Dora's approach to everything really.

"David!" she exclaimed enthusiastically, "Please pass me the courgettes!"

To my shame, I didn't know what a courgette was. I thought it might be some kitchen implement like scissors, a plural word for a single entity.

Perhaps they were for straining the mixture of onion and tomato. I looked around blankly for any kitchen implement that I couldn't put a name to. Nothing sprang out at me from around the kitchen, no metallic implements or mashers, dicers or sprinklers.

"Sorry Dora?" I said, feigning deafness and hoping she'd be a little more specific by pointing in the general direction of the courgettes. True as always, Dora pointed to the anonymous brown paper bag on the draining board. I picked it up and looked inside. It appeared that Dora had done a deal with the grocer to purchase under-grown and probably under-ripe cucumbers. Perhaps there was a secret organization of grocers into which she had been inducted by her dad. God knows what they'd taste like and why would she want these now, as we clearly weren't having salad?

To my surprise she chopped the *so called* courgette as deftly as she had the onion and tomato. I noticed that the skin was more like a marrow than a cucumber, clearly a different cucumber variety and, unusually for Dora in the cooking arena, she had cut them thicker than I would have liked or expected. Still, as a guest, it wasn't for me to question the way she prepared the food that she had graciously invited me to share. I was ready to field the mini-cucumber and place it in the fridge so that it would be proverbially cool when we were ready to eat it, but to my horror, Dora scooped up the lot and added it to the bubbling pan.

Although this might be perfectly acceptable in Greece, I felt an involuntary shudder and could feel my face screwing into that look of revulsion my mum made whenever anyone mentioned foreign food. I hoped Dora wouldn't look at me at this precise moment.

"Do you like ratatouille?" asked Dora.

I wanted to appear non committal, and tried to work in the Kipling joke – do you like Kipling? I don't know I've never Kipled. I realised it wouldn't work with ratatouille.

"I don't know, I've never tried it," I replied honestly.

"It's gorgeous, I could live off it," she enthused.

So that night the three of us ate royally off ratatouille, with my contribution being the freshest of fresh French sticks from the bakers and a pack of Lurpak butter to set it off. It felt like picnicking in the house, and I even took to the mini cucumber things which had soaked up the olive oil so effectively.

Yet again I was on my uppers that summer. With a job failing to materialise, I had been forced to sign on and presented myself once a week to the job centre to see if there were any vacancies and to be officially recorded as among the list of the unemployed. It was a miserable experience and the thought that I was not doing anything productive was really frustrating. I determined that I would never be in this position again.

There had been considerable delay in sorting out my benefit payments and when a postal order finally arrived for £39 for the six week period I was mightily relieved. The postal order also gave us an opportunity to get one over on the shopkeeper who doubled as the local postmaster in the shop down the road. When we had had the unfortunate experience of going into the shop to buy stamps or a paper, he could be heard, holding forth to all and sundry about what was wrong with the nation, how the death penalty should be re-introduced for shoplifting, how he would personally pay for the boat, and consider it exceptionally good value for money, to repatriate every foreigner from the country. We hated entering his shoddy little shop to see his ugly, moaning face and unwashed shirt glaring at us.

Knowing we were students seemed to incite him more and he grudgingly passed our change out, one coin at a time under the metal grill behind which he was imprisoned. I therefore waited until all three of us were available before going down to the post office to cash my giro to the astronomical value of £39.

"I'd like to cash this postal order from the government please," I started and watched as his hands involuntarily clenched into a fist.

"So," asked Colin, "what are you going to do with all the money the government has given you?"

"Sex and drugs and rock and roll! The rest I'll probably fritter away," I replied in words calculated to push the postmaster to the brink of apoplexy.

"A barrel of beer, we could buy a barrel of beer or two and spend the week drinking it!" added Dora uncharacteristically as she didn't even like beer.

"I like your thinking," I replied.

"So, run it past me again, how did you get all this money?" questioned Colin.

"Mostly it involved sitting on my arse not doing anything, then going to say hello to a gorgeous girl at the Jobcentre once a week – easy peasy," I said firing for effect at the hapless postmaster.

He did everything he could to try and prevent payment, ensuring that I had a valid giro by holding it up to the light and examining it in minute detail.

He was in physical pain as he counted out seven crisp fivers, three pound notes and a variety of small change to try and inconvenience me. I equally slowly counted each note he handed over, the slower he went, the slower I went.

Customers in the shop could clearly see the game and were chuckling, their shoulders lifting up and down.

"Now get out of my shop, you're barred you bloody sponging students, you're barred! To think…"

I just know he was going on to say "I fought a war for the likes of you" and I moved in quickly to add, "To think, my dad fought a war to eliminate small-minded, racist, fascists like you from spouting their bile. Luckily the post office has provided you with a cage from which to spout your pathetic, ill informed views!"

I thought the use of racist and fascist in the same sentence was a little superfluous, but what the Hell. We turned and headed out the door laughing.

We heard "Bloody students!" called after us and ran home laughing down the street.

Chapter Six
BOO

Being a relatively small university, York could not attract the biggest of bands for concerts. Whilst each college hosted reasonable sized local and even national bands at the May Balls and Central Hall had the likes of bands like Lindisfarne, and the legendary Horslips, ours was not a venue as enticing to the big bands as Leeds for example, where we regularly watched Thin Lizzy.

York made up for this by having an interesting range of speakers from Politics and other fields. There were speakers from British Nuclear Fuels, arguing the case for nuclear power. I asked a question in their presentation that had people congratulating me at the end of the talk. Their spokesperson had deflected questions about nuclear safety by explaining the odds of a nuclear meltdown. Calculations were brought forth freely which estimated the chance of the occurrence as being in the order of a million to one. Other potential disasters such as terrorist attack and earthquake were, we were reassured, as, if not more, unlikely. It all began to sound rather complacent, so I asked my question.

"If we assume your analysis is correct in terms of the likelihood of a disaster occurring, what contingencies have you got in place for the inevitable day when something does happen?"

The man stopped in his tracks, and began to reiterate the likelihood, by event, of a disastrous event occurring.

"I'm not asking about the probabilities, but the contingencies when one of these events occurs."

The man went back to talk of the odds of any individual disaster and the chairperson brought the proceedings to an early close. Some of the radical anti nuclear faction, came and patted me on the back for having cornered the spokesman, when they had failed in their posturing. It actually worried me that the basis of the safety policy was a mathematical model which suggested anything untoward was "unlikely to happen". It seemed like putting a scientific veneer on an argument that was clearly untenable. The argument put forward had no greater validity than the odds on a horse winning the Grand National! I was suspicious of the nuclear power industry after that.

We had a visit from Ted Heath, by then in his twilight years, having been eclipsed by the Grantham grocer's daughter. I was hugely disappointed by his talk that seemed to point to a world recognisable only to him. He used a phrase several times which he had clearly picked up on his travels, to deflect any questions he did not want to answer.

"You seem to be suffering from a misapprehension, I fear you may have been suffering from it for some time!"

It drew a laugh from the Tory stalwarts but it was too well rehearsed. It was a glib and self-serving response and a glib and self serving talk. I wondered how people like that rose to high office, seemingly unrestricted by creative thought or charm and full of erect smugness. In short, he confirmed my suspicions about the Tory hierarchy, although technically, Heath could not be considered a Grandee, being a Grammar School boy.

An eagerly awaited talk was one given by ex convict John McVicar.

It took place in a relatively small lecture room in the Physics block with no more than thirty people scattered about the seats. Clearly McVicar had had less effect on others than on me. To the right, physically and politically, sat a phalanx of Tories, come as a mob to tame the former public enemy number one.

I must admit I chose to sit a few rows back from the front. Having vivid memories of one John Mc Vicar mugshot, appearing, sneering and growling out of the black and white television set in the sixties. He was always being sentenced for some hideously violent criminal act or staging an audacious escape from a maximum security prison like Durham.

Professor Taylor had recounted how after one of his visits to the prison to deliver a course to prisoners, McVicar had come forward to thank him for the course, which he had found most enlightening, and to apologise for not being able to attend the remainder of the scheduled lectures. Professor Taylor had thought little more about it, assuming that McVicar was being transferred again. That week John McVicar escaped from the maximum security wing.

Across the country and on television the same picture always appeared. It reminded me of Tim the Alsatian dog who would have savaged me as a child had not the rickety wooden fence prevented it. This was McVicar, wild, dangerous and unrepentant.

Professor Taylor having completed his introduction, I waited for the doors to open to reveal a snarling Mc Vicar, like a manacled King Kong. Behold, the criminal wonder of the age!

An academic rose on the front seats and adjusted both his reading glasses and the papers he held in his hand. The man was nondescript and slightly vacant, the way serious lecturers are. He wore jeans and a cord jacket in a biscuity shade. He turned to the gathered throng, took off his glasses, and announced in a London accent how glad he was to be there and invited questions. None of the audience had recognised this person as McVicar and he had been there all the time we were waiting for the lecture to start. Indeed, had we been told that this was **the** McVicar, we would probably have laughed and denied the possibility.

A thick set and sweaty Tory boy, with a tartan tie, egged on by his friends launched into a tirade of condemnation about McVicar's crimes and the remorse he must now be feeling and how prison had tamed him and acted as a sharp deterrent.

McVicar smiled at what must have been an habitual question for him. He adjusted his glasses one more time and replied with a measured response.

"Well," he began, "the picture you have of me as a highly successful criminal who stared out at you from wanted posters (and he seemed to be looking directly at me) is all very well. But I would dispute that picture of me as a successful criminal. I've spent a fair proportion of my adult life in jail and I came to the conclusion that I was not that successful as a criminal so I decided, of my own volition, that I was going to give that life up and begin a new career as a sociologist. To that extent I am not reformed, I have simply chosen a different path in life."

The Tory cabal was both frothing and speechless at the same time. They had expected to be able to bamboozle the London mobster McVicar with a tirade against him and his kind and the need for a short, sharp shock approach to law and order that would put people like McVicar in his place. He had disarmed their arguments in one sentence. The talk explored in some detail the origins of criminal activity, penal reform and punishment and rehabilitation.

I still tip-toed out at the end, anxious that the mild mannered raconteur and serious academic might turn, werewolf-like back into the snarling villain of old.

Chapter Seven
BLISS

We didn't know it at the time, but the summer of 1976 was to prove a scorcher. Talk of hosepipe bans was not cause for alarm, nor the beginning of a global overheating catastrophe, but merely the symptom of a long spell of fine weather.

My Part 1 examinations had finished a few days before and, like those who had finished before me, I now took my place on the falling piece of grass that edged the lake behind Goodricke C block. We must have looked like pink sated crocodiles gathered there, too lethargic to move, drinking in the sun's rays.

It had started three days before when the biologists had completed their exams and had taken up their place next to the watering hole. There must have been sixty of us gathered there now, all lying on the brown and orange checked top covers of our College beds. The space between us was slowly reducing as more exams finished and I foresaw a time, like in the African wildlife films, when one overheated crocodile would snap and there would be mayhem on the banks of the lake.

Not that we would enter the lake as we had all heard the stern warnings of the campus authorities about the lake not being a suitable venue for swimming. Simon, complete with white coat and wellingtons and looking like the traditional "man from the ministry" had done an analysis of the water. What he had found had shocked even him in its biological toxicity. Even the massive carp were lazily shimmying across the surface of the lake, desperate to take on board more oxygen than the murky depths afforded. I swear I heard one of the fish coughing in the centre of the Lake.

A philosopher, complete with a small pencil case and a sheath of last minute revision notes hastily crossed the bridge heading for the examination venue in the spaceship that was Central Hall. He received an ironic cheer from the sunbathers behind Goodricke C block and made an appropriate hand gesture in response. Simon started on a loud, beer-fuelled slow chant, "Phil-----os----o---pher!" and everyone but the philosopher started laughing, only too conscious that a day or two before they were the one's hurrying belatedly to the exam room. I recognised the late student through the blur of my badly applied sun cream as Vinny, a dour lad with a beard, from the depths of some Birmingham suburb, with a drooling accent and melancholic take on life and everything really. He called all the girls "Chick" and used the word "Yam" effusively, and not to refer to the tropical vegetable.

He was dressed in his habitual green corduroy jacket, brown cord trousers and black Chelsea boots. He looked warm in the middle of winter, but what had possessed him to dress like this for the heat of a Central Hall examination grilling was beyond me.

I said he came from Birmingham, but that wasn't strictly correct. A term or so earlier he had button-holed me in one of the college bars and we'd had an animated conversation, as only student conversations can be, about accents and class.

He had been really put out about me describing his accent as "Birmingham", more put out than even our beer intake should have warranted, and he took me aside, like the Ancient Mariner with the Wedding Guest, to put me straight on a few things.

He gave me a social geography lesson on the Black Country, of the long chain making, colliery and saddlery traditions of the various constituent towns in the Black Country. He talked of the land of the "Yam–Yams" and other things that left me confused. Pies and Methodism he declared as the two constituent parts of his Black Country heritage. He described a land not unlike Sparta, in which strength and physical prowess was prized above all and insisted all Black Country women looked like Ursula Andress emerging from the steamy Caribbean in that Bond film, although he admitted that there was a fair probability that their blond hair was as likely to be from a bottle as to be natural. He said the sexual voraciousness of the Black Country women was legend, but that the local Methodist elders had tried to suppress this reputation and had largely succeeded.

He was glad, he said earnestly, that he had done well enough in his A levels to have at least three years respite from their persistent attention. In fact, he felt that had the exam results not gone in his favour, he might well have had a banishing order placed upon him. He then took a long swig of his seventh pint of Guinness and fell silent. He sucked me in, and in the pregnant silence of a few seconds I had to ask the question, "What banishing order?"

"Well," he started conspiratorially, "I fell out of favour." And he scanned the room conspiratorially, to make sure no-one else could hear his words.

He explained that he hailed from the epicentre of the Black Country in Tipton and in fact had grown up on an estate so impenetrable to outsiders that it was known as 'The Lost World'. Things worked differently in the

Lost World and growing up he had had fine physical prowess, was fleet of foot and strong of arm. I looked him over sceptically. He countered my scepticism saying that he had been one of the Harriers – the absolute physical elite of Tipton. I looked non-plussed.

"The Harriers – Tipton Harriers – elite Sports club – green and white hooped vests – always winning races in the Triple A championships. Roight!"

I slowly cottoned on, nodding open-mouthed, in partial recognition.

"It was the A levels that did for me, all that studying. I started missing training sessions but I kept up the high protein diet of Black Country pies. I slowly metamorphosed into the fat bastard that stands before you," he stated flatly.

"I've a lot of gym based work to do if I ever want to return to Tipton!"

As it happens Vinny was on for a triumphant academic return to the Black Country if the result of an earlier examination paper, sat just before Christmas was anything to go by. The question had been put in a Philosophy/Semantics paper:

Discuss the proposition that the number of bears is three?

He swore that in reply his truncated answer had read: *God Knows!*

And he had received a 2i for that insight! That conversation more or less summed up the problem of engaging philosophy students in any type of discourse as they wove such a complicated web with words that it was impossible to glean fact from fiction.

Vinny had disappeared from view now, his flat footed lope, which had left the metal framed bridge vibrating, receding into the distance. Two and a half hours of intense sunlight had left me wondering whether he had ever really existed or whether he was a figment of my imagination.

The bank fell silent, apart from Davy's tape selection which was, as if by auto suggestion, currently playing Lou Reed's *Perfect Day*, and it was. Or rather it was until Sandra, a long curly haired streak of a hyperactive girl, in the middle of the dulcet line 'You're going to reap just what you sow,' shattered the mellow mood with the unhelpful question, "Does anyone want a cup of tea – I'm going in to make one so I can easily make more than one. Or coffee, I can do coffee just as easily. I think I might have some biscuits as well. I think the bourbons have gone. Jeff, have the bourbons all gone? Did you finish them last night or did you leave any? It doesn't matter though because I bought a packet of digestives two days ago at Hillards – do you remember Jeff, because that old lady said, I'll never forget this, she said that she hadn't seen hair like mine since the war. Didn't we laugh Jeff, Jeff didn't we. Right, I'll go in and put the water boiler on and I'll come back with a pad and take orders."

"You can take mine now Sandra – just bugger off and shut up – not necessarily in that order," said an anonymous voice from the bank that sounded suspiciously like Marco's.

"You are so cheeky!" riposted the irrepressible Sandra. "Isn't he so cheeky Jeff! He's always saying things like that to wind me up!"

But everyone knew the truth. Sandra was one of those insufferable people who meant no harm but in whose company nobody felt relaxed. Jeff was a saint among men to put up with her, her endless fidgeting and tidying, her incessant need to fill any silence with mundane drivel and statements of the obvious. Despite this, we would all defend her against anyone from outside the group who pointed out her shortcomings. That was the nature of friendship in Goodricke. I was thinking this benevolent thought when she appeared in the window of a ground floor room.

"John, John, I hope you don't mind but I'm in your room, it's just that I can't serve the tea and coffee from my room because it is on the second floor, so I thought I'd come into a ground floor room and open the window so that I can take the orders and serve them from the same place. This way I won't have to walk all round the block and risk spilling the drinks, they'll also be hotter as well. It could also be dangerous on the bank, carrying hot drinks on that slope, I might lose my footing and then where would we be – casualty with second degree burns no doubt! I certainly don't fancy a trip to casualty in this weather – it'll probably be full of people who are badly burned because they didn't put on some sun cream in this intense heat. And she nodded almost imperceptibly at Kim who had, as Kim always did, gone for the instant suntan, courtesy of extra virgin olive oil. Another use for olive oil, I thought casually, although I wondered if anything but 'extra virgin' might be more appropriate for Kim.

"So John, I hope you don't mind me using your window like this John. I promise I won't spill anything on your carpet – and if I do I'll clean it up straight away because I got some cleaner and disinfectant whilst Jeff and I were at Hillards the other day. It isn't specifically for carpets, but I'm sure it would stretch at a pinch – you might have to dilute it with water though."

The anonymous voice ventured that he'd like to dilute her, Sandra, with water, a lot of water! In fact to the uneducated eye it would look like she had been drowned.

Sandra droned on, "I've brought my milk and tea and coffee down from my floor – I won't be using any of yours – I can't be doing with people who use people's food and drinks without asking first."

This was very true. Sandra, when not talking the hind legs off a donkey could be equally irritating with her notes:

This Strawberry and Passion Fruit Yoghurt belongs to Sandra and her lovely Jeff. Please be so kind as not to eat it when you come in late at night with a bad case of the munchies and we will both be very grateful.

This was written on a square of strawberry coloured note paper and held in place around the yoghurt pot with a matching red elastic band from her companion writing and stationery pack. The writing was in distinct copper plate executed with fountain pen.

Sandra would have been livid to have found that, despite the use of blotting paper to dry her missive, the damp conditions in the fridge had led to her beautiful writing running. She need not have worried about that though as what she found in the morning was an empty yoghurt pot with a new note scribbled in pencil which read, *Yummy, Cheers Sandra!* which started the investigation of the handwriting of all the inhabitants of C block. She never did realise the early morning feaster was none other than Jeff in an increasingly rare act of rebellion.

"Don't tell her it was me! Don't tell her it was me!" he later begged us, rocking backwards and forwards in the plastic chair in the kitchen, his hands clenched white above his head.

I'm not even sure which is yours anyway" Sandra continued on, "and, by the way, you should know that there is some milk that is past its best in your fridge. Well past its best!" she added with more than a hint of disgust. "I've got my pad with me so I'm taking orders now."

"What colour pad are you using for taking the orders?" asked Ann in playful mood.

"Well it is very thoughtful of you to ask Ann. I did toy with blue, but I thought the sunshine yellow better captured the spirit of the day – so I went with that!" The intense deliberation that had preceded this choice of paper colour explained Sandra's ten minute absence from the scene.

"Right who is for tea?" and she proceeded to write down the names, in full, of all those whose hand was up or who had shouted out, double checking the order after every second entry. She wrote in her copper plate script, *John L, tea with two sugars,* adding a final full stop with a flourish normally associated with primary school girls when they have completed a poem.

John P, tea with two sugars. (John from Chorley with skin problem.)
She added to avoid any confusion with the other John. She had added the words *with skin problem* because she couldn't bear to utter the word acne except in a mouthed whisper like Les Dawson used when he chatted over the fence in his sketches as a Lancashire mill woman.

"Can't you just tick a column called tea and put a cross equal to the number of sugar someone wants?" asked Marco helpfully, "and we might actually get to drink it before the day is out."

"Noooooooo!" retorted Sandra dismissively, rolling her eyes to the heavens. "Just think for ONE minute about the capacity for confusion! And there is nothing worse than not getting the beverage you ordered when you have had time to savour its arrival!"

This was the latest in Sandra's list of things that there was "nothing worse than". Having given up the receding prospect of being able to drift off on a sun-induced nap I piped up.

"Dysentery."

"Dysentery what?" enquired Sandra suspiciously.

"Dysentery, thank you," I added, making out that my answer had fallen below the required level of politeness and placing Sandra in the position of the disapproving school ma'am that she so relished.

"No, what do you mean dysentery?" she enquired, seeking clarification.

"Dysentery – dysentery is worse than not having the beverage you ordered, I think."

The crowd caught the mood and added their own thoughts about things worse than not getting the beverage you ordered.

"Syphillis."

"Childbirth."

"Crabs."

"Being crushed by an anaconda."

"Being kicked in the Balkans."

"Being torpedoed in the Baltic."

The increasingly hackneyed replies came and the mood subsided into quiet giggling.

"Trapping your willy in a vacuum cleaner!" chimed Animal, a little too stridently, "I should imagine," he added as if to clarify that this had not, in fact, happened to him, which did not dispel the mental picture everyone now had of a dispirited Animal presenting himself and his mother's upright hoover at Casualty on a lazy Sunday evening and juggling whether to use as explanation 'I tripped and fell onto it' or the more truthful 'I haven't got a girlfriend'.

"You lot are so naughty, I don't know why I bother, I really don't," giggled Sandra, not picking up on the irritation and almost murderous intent in our teasing.

We knew we would all be the verbatim subject of Sandra's diary that night and that the beverage list would replace the yoghurt message in pride of place on the notice board in her bedroom – another of Sandra's golden memories.

Over the lake in Wentworth College, someone, and it was probably irritating Nick, had filled a Fairy Liquid bottle with water and was squirting cold water over the girls in their bikinis. They rose up in real irritation but Nick carried on regardless, like a six year old miscreant on a public beach. My thoughts turned to sniping rifles and cross hairs and a single shot echoing off the lake and the CLASP and breeze block walls and then…silence.

Perhaps Sandra, well meaning, intensely irritating Sandra, was not so bad after all.

"Do you think she can stop herself?" asked Marco.

"Who, Sandra?" I clarified, "No, I really don't think she can."

"It's like an illness with her – this constant need to say what's in her head." continued Marco, "She left a message in our kitchen last week that read *Don't make any plans to use the kitchen between 7pm and midnight as Sandra and Jeff will be entertaining and will not be requiring any more guests that the scintillating company invited! You have been told!!!*"

Sandra was, if not a red rag, a pink gingham tea towel to Marco. Then again they had shared the same corridor and, therefore the same kitchen for two years. She was slowly driving him nuts. He had inflamed the situation by scrawling – *We have been told but have we been ASKED!!!* on her note.

This had gone down very badly and had ended with Sandra, usually immune from hint or personal insult, reaching into her cupboard and throwing a full bottle of peanut butter at Marco. Marco had sidestepped and it had hit me in the hip. I hate peanut butter at the best of times, but this assault with a peanut grenade had stung actually and metaphorically.

Most of the sunbathers were now too tired to speak and, eschewing any form of sun cream, save for the few hard core sunbathers like Kim, who had doused themselves in a liberal emulsion of olive oil (a trick they had learnt on holiday in Benidorm), were lying there burning as if on a voluntary rotisserie. There was very little movement save for the habitual squabbling between the coots and the moorhens, and the involuntary out breaths of the bathers as they hauled themselves from side to side or back to front as the heat of the sun began to burn.

A dozen transistor radios played low and Davy, completely in character, had hooked up his stereo system through adjacent bedroom windows on the second floor to provide a full stereo experience shoehorned onto a series of his famous compilation tapes. Apart from the prospect of the sleepless night to come I knew my burning skin would afford me, I could think of few times when I was happier. I lay squinting in the relentless sunlight and thought of equivalent blissful days.

One immediately came to mind. It was the Thursday of our last week in primary school and we had been marshalled from Victoria road over the Vale Road Bridge to the outdoor swimming baths next to the Floral Hall on the promenade. For once, as we entered past the turnstile the temperature indicator was set at 72 F – this was almost tropical compared to the 47 F with which we had started our weekly swimming lessons some six weeks earlier. We actually enjoyed being in the water this week and there was a general feeling of bonhomie amongst teachers and children based on the shared knowledge that this would be the last occasion we spent such informal time together, for tomorrow would be Prize Day and sad goodbyes to Emmanuel and all that we associated with our fantastic school.

As we were being marshalled together, and the last kids who had risked lacerating their tongue with the exceptionally salty crisps that were sold in the little tuck-shop at the near corner of the pool joined our crocodile, I looked around my classmates; everyone was brown, smiling and animated. The sun, ricocheting off the blue water of the pool, made them look an angelic host, if you squinted. Collectively we looked like the cover of a Beach Boys album extolling the virtues of surfing and for a few seconds, despite this being north Wales, we were all California boys and girls….

At that moment, a blue Frido ball with the pimples that dug into your foot when you kicked it and a game of football under the pier were all that were needed to attain perfection. A young Lou Reed, penning *Perfect Day*, would at this point be reaching for his rubber (or eraser as our American cousins would have it) and trying to find something that rhymed with Frido. My patch of blanket behind Goodricke College was undoubtedly another one of those days.

It was at this point that Barry arrived fresh from whatever had detained him on this beautiful day. Whatever had detained him must have been a reasonably formal occasion as he was dressed in his habitual grey jacket, jeans and trainers when everyone else had made the effort to accommodate the sun. "Wotcha!" he announced to no-one in particular. There was a collective muttering of welcome which was as much as we could manage in the enervating heat.

"Barry, aren't you a tad hot?" asked Ann as he slowly barbecued in his jacket.

"No, not at all actually, I've read up on yogic temperature control and I've mastered the art of regulating my internal body temperature by separating my mind from my physical body."

I waited for Marco to come in here with some pithy words but he was silent, either sleeping or squawked out from the recent encounter with Sandra.

No doubt Barry had, once again, been in the more obscure sections of the JB Morrell Library. I admired his thirst for knowledge; nothing was too arcane for him to taken an interest in it. In fact, the more obscure, the more interested he was in studying it. Last week he claimed to have mastered yogic flying with a guy with a beard called Trevor. He claimed it was an out of body experience in which they flew around Trevor's bedroom until the positive karma left them and Trevor knocked over his stereo system which had brought them back to Earth with a bump – literally. He talked with an intensity which was sincere and disarming, illustrating his experience with liberal use of adjectives and sometimes pausing with gravitas to conjure up just the right word to describe a phenomenon.

Mischievously, I'd suggested the same sensation could be obtained from a quickly drunk bottle of Don Cortes, several snakebites, or our old favourite, football, a long, hot sauna and a couple of pints of shandy. Barry had insisted his had been a deeply religious and that Trevor was, rather implausibly, his Yogi. I resisted the temptation to add "Bear?"

Trevor had never struck me as the yogic master type. He appeared to have problems simply getting dressed. His thick black beard and black framed glasses were most usually associated with a red patterned lumberjack shirt and dirty jeans. Trevor had the habit of starting every utterance with the exclamation "Ha!" as in the way he had accosted me in the junior common room once when I'd been happily reading the sports page of *The Guardian*.

"Ha! What **you** seem to be forgetting is that I come from that part of the Wiltshire Dorset borderlands in which a deeply traditional conservatism can be squared with an enthusiasm for Europe based on historic patterns of trade dating back to medieval times!"

Clearly I was being sucked into a vortex of one of Trevor's internal conversations here. This statement was delivered as if it had been the latest in the list of conversations we had had on the subject. He had positioned himself so that I was not able to simply get up and walk away. He seemed to delight in doing this, and in breaching the social distance that was kept when you spoke to someone in this country. Many of the girls had been unnerved by this as he spoke too loudly and too close to them. It was difficult to decide if he knew the social rules and was deliberately pushing his luck or was genuinely unaware of the social niceties. No doubt in years to come this would be described as a 'syndrome' but at the moment it was simply Trevor being annoying.

"Ha!" I replied mimicking his openers in an attempt to open up a channel of communication on a level that he would hopefully understand, "What *you* are forgetting is that I've never had such a conversation with you and am not remotely interested in any aspect of Conservatism, except its early demise!"

It went quiet then as he processed the information and I genuinely did not know how he would react. The potential range of reactions clearly lay beyond what anyone could normally expect and a fight might not be out of the question.

The reaction when it came was preceded by a significant period of blank faced conjecturing which was again longer than the socially acceptable time to have a bearded man staring at you.

"Ha! Bravo, good point. Ed 'Stewpot' Stewart – genius or buffoon?" Trevor ventured, as if he was trying to lighten the atmosphere and move the conversation onto a more socially acceptable subject, although his thesis seemed too close to the heavy historical books he was prone to devote an unhealthy amount of time reading.

Ed 'Stewpot' Stewart was the avuncular host of a Saturday morning radio programme in the days before television stretched throughout the day. The show consisted of children writing in to request an unlikely selection of 'children's favourites' which all had the ring of the sort of 'tunes' parents would request on their child's behalf. In many respects, this programme was as niche as the output of John Peel in his desire to promote new bands. Ed 'Stewpot' Stewart was preserving a comfy parent friendly vision of fifties middle England populated by the witterings of middle of the road comedians and their inane novelty records.

Whenever I heard the theme music for that show I could see, in hues of greens and browns, with which I always associated the Fifties, a father sitting, smoking a pipe and wearing brown trousers and a green sleeveless pullover with rolled up shirt sleeves reading the paper in his well upholstered chair adjacent to the fire. A boy and a girl snuggled on the rug at his feet. The blonde haired girl was reading a hardback book – Black Beauty or something of that ilk, whilst the tousled haired boy, who was invariably, named Richard or Anthony, giggled at the antics of Desperate Dan on the cover of the *Dandy* and took occasional licks of his sherbet dab.

The white highland terrier, Rags, snoozed unconcerned in the range of the radiated heat from the fireguard, and dreamt of whatever moved a Highland terrier to contentment. Mum could be glanced through the open door to the kitchen, smiling inanely under her immaculate coiffeured hair, and her tidy floral pinafore dress, wearing an unfeasibly high pair of stilettos for the task in hand, which was cake-making.

None of this rang true for my household and I deeply resented such a comfy picture being applied as a stereotype for a lifestyle I'd never known.

While I was conjuring up all these associations Trevor had started on one of his legendary lists. This one was of the records that constituted the oft repeated playlist of Stewpot Stewart. I was clearly meant to comment on each record in turn….

"Ha! Three Wheels on my Wagon, original song by Burt Bacharach and a collaborator, recorded by the New Christy Minstrels"

"Jolly, but essentially crap." I replied.

"Ha! Agreed." replied Trevor, before embarking on his next tune, "Max Bygraves *You're a Pink Toothbrush, I'm a Blue Toothbrush*, written by Irving Halfin, Dick James, David Ruvin and released with the Children's Choir in 1959," said Trevor as if he was reading from a book rather than recalling this from memory.

"Essentially crap and not at all jolly," I opined confidently.

"Ha! Wrong!" interjected Trevor without further explanation. I couldn't believe that Trevor, with his classical music leanings (he was often interrupting the Sunday Night Goodricke disco by talking loudly to the wall about specific movements in Beethoven Concertos, (until the DJ played the Moody Blues *Go Now* and everyone joined in and pointed at him until he took the hint) could consider any merit in this monstrosity of a fabricated song. Clearly there was some emotional association, perhaps to a childhood time, when the weight of his encyclopedic knowledge had not hung so heavily on him. He wasn't sharing any such insights though and proceeded to the next song.

"Ha! *Hello Muddah, Hello Faddah* by Allan Sherman released in 1963 it reached number 2 on the Billboard Top100 on August 24th?"

"I thought that was called *Camp Granada*?" I said.

"Ha! No it wasn't, but a board game was developed from the song called *Camp Granada* that was released in 1965.

"I loved this song – always made me laugh," I added and began to quietly sing the words.

"Ha! Correct!" replied Trevor who was already moving on to his next little pearl, with no interest in accompanying my singing which had now reached the refrain *Take me home. I beg you*….

"Ha! *Side Saddle* by Russ Conway?"

"A pleasant enough tune but it has no place on a children's request show – that is something for your old auntie!"

"Ha! An interesting thing about *Side Saddle* was that it was released in February 1959 by Russ Conway on Columbia Records and spent thirty weeks in the charts with four weeks at number one."

"Ah! But Trevor can you tell me its catalogue number?" I asked seeing if I could derail this musical Juggernaut with a carefully placed pothole.

Trevor thought for no more than a couple of seconds, as if a lady librarian in pearls and a twin set was thumbing through a card index and came up with the answer which Trevor stated loudly and with enthusiasm, "Ah! Columbia DB4256."

I had no reason to doubt him.

This session continued for another half an hour until Trevor came up with songs, which were even beyond my recall in childhood – Trevor was still going strong though, like a marathon runner on steroids.

"Ah! Pinky and Perky, puppets created by Jan and Vlasta Dalibor for the BBC in 1957. Sang lots of songs. Mike Sammes was the voice on the records."

The name Mike Sammes brought back horrible memories of late Sunday afternoons with Mike Sammes and his legendary singers 'Singing Something Simple' to appeal to my parents. It sounded like treacle covered in custard and then wrapped in toffee apple toffee and inserted in your ears. I hated those cloying melodies and the accordion changing key from one tune to the next with a vengeance. My mum and dad couldn't get enough of them though. I abandoned all though of the saccharine coated Mike Sammes and tried again to stop Trevor's verbal onslaught.

"But Trevor, which one was Pinky and which one was Perky?" I asked thinking this would send his brain into meltdown.

"Ha! Perky usually wore a hat."

I let thoughts of Trevor drift away and slowly fell asleep with Davy's summer sunbathing selection playing in the background and a contented Sandra slurping her tea. Life really could not get much better, examinations over, a sunny summer ahead of visiting friends across the country and a second year at university beckoning so long as I had mastered that Statistics paper.

The euphoria was broken by waking suddenly with my body on fire and my skin stretched tight in all the wrong places. I really should have taken up Sandra on her offer of sun cream.

Chapter Eight
MEDICAL

I'd always had a general disdain for the medical profession. I'd been more than happy to consult them in an emergency, but for more routine affairs I'd always worked on the premise that if the old bod was generally in good repair 'if it ain't wrong, don't fix it!'

I'd been spoilt as a lad because our family doctor was Tommy Lamb, who had gone through school with my Dad, where their career paths, despite starting in the same class in grammar school, had veered off in different directions. Tommy had gone on to medical school and my Dad had been forced to leave at 14 due to the Great Depression. Nevertheless, they were reunited when Dr Lamb had set up practice in Rhyl. All our family were registered with him at the practice surgery in the grand Victorian house with the stained glass windows opposite St Thomas' Church on the corner of Bath Street and Russell Road.

I was always fascinated when we visited the surgery to walk on the parquet flooring in the waiting room, which my dad always reminded me had been laid by my grandfather. We'd wait in line at the counter and whoever was accompanying me would give our name and address to one of the three well-manicured ladies who would riffle through the medical notes in their severe buff envelopes. If you had arrived without making an appointment by phone there was always much tutting and muttering under breath, for that made you one of the spanners that clogged what was otherwise a well-oiled machine.

Having braved the receptionist and been mustered onto their list, you were beckoned to sit down in the seats that lined three sides of the room. It was a large room that had quite clearly been the sitting room or 'front room' when Clarence House had been a private residence.

In one corner of the room, what had once been a doorway had been glassed in with decorative frosted glass. It seemed, improbably, to lead into some sort of garden with ferns and foliage. It left me with the impression that it could be the portal to enter Narnia or that, at night; the grandfather clock in the hall might chime thirteen. I always aimed to sit on the seats nearest the frosted glass and this was not just fancifulness on my part. Admittedly a glimpse of Aslan or some other mythical character or creature had first motivated me to sit here, but the glass doorway was the only part of the wall perimeter which did not have a chair against it. That meant that the person sitting there only had one other ill person sitting next to them.

This was a major consideration when the room was surveyed, especially in winter, for all the usual suspects were in. There were overweight fifty year old men with rasping, rattling coughs who we'd pass at the entrance to Clarence House feverishly dragging on a Senior Service cigarette before pinching them out between brown nicotined finger and thumb, ready to light up again as soon as the ordeal of the medical appointment was complete.

"It's me chest, doctor, I seem short of breath, can't understand it, think it might be the ole' bronchitis playing up again. I was right as rain last week!" they'd wheeze, genuinely surprised that there might be a link between their forty a day smoking habit and their colander lungs. Still, they'd grown up at a time when adverts had extolled the virtues of smoking as medically sound.

There were little old ladies in headscarves and faded patterned coats in mustards and browns whose reddened eyes were barely open with tiredness and who cocked their heads over to one side to control the throbbing pain from their ailment.

Harassed mums with tousled hair struggled to control piercing, monotone, crying babies who lay lie starfish in their fleecy one piece suits, red cheeked and snot bubbling.

Discreetly buried in one of the woman's magazines which they had carefully selected from the stout dark oaken table in the centre of the room would be the girls in their twenties in their improbably coloured shoes and fashionable coats and meticulous hair. They didn't look ill to me and I remember being hushed up when as a very small boy I'd asked, "Mum, what's that lady doing here she doesn't look ill to me?"

My mother went red and hushed me and I could tell from her sharp, narrow-eyed expression that my legs would have had a slap had she thought she could get away with it.

Some people made their ailments particularly obvious with bandaged fingers arms and legs that I imagined hid hideously fractured bones or suppurating gangrenous wounds. It was only later that I realised that in my head, part of me lived my imagination in a Hieronymus Bosch landscape of unmitigated horror. I was never closer to this image than when I was in the Doctor's surgery.

If we were particularly unlucky, and we habitually were, we'd end up sharing the surgery with Mrs MacColoran and one of her brood. Mrs MacColoran lived on the estate and was the epicentre of the earthquake that was the MacColoran family. A small lady with thin wiry features, darting black eyes and jet black hair, she was never at rest. The MacColoran family numbered…to be honest I don't know how many children it numbered. In no particular order there was Ciaran, Gregory, Declan, Niall, Vincent, Sean, Terry, there was an elder girl called Consumption, or something like that, and who had left home to go to a convent, Peter, Adrian, another girl who always winked and blew kisses at me whenever she saw me whose name when written down looked like Raisin, but was pronounced Rosheen, Barry, Dermot and Brendan. There were also the dogs – three retired greyhounds that always accompanied the children and were called Fergus, Carrick and Enya. Fergus was a brindle, Carrick was missing part of his ear and Enya was a beautiful honey colour.

When Mrs MacColoran called the family into dinner from their play on the estate she made no distinction between the children and the dogs.

"Brendan, Róisin, Declan, Enya, Ciaran, Barry, Peter, Carrick, Vincent, Dermot, Adrian, Sean, Fergus, Niall, Terry, Gregory – your food is on the table and going cold!" she'd shout from the entry between the two houses so that her voice projected outwards and upward and across the estate in a surprisingly angelic lilt.

Whether they were huddled in dens near the allotments, crouched in conspiracy in someone's shed, playing football on the clinic field or fishing in the Cut, it was always, surprisingly, Róisin who heard the note first, closely followed by the dogs who would sniff the air to determine the direction home and they'd all be off and running in a MacColoran stampede.

Today the surgery had been graced by Vincent who was the most diabolical of the clan. He sat directly opposite me, blocking out my imperfect view of the passing traffic and the church opposite through the net curtains.

At the tender age of six he had dedicated himself to total and unconditional mischief. I knew from past experience and my mum's advice, that the thing to do, but the very hardest thing to do, was to totally ignore him in the hope that he would get bored and move on to torment someone else.

I tried desperately to look anywhere in the room but at him, but eventually I was drawn in. I tried to focus past him but he was like a target on a radar scope. Eventually my eyes focussed on his crew cut head and flashing eyes. Whatever ailment had brought him to the surgery had not dampened his spirits. He smiled at having caught my attention and pulled a series of faces, screwing up his nose and squinting through narrow eyes. I managed to look away and earnestly studied the public health notices that were neatly arranged as small posters on the pinboard above the ornamental wooden mantelpiece under which a large gas fire hissed a monotonous note and spread soporific heat and fumes into the waiting room.

Apparently, coughs and sneezes still spread diseases and immunisation was the way forward in defeating the childhood scourges of polio, whooping cough and measles, mumps and rubella. Nothing had changed from the last time. My attention wandered in the gaseous heat and before I knew it I was back in the basilisk stare of Vincent. This time he was sniffing hideously to keep my attention and giving me the V sign alternatively with his left and right hand.

I appealed to my mum, sitting next to me, hoping my facial gesture would alert her to the miscreant's antics but she was deep in some recipe in *Women's Realm* and would not re-emerge until our name was called on the tannoy. I realised I was on my own to resolve this situation.

At that moment, the tannoy crackled into life and I prayed that my or Vincent MacColoran's would be the name called out.

"Thomas Edwards to Dr Parry" came the call and the torment went on.

Luckily for me, Thomas Edwards had vacated the seat the other side of my mum and I now gave up my corner quarantine seat to quickly occupy it. This quick thinking had put the aspidistra plant on the oak table between me and Vincent's stare and I savoured my victory. Although I could no longer see him I could savour his discomfort and he tried to compensate for not being able to see me by setting up a loud and hideous coughing fit in which I feared he'd cough up his entrails if he felt he could better me. This brought a timely and loud rebuke from Mrs MacColoran,

"Vincent, yer little bugger, will you stop that silly coughin' now!"

I couldn't resist it. I craned my head around the side of the aspidistra and smiled with some satisfaction at the now silent and rebuked Vincent who was red-faced and bloodshot of eye from his coughing exertions. He glared daggers back at me and I knew that this was not over.

The tannoy crackled again and I listened for our name. It was Doctor Lamb calling the young girl, who got up and rushed out of the waiting room faster than I thought necessary. This was bad news indeed for we would be left in the room for at least another fifteen minutes whilst the girl, who did not appear ill, spoke with the kindly Doctor Lamb.

The tannoy crackled once more and the elderly lady to my right was summoned on creaking knees to her appointment. She turned and levered herself up the frame of the chair to bring herself up to a standing position.

She was obviously in great pain. I thought myself very lucky that I'd never be that old.

To my horror Vincent was on the move, first to the oak table and then to the box of wooden toys underneath it. He edged across the room, coming in and out of eyeshot like some hideous serpent, making his way inexorably to the seat that had just been vacated. Armed with a cartoon book and a wooden toy he sidled onto the seat, feigning disinterest in me. I looked to my mother, miles away in the *Women's Realm* where a particularly natty Fair Isle jumper knitting pattern had captured her interest. Across the room, relieved to be briefly alone, Mrs MacColoran was deep into some tale of woe on an agony aunt page of *Women's Weekly* – as if her life were not troubled enough – somebody else's misery relieving her of her own. It was just me and Vincent and a roomful of disinterested sick people, and now he was smiling malevolently at me.

For a while he just grinned like a maniac and then he slid down the canvas seat, of the sort we had in the Hall in school, and sat on the floor feigning to play with the wooden toy. I stared resolutely out of the net curtained window opposite.

I couldn't help myself; I looked out of the corner of my eye and saw him placing the book next to my leg so as to conceal his intentions from the rest of the room. Silently I looked at my mum and at him several times to alert her to his foul intentions. She was busy knitting one and pearling two in her mind's eye and had no time for the trepidation her son was in.

Then two dirty fingernails closed on a hair on the back of my leg and pulled. It hurt. Not in a fatal, agonising sort of way, more the shock of an unprovoked assault on my person. I turned and looked at my mum in an incredibly pained sort of way but she was sorting out the intricacies of the patterned side panel of my latest woollen jumper and was toying with the idea of complementing it with a matching balaclava.

"Don't react to provocation, and above all, don't ever make a scene!" had been a homily my mum had readily delivered to me despite my incessant 'Buts' and 'What ifs'.

"But what if, by saying and doing nothing, someone got run over?"

"That is hardly likely to happen." countered my mum, with a note of finality.

This would be the test of her advice as Vincent, disappointed in not having drawn a reaction from me, moved to pinch me again, no doubt harder this time. This is what happens when you ignore someone, I'd be able to trumpet. Had I been old enough to have been familiar with it, I could have run out the failed argument put forward by the appeasers in the 1930s.

He pinched again, harder to ensure he drew blood this time and I whelped loud enough to be sure that my mother and his mother would have to react. My mother lifted her head from her knitting pattern and frowned at me for showing her up in the waiting room mouthing "Ignore Him" through tight lips.

From across the room, without even seeing what had happened or raising her head from her magazine, Mrs MacColoran, correctly sensing that her child was the centre of some kerfuffle shouted melodically, "Vincent, whatever it is you are doing, stop it immediately you irritating devil!"

Vincent quickly sat bolt upright and made to be deeply engrossed in reading the book, looking over with wounded innocence towards his mother, in what was clearly his standard response to a rebuke.

There followed a tense impasse in which I knew he was going to strike again once the fuss had subsided. The room fell silent with only the hiss of the gas fire and the occasional coughs of the old smokers and the young baby who had given up his struggle and was being rocked into almost peaceful sleep on his tired mother's knee.

Vincent bided his time knowing I was going through traumas in the waiting. I had moved from passive acceptance of this fate now, and was calculating whether I could angle my leg to kick him in the face and legitimately claim it as an involuntary spasm brought on by the shock of being pinched. I decided that it was worth a try.

He pinched, I kicked out, and all hell let loose.

He really pinched hard this time so I felt fully justified in lashing out with my right leg. He had the foresight to be moving away from me so it was the sole of my new Clark's Wayfinders shoes that caught him flat on the face propelling him faster than he had anticipated into the horizontal position which he was trying to assume to put distance between his hand and my leg so as to feign no knowledge of what had happened to me.

It was a real stroke of good fortune that my Clarks Wayfinders were new, as the animal footprints moulded on the sole were still intact. His left cheek had the distinct impression of a red fox's paw welting up on it and I had every reason to be pleased with my nature related handiwork.

Vincent looked genuinely shocked and unsure how to react. One of the old men looked at me for a few seconds and I thought I must be rumbled, but then he winked in appreciation.

Vincent had now set up a loud howl, not unlike that of a fox, I imagined, in appeal to his mother. His mother was not about to find her son appealing though. In a shrill banshee cry she screamed, "Vincent, you little bugger, I'll be taking my hand to your face any minute now!"

And Vincent cried all the more.

I was able to savour his demise for no more than a couple of seconds before over the tannoy crackle the reassuring tone of Doctor Lamb rang out.

"Mrs Hughes and David to Dr Lamb please!"

I was relieved to be able to leave the room before my mum could ask any searching questions and before Mrs MacColoran had time to reconsider her apportionment of blame. My hand was on the ancient wooden door handle and out onto the intricate pattern of the tiled floor in the Hallway at indecent speed and I did not wait, as I usually did, for my mum to pass through the door first.

Dr Lamb's surgery was everything you would expect it to be. An ancient roll top oaken desk was set along one wall and on it were arranged an instrument for taking blood pressure that I never got to have a go on, a beautiful fountain pen, two piles of patient notes in thick sepia envelopes being moved after each consultation from one pile to the other of which my mum's and mine were now displayed in front of him, a crisp white pad of prescriptions ready to be crafted with the fountain pen, one of those torches with a cone on top that they looked down your ears with, and an ashtray with a cigarette sending coils of smoke up to the ceiling.

In the wooden divisions of the roll top desk were papers and Quink ink, documents and assorted medical magazines, each division performing a function and full to capacity with material. On top of the desk was a large jar, half-full with dolly mixtures and I looked forward to choosing one of the jelly drops at the end of a successful medical examination.

Behind the desk, and thankfully obscured from view near the full size window, was a glass and metal cabinet on wheels with a range of medical instruments and a metal kidney dish on its top. This was for serious medical stuff and I went to the surgery on the strict understanding that I was there for an 'Open wide' and AAAAH as I gagged on the lolly stick thrust to the back of my tongue; the woodpecker tap on the front and back of my chest; the cold stethoscope repeat of the tapping whilst breathing in and out and a swift look in my ears, nose and throat with the conical topped torch. Doctor Lamb would nod sagely, let my mother know that it was nothing to be concerned about and raise his half-framed glasses to write out the prescription in a flowing but undecipherable script which always translated into sticky strawberry flavoured medicine, two tspns, four times a day.

Fear of the medical kit obscured from view behind the desk always meant that, no matter how ill I had been, my symptoms were always subdued by the time I arrived at the surgery. I once arrived, accompanying my mother who had a long standing appointment and complained of a tight feeling in my shoulder. Doctor Lamb could see my discomfort and asked me a few questions about this pulling pain before suggesting I remove my shirt.

To my horror, as I took off my grey primary school shirt, the problem revealed itself. In my rush after games in the Hall that morning, I'd been so keen to get dressed to go for our Friday fish and chip school dinner, that I'd put both an arm and my head through the sleeve of my vest. My mum was embarrassed but Doctor Lamb rocked with laughter and raised his feet from the ground in order to rotate back and forth on his swivel chair.

Today was to be different though. I'd never been summoned to an appointment at a hospital before and the result of this thorough medical examination would have implications stretching far into the future. Neither mum nor dad would be accompanying me and the medical examination would not be carried out by friendly Doctor Lamb.

The letter had been officious in the extreme – *Report to… Assess your medical condition and suitability to become an 'accredited teacher'*, even going as far as *Right to appeal*. This felt like a serious appointment and I determined to arrive calm and in plenty of time for it.

Anxious to know the format of the examination I'd sought Davy out (he'd gone through the medical at the beginning of the previous year) and had found him in the JB Morrell Library of all places. We made our way down to the snack bar for a pack of three Jaffa Cakes and a cup of tea and he enlightened me to the mysteries of the official DES medical for teachers. As anticipated he started off with some horror stories of large syringes and all too intimate examinations before realising that I was not rising to the bait.

"It's pretty straight forward really, ear, nose and throat, chest examination to make sure you are not a raging consumptive and Bob's your uncle except—"

"Except what" I pressed, although sensitive to another wind up.

"Well," said Davy, "the doctor was a young woman who did not look any older than us and she had been quite chatty all the way through the examination. We were just about finished and I was buttoning my shirt up after having the cold stethoscope treatment when she asked what subjects I would be teaching and when I said Social Studies, the mood changed and she asked me to drop my trousers!"

I studied his face carefully for any tell-tale signs of a smirk but he seemed genuinely baffled by her request and didn't seem to be making it up. I thought there must be something about his Belfast accent that might have provoked this, or perhaps she had fallen for his boyish charms and had taken advantage of him, in her medical capacity, but he added no more to enlighten me and we both returned to our Jaffa Cakes, deep in the enigma.

If it's worth doing, it's worth doing well and if it's worth going to, it's worth arriving early for! These were two of my dad's favourite homilies.

"Six years fighting for King and Country and that was about all I learnt," he'd tell me on a regular basis.

That and, "Up there you want it (tapping his head) and down there for dancing (pointing at his feet)! "

"These were the things it cost me six years of my youth to learn, and here I am sharing them with you for nowt!"

"I learnt about timing on the medium Ack-Ack, on the predictor of the 3.7 QF."

And he regaled me with stories of his time in the war, firing the QF – Quick Firing Anti Aircraft Gun. How he sat next to the gun and calculated the speed, height and direction of the target on the predictor, by all accounts a primitive computer, and shouted out smartly for the gunner setting the fuses. Always best to be ahead of time, whether it was when dealing with the Luftwaffe, any form of transport arrangement or interview. I imagined my dad blazing away over eastern England, whilst the Luftwaffe crews were still tucking into their breakfasts on French airfields.

"Thing is," said my dad, "you fire ahead of them and you are going to put the willies up them and they are going to miss their bombing run calculations, whether or not you hit them. Fire behind them, and you hit bugger all! Which is why the early bird gets the worm!" he stated, spectacularly mixing his metaphors, but making a surprisingly coherent point.

Nevertheless, and despite myself, I found that I had adopted the same attitude to punctuality at appointments.

So it was that I arrived forty minutes early for my medical appointment in the hospital in Bootham. I was so early in fact that I thought it would come across as a little obsessed to even register at the reception desk so I contented myself sitting in a faded plastic chair thumbing through back copies of *Horse and Hound* and *Yorkshire Life* which were spectacular in the dearth of interest they held for me.

Every few minutes I had an internal dialogue in which an insistent voice, which sounded rather like my dad's, suggested I should go and register and a second voice, more like my own, suggested I relax, remain calm and register as close to the appointment time as possible. After all I was in the right place – how long would it take to register. As always, I eventually gave way to my dad's voice.

I approached the desk and, with my best smile, passed my letter to the lady in the pink cardigan and the horn rimmed ornamental spectacles. All the secretarial type ladies seemed to wear a cardigan and ornamental spectacles. She smiled back and surveyed the letter. She looked at me, smiled again and reread the letter. She then removed her spectacles and let them hang at her chest by a leather thread and held the letter at arm's length. This seemed to do the trick as a light went on and she retrieved the spectacles and placed them back on her nose.

"Right time, wrong place, my love. This is Bootham, you want Monkgate. That's where they do the vocational medicals. Do you know the way?"

I was unsure and realised I had to wait and hear her reel off the instructions, giving me alternative routes and a travelogue, including places of interest and tea shops along the route, one of which, she did not mind admitting, did the best sultana teacake this side of Betty's! It was this shop that she and her sister, who came in once a month from Knaresborough, on the train, always more of an adventure on the train than on the bus, a sense of occasion, would meet up in before they went off on a shopping expedition. Well, they called it a shopping expedition, but it was more of a browse and a hunt for knick-knacks really, there were some Saturdays when they ended up back at the tea shop for an afternoon tea and cream cake without buying anything and wondering where the time had gone!

As indeed was I, who had the misfortune to be listening to this tale of inconsequential information whilst a large clock ticked off the seconds behind her. She still hadn't got to the Monkgate Hospital which was where I was due to be in less than two minutes now.

My dad's voice could be heard mouthing complacently, "Now if you'd only listened and reported to the desk as you arrived, which I'd suggested, all of this unpleasantness could have been avoided."

"Shut your face!" my internal voice exploded rather rudely.

I made a mental calculation that it was about a mile to the other hospital and I had less than two minutes to cover the distance – twice the pace that had left Roger Bannister – Doctor Roger Bannister – a crumpled heap on a cinder track. I would not have Chataway and Brasher as pacemakers, nor would I have the benefit of even primitive running shoes. As luck would have it, I was wearing my blue suede loafers, which, if truth be told, were not a shoe given to cruising along at high speed, more for loafing around in really.

"Got it!" I shouted to the bumbling receptionist who was now describing some enchanting floral print curtain material which her and her sister had seen in a back street haberdasher's somewhere along the route to my appointment and which her sister had said was very reasonably priced given the quality of the print and the weight of the material – you won't need lining material with those she'd said, and she was right.

"Must dash!" I added by way of apology for my hasty departure and turned on my heel to run the race of my life.

The first quarter of a mile was back down the entrance road with parkland to my right and an avenue of trees to my left. I'd set out at a tremendous pace, and it now transpired, without the letter! Would I need the letter, possibly not so I could press on. But this was foolish thinking – of course I'd need the letter – without it I could be any Tom, Dick or Harry turning up claiming to be me! Whilst thinking this thought I'd taken another twenty paces which I would now have to retrace back to the receptionist. I turned on my heel, cursing my inability to get even the simplest decision right this morning. And it had all started so well, if only I'd taken one of the forty minutes to read the letter carefully, I'd have had time to realise my mistake, shared the joke with the receptionist and saunter in my loafers down to the other hospital, perhaps pausing to window shop at the Monkgate Bar Model Shop on the way.

I retrieved the letter that the receptionist brandished whilst wagging the finger of her other hand in mock rebuke and tut-tutting. I didn't need mock rebuke, I didn't need finger wagging, quite frankly, middle aged woman or not, had I had the surplus energy to waste I'd have quite happily have punched her at this point in the game.

I went back down the avenue of trees and the parkland, slightly slower this time, and through the ornamental wrought iron gates, left onto Bootham and back towards the city.

I mentally rehearsed the route as I dodged wheelchairs, road sweepers, prams and people standing talking with bicycles slewed across my route –

all seemingly hell-bent on delaying me. A couple of hundred yards down Bootham I'd have a decision to make – straight on, through Petergate and bear left past the Minster or turn left and head down Gillygate. Which was shorter, no, which was faster? Gillygate would be less crowded that Petergate and the Minster environs which had a less than heavenly throng of aimless tourists all year round.

Gillygate, yes Gillygate it was then, obvious choice and I veered left off Bootham thinking that despite my feverish brow from the laboured running, at last I'd made a right decision. Then the doubt hit me, it was in fact significantly further along Gillygate and then right onto Lord Mayor's Walk than straight through the city and past the Minster – you'd said as much when you had taken your dad to the top of the Minster – you distinctly remember saying that from above you got a different view of how far the walls protruded out in straight lines to form apexes rather than right angled turns and if that was the case and Gillygate and Lord Mayor's Walk, which followed the route of the city walls was bound to be a significantly longer route.

I immediately thought of turning round and retracing my steps back to Bootham and left under Petergate Bar. I began to slow my pace gradually to protect my heels which were now blistered. I turned to retrace my steps, and to my horror, coming towards me were school children, hundreds of school children forming an immense crocodile heading for swimming, or on some cultural tour of the city. Whatever the reason for their being there, they were completely blocking my path. I turned again, my shoulders, back and trousers now drenched in sweat and continued on my erstwhile course, almost crying with frustration.

I finally made the sharp right turn of more than ninety degrees (my suspicion had been correct) into Lord Mayor's Walk. I was half running, half limping now, blisters and oxygen debt betraying me, and had the misfortune to be recognised by a gang of York St John's students who sang out their usual insult to the University students. I had neither the breath nor the inclination to send back the usual riposte of "Your dad works for my Dad!" which always sickened my sensibilities. This was a reference to the fact that the University of York had a reputation as home to a large public school contingent, to whom I was not very sympathetic.

Almost there, almost there, I thought feverishly. I was stopped by adverse lights at the Lord Mayor's Walk/Walmgate Junction and had thirty seconds to regain my composure. It was not nearly enough time and merely made me more aware of the sweat which encapsulated me. The lights changed to green and I hoped that the reception area to which I had to report would be well signposted as I fell staggering into the road.

Why? Why? Anytime in the last week I could have read the letter and sorted out the correct address. I made a mental note to double, no triple read any communication ever put in front of me that entailed appointments and addresses.

I was there. I was there, at the hospital, in through the main entrance. I was confronted with a dancing wall of directions to departments, such was my dizziness - Gynaecology, STD clinic, X ray, Psychiatry. It must be there somewhere.

"Can I help you?" asked the receptionist in a pink cardigan and ornamental glasses.

"Yes," I said, with a sense of déjà vu, hoping that cream teas and haberdashery would play no part in her answer.

"Teacher Medicals?" I breathlessly rasped.

"Down the corridor to the right, second door from the end," she ventured, not wishing to engage any further with the drug addled wretch before her.

"Teacher Medicals indeed!" she muttered under her breath, "What is the world coming to!"

I fell through the door of the clinic reception area brandishing a grubby and sweaty letter, "Hughes, David" was all I could manage to say.

"You're late Mr Hughes! I'll see if Doctor Marriott is prepared to fit you in – she doesn't have to, as your allotted appointment time has gone!"

I grimaced and indicated by international sign language, as words had now, quite literally, failed me, that I would just pop to the toilet.

A full bladder and a long sprint were never hearty bedfellows and I relieved myself with the exquisite joy that only a man who had run a mile in blister inducing loafers, carrying a gallon of liquid internally could appreciate.

I exited the cubicle and found myself washing my hands looking in the mirror at a sweating mess. A dainty squirt of the hand soap was not going to sort this wreck.

Off came the sodden jacket and the limp shirt underneath it and I set to with as many paper towels as I could muster to quench my leaking body. It was no use, the super-absorbency of the towels was no match for my sweat glands, no sooner had I wiped one swath of me dry than I was perspiring again. A middle age man entered the toilets, took one look at me and turned on his heel.

I tried washing my matted hair with cold water but it insisted on hanging limply to my forehead. In the end I placed my shirt over the radiator and stood near the open window hoping for no more than damage limitation.

I realised after a few minutes that I could not stay here indefinitely and shaking my shirt to try to maximise the drying effect, I was forced to redress. My saturated jacket now felt twice its normal weight. I could either wear it, wet look, which is a strange look for a wool worsted jacket to pull off, or drape it nonchalantly over my forearm. I decided on the latter look. Unfortunately this highlighted the clamminess of my shirt, and particularly my mangrove armpits.

I'd always had a thing about sweaty armpits and would do anything to avoid even giving the impression that I was anything less than underarm arid. I'd walked like a robot in examination rooms rather than reveal an indecent moistness. Today I'd just have to brass it out.

I was met as I re-entered the reception area of the clinic by the receptionist, gesturing towards the open door of the doctor's surgery. A white-coated short, pretty doctor was standing there with a less than sympathetic look on her face.

This was the Dr Marriott Davy had described. I followed her into the room unduly conscious that even my ears were sweating in that way that I'd only witnessed when Davy and Marco had tackled the fiery Ceylon curry. I thought a dolly mixture at the end of the examination was probably out of the question today.

Dr Marriott opened the discussion with some questions about my general health. Although panting still and able to string no more that a third of a sentence at a time I confirmed that I was in extraordinary general health, that I did not suffer from shortness of breath or palpitations and had never had any heart related problems. She seemed surprised.

She wrapped the rubber sleeve of the blood pressure thingy around my arm and proceeded to inflate it to the pressure where I though she had induced a heart attack. Still she inflated and still my blood coursed through my veins. Had I ever had problems with blood pressure? I gestured no through gritted teeth, unable to catch my breath.

I decided that I must fixate on something in the room and concentrate on it as hard as possible in an attempt to lessen my blood pressure and reduce the sweating. The sunlight raining through the window was shining on a silver kidney bowl on the doctor's desk and this was what I focussed on. The dish was full of liquid, yellow liquid. The kidney dish was full of urine! At this moment that was the most unwelcome liquid I could have imagined. Urine, on her desk like that! Disgusting!

"I'm just going to listen to your chest, can you take your shirt off please Mr Hughes." said Dr Marriott in an anodyne way.

As I unbuttoned my shirt she retreated to her desk and dipped her hands into the urine filled kidney dish. She caught sight of my look of disgust and said, matter of factly, having caught my train of thought, "It's disinfectant."

I feigned knowing that all along.

The stethoscope was refreshingly cold on my back but did little to quench the heat that was still radiating from my body. Clearly, the evidence was stacking up against me and she looked at me strangely and turned over my medical notes twice before writing down the latest piece of damning medical evidence on the form. She proceeded to a cupboard at the far end of the room.

"I'd like you to fill this."

She held a small plastic container into which she wanted me to present a urine sample.

It was all I could do not to repeat the words of Ronnie Barker in the new situation comedy that had aired a couple of weeks earlier, "What, from here?" but I thought better of it. The medical evidence was damning enough, no need to give her any further ammunition.

I must have looked somewhat nonplussed because she added, rather unnecessarily I thought, "I want you to go to the toilet and provide a urine sample and then bring it back here."

Clearly she had me down as both a physical wreck and a mental imbecile now. Nonetheless, I headed out of the consulting room and back to the toilet carrying the urine sample container with as much care as I used to carry the wine, as a server, at communion.

Peeing to order is always difficult. Peeing to order in a totally dehydrated state was next door to impossible. The more I got myself worked up about not being able to perform the worse it got. Everyone outside knew why I'd come in here. What was a decent period in which to decant a sample? I'd no experience of this sort of malarkey. A couple of minutes, five minutes? Surely ten might suggest some acute renal problem. I'd now been here fifteen and no amount of stomach muscle tensing was having any effect. I'd taken my shirt off again to cool down as much as possible and it was looking as if I was stopping sweating at least. Internally I was probably now as dry as a desiccated coconut. The omens did not look good.

After twenty minutes Dr Marriott and a porter entered the toilets.

"Mr Hughes? Mr Hughes are you OK? Why have you taken your shirt off Mr Hughes? Is there anything I can get for you Mr Hughes?"

There was genuine concern in her voice, which, in turn, concerned me. Why would a doctor be so concerned?

"Mr Hughes, is there anything I can get for you?"

Like a three year old I responded, "Can I have a drink of water, please."

Ten minutes later I was back in the surgery. I had provided one dilute urine sample and explained my dishevelled arrival. In the circumstances, explained Doctor Marriott, she felt it best that she tear up the form she had been so assiduously filling in on my behalf. She admitted to being perplexed at the way I had presented and was working on a hypothesis that I was suffering from either dengue fever or malaria. How we had laughed, me perhaps rather more than I should have.

We repeated the inspection and yielded a series of results within the spectrum of normal. I was both relieved and happy to have made her acquaintance. I buttoned the last button at my collar and was reaching for my jacket when she enquired which subject I would be teaching.

Not without some pride I announced, "Social Studies."

"Drop your trousers Mr Hughes," she responded in a hard professional tone.

Chapter Nine
OBSERVATION

"**R**ight *Mun*, great to have you on board, we'll have some fun in the next few weeks!"

Such was the introduction to Ieuan. Like me, Ieuan was part of the great Welsh cultural export to England. I immediately felt at ease with him as he sounded like all my south Walian relatives with a view on the world and a generosity of spirit that was infectious. As coincidence would have it he hailed from Treorchy, just up the Rhondda Valley from my relatives in Tonypandy.

"*Duw Mun*, we're practically relatives!"

That was the introductions out of the way and now it was down to business.

It had been eight weeks since I'd made the bus journey across York to Clifton Without primary school to ask the Head if I may attend the school at the beginning of the new school year as part of my observation period prior to starting my PGCE in October.

The Head had been a kindly man, hidden behind masses of paperwork on his desk. We had talked educational philosophy with the distant hum of young children enjoying morning break on a sunny summer's day. I could hear the half forgotten chants of games I'd played some fifteen years before.

Some girls were playing *Queenie O Cocoa Who's Got the Ball?* Others were doing French skipping using what I assumed was knicker elastic framed around two stationery girls' ankles whilst a third wove intricate shapes out of it, like a weaving machine, before jumping out of the elastic.

Mixed groups were playing tag, with the boys, all crew cuts and short trousers, being over boisterous as always. On a Victorian wall, for this was the age of the school, a neat grid of numbers had been painted in contrasting colours and a couple of boys were throwing a tennis ball, trying to hit each number in turn. They threw the ball as hard as they could, for the next person had to throw from where he retrieved the ball. If he failed to hit the wall, or the right number, there was clearly some forfeit in order, although I could not work out what that was. A crowd of onlookers were admiring the good shots, and deriding the poor ones, whilst waiting their turn to be summoned to play the winner.

The same coloured paint that had been used to decorate the wall with numbers had been employed to paint in a hop scotch grid and this was being well used by whirring and impatient girls with long hair and skinny frames.

Other girls gathered in tight knots to talk conspiratorially, alternatively grouping together so that their heads touched and whispering or shrieking out loud as someone made some comment, probably, I thought, about who fancied whom.

Standing alone near the bins was a plump boy, tucking into his lunch box with a fixed and determined stare. All the revelry seemed to pass him by. He was onto a packet of crisps now, having seen off his sandwiches with relish. I was unsure from this distance whether he had relish in his sandwiches, but he had definitely demolished them with gusto.

Several pairs or trios of boys were clearly in intense negotiation. They produced a wad of what appeared to be banknotes from their pockets and it was only then that the penny dropped that they were exchanging card collections.

Practice in this area had moved on from the Brooke Bond cards I would have collected with Animals of the World, Cars, Aeroplanes and Space Exploration as themes. I'd remembered the 1970 World Cup coins that were available from petrol stations, as were the complete list of FA Cup Winners coins – including the elusive Cardiff City –victors in 1927 over Arsenal.

The Brooke Bond cards were a doddle for me as Auntie Betty and Auntie Glad worked in a large café on the promenade in the summer and were able to get me huge stacks of cards from the catering packs of tea and coffee that were used there. The thirsty holidaymakers fed my collecting, so long as I could abide the strong, astringent aroma of industrial strength coffee, I could amass a complete collection with swaps in next to no time.

The coin collections provided with petrol were more problematic, as we did not own a car at this time and, but for the occasional donations from uncles, particularly those with no, or very young, children, I had no legitimate way of obtaining the coins to place in the holders of the cardboard presentation file.

I wondered what they were collecting now. I remembered in the late sixties cards started appearing with a thin sheet of chewing gum. It struck me that this was quite a change in our card collecting habits. Before, the cards had been the result of an incidental purchase by our parents, more often than not, tea, coffee, breakfast cereal with Hong Kong made plastic figures, and then petrol.

Now we were being asked to fork out directly on sweets, not that I would ever pay money for chewing gum in any of its forms. Ever since Mallie Jackson had shared with me the story of the lad who had been brought into hospital, when he was there having his tonsils out, because he'd swallowed bubble gum rather than spitting it out into a waste bin I'd never eaten chewing gum in any of its forms.

Mallie had said this was true, right, that the chewing gum had expanded in his guts and gone rock hard and no food could get past it. The lad had not gone to the toilet for a fortnight and all the food he had eaten had backed up so that although he had lost weight his stomach had swelled up enormously with rotten food and you could smell it all over the hospital ward. Mallie said they'd sliced him open that very evening as they thought he might explode if they didn't act quickly. He said that the boy's breath smelt of rotten fish and bins and that you could smell him all over the hospital when they did the operation and that no-one could sleep that night because of the smell and that some of the kids on the ward needed oxygen masks to keep the smell from them.

It sounded preposterous now but when I first heard it when I was seven it had made an impact and I was worried sufficiently never to eat chewing gum.

The content of the cards changed now as well. They were no longer in any sense educational. Most were American in inspiration and related to TV series or films that I had not seen. Had they been about *Batman*, *The Monkees* or even the *Banana Splits*, that would have been okay but *The Twilight Zone* and *Invasion of the Bodysnatchers* meant nothing to me. I made a mental note to check what the boys in the playground were collecting.

A crescendo of irreverent noise had attracted the Headteacher and he had made his way to the window. I had failed to register any change in the pitch of the general playground frenzy but the Head had an attuned ear. Stood there, magisterially framed by the window, he gazed on his domain. As if by magic, a ripple had gone out across the playground freezing all the children like statues in the game as it radiated outwards from the Head's presence in the window.

The noisy lads suddenly looked round, although it had been unclear who or what had alerted them, and froze on the spot. The Head smiled and wagged the forefinger of his left hand. The rebellion subsided and the group dispersed across the playground and spilled out onto the field.

"British Bulldogs!" explained the Head. "Strange really, we play Rugby League here – there is a local tradition and it is a safer and more comprehensible form of the game for the lads to get to grips with than Union. British Bulldog captures exactly what we want them to do in terms of tackling and evasion but they will insist on trying to play it on the tarmac. We've had a couple of broken bones which we'd prefer to avoid."

We returned to conversation about what I could achieve in my two weeks observation. It was clear that the term 'observation' was a misnomer. Any thoughts I had about sitting quietly at the back making notes were quickly dispelled. I'd be involved in the life of the school and would be expected to take part in the duties and after school clubs.

"It's valuable experience for you and takes a little pressure off our hard working staff as well. More fun than sitting in the back taking notes as well!"

"Absolutely!" I replied, unsure of my ability to handle groups of thirty children or present them with anything educationally meaningful with which to occupy their time. Strange, I thought how he had managed to read my mind.

I could enthral them with my MA thesis work of the last year, on the UN Arms Embargo on South Africa, but I couldn't help thinking that this would be of limited appeal. Similarly my forays into Macro and Micro Economics from the big Alchian and Allen book seemed lacking in colour. The work I'd completed with Jones the Industry on the French social historian, Emmanuel Le Roy Ladurie on the Peasants of Languedoc certainly had colour but was a little removed from the traditional primary school syllabus. I had a summer to become interesting, interesting enough to engage large groups of easily bored ten and eleven year olds. It seemed something of a tall order.

I glanced beyond the fish tank that had been turned into a worm habitat. I was sure there was a name for this but I couldn't for the life of me remember what it was. Across the playground the ringing of the bell by the duty staff had heralded the end of morning break. I wondered if I was making a huge mistake inflicting myself on the young minds of Clifton Without Primary School.

The Head, it appeared, had no such doubts and he popped up out of his office chair and ushered me out of the room to meet Ieuan Morgan, who was just starting a preparation period as his class were going over to morning assembly where the Head would corral them.

"Hiya, Davy boy," Ieuan opened, shaking my hand in his bear-like paw. "Good to meet you."

When he heard my pronunciation of Ieuan, he stopped and eyed me suspiciously...

"Not Welsh are you – most people struggle with my name?"

I confirmed that I was and that I had grown up next to a Ieuan and that my mum's family were originally from Tonypandy.

Tonypandy is a sort of watchword in Wales. To be from Tonypandy in the Rhondda Valley with its coal and radicalism was to be at the epicentre of working class Welsh culture. In Tonypandy, Winston Churchill is remembered more for his part as Home Secretary in sending troops to break a strike in 1910 than for his efforts in the Second World War. I was always proud to be associated with this history, as it appeared was Ieuan, who was from the next community up the valley.

"A fellow Socialist then? I'm telling you *mun*, come the revolution we'll bring the English education system to its knees. If every Welsh teacher in England withdrew their labour every school would be crippled – they'd be a nation of ignoramuses without us. The buggers have had our coal and our water, it's payback time!" and he laughed an unrestrained laugh that echoed down the Victorian corridors of the school,

"Only joking, mind," he added in mock seriousness as his laugh subsided, and not before two teachers' heads had appeared out of their doors to investigate the uproar. "Haven't got time for Nationalists me, too small-minded and chauvinistic for my liking – I'm a nationalist for eighty minutes when we play rugby and ninety when we play football and that's my lot! Right, come on over to Learning Central – that's my classroom, and we'll get this gig on the road."

This, my first encounter with Ieuan, proved typical of the man.

Learning Central was a mobile classroom which, from the outside, had clearly seen better days. There was rot where the glass met the window frame and the sage green paint that was always used to decorate the panels of mobile classrooms was sun-bleached and flaking in places. All in all it cut quite a forlorn picture as a seat of learning and I wondered if Ieuan had been quarantined out in the furthest corner of the yard in an effort to contain his infectious enthusiasm.

We entered the vestibule and Ieuan attempted to close the warped outer door in an effort to keep out the latest shower. Along the outer wall of the vestibule were the names of every child above the appropriate name peg. Each child had decorated their coat peg in a way that reflected their interests, there were trains and aeroplanes for the boys, business suits and, what I took to be pop singer garb for the girls. Someone called Cookie had broken ranks and opted for a remarkably accurate scaled drawing of a concert piano.

Ieuan stopped at the entrance door to the classroom and theatrically drew my attention to a large wooden sign with beautifully executed Gothic script on it,

Tremble all those who enter this Learning Room!

"Better explain this…" said Ieuan. "Truth is you've got to set a tone and have them treating the room with respect. The buggers need to know this is where the serious action takes place, We're not messing around when we enter the room. You are meant to leave it somehow better than you came in. So we have a little ritual like, where we all stop and tremble before we enter – gives a little pause for thought and no-one can say that they don't understand what we are about beyond the door."

He stood stock still as if transfixed and then started to shake his hands and ululate building into a crescendo after about five seconds and sharply truncating this with the word "Learning!" and a flick of the fingers of the left hand.

"I know it seems daft," he continued, "but it is the best way I've found to get everyone focussed and it means that they have fewer excuses to mess about once they cross the threshold. I came up with it because kids were turning up late with the wrong attitude. This way, everyone wants to be there for the Learning chant and they enter the room calm. If you are late you just get to say "Learning" and touch the door frame – not half as much fun. Do y'know, I reckon it is worth one to two minutes of what would have been wasted time at every break. My varmints are always first off the playground because of it. Lateral thinking see!" and he made the gesture that I'd only ever seen my dad use – tapping his head he said "Up there you want it!" and pointing to his feet, "and down there for dancing!"

"Look," he continued, "I'll not insist on it now but don't let me down on this – it works because we all take part in it so I'll need you to go through our little ritual every time you enter the room."

I liked the idea, just as one might appreciate a West End show, but I had no real desire to take part in it. It looked like I wasn't going to have an option. Clearly my 'observation' was going to be far more active than I'd hoped.

As we entered the room a lad jumped up from the piano, clearly he had been responsible for the intermittent notes I'd heard as we crossed the playground. My first thought was that he was in some form of detention but his words belied this.

"Cup of tea for you and our guest, sir?" he asked smiling.

"Smashing Cookie, that's the ticket!"

"How do you like your tea sir?" Cookie asked.

"Milk, no sugar please," I replied trying to define how I should react to a pupil.

"This is Cookie, our resident genius, he mouths the answer to me when I'm left flummoxed. I've had him propping me up for two years now. I really don't know what I'm going to do without him."

Cookie was busily mashing the tea into three school mugs and I wondered who the third one was for. He was quite a slender boy with a winning smile and the beginnings of laughter lines at the creases of his eyes. His eyes were his most prominent feature, deep brown disks with almost luminous whites of the eye. This gave him both lightness and an intensity. His hair was styled in what I'd once been reprimanded for as a 'Beatle Cut'. This style seemed to be contrived to hide as much as possible of his rather low slung and protruding ears. The fringe crossed his forehead about a quarter of an inch above his eyebrows in a style that I'd once been warned would provide 'a breeding ground for spots where the greasy hair met the greasy forehead!' Cookie still had a few years to go before having to worry about the onset of puberty and greasy foreheads I surmised, the lucky lad – all those bodily changes to look forward to!

His clothes were particularly neat and tidy – grey shorts, similar to the ones I wore as a child, and a crisp white shirt which had obviously been lovingly engaged to a fastidious iron for some time. He rested the third cup of tea on the desk next to the piano and went back to tinkering with the keys and making changes to some music which was propped up on the stand. I looked quizzically at Ieuan, not sure how openly I could talk with a pupil present. He picked up on my nervous eye movement.

"Don't mind Cookie, he's my oppo, my trusty lieutenant, aren't you Cookie?"

Cookie smiled and nodded distractedly as he made another amendment to the note sequence on his music sheet.

"Besides," said Ieuan, "he needs to crack on with the music for next week's concert. Bit of a musical genius is our Cookie, well all round genius really. He has written the Autumn concert for us and he just needs to fettle some pieces for the soloists. Great idea as well – *The Life and Times of Guido Fawkes* – really topical as well as he was educated just down the road like. Give Mr Hughes a blast maestro!"

I braced for a nursery rhyme chant and was met by what was clearly a full orchestral piece. After thirty seconds of what I would have sworn was the work of a Beethoven or Liszt, Cookie came to a crescendo and sat still, his fingers spread over the combination of keys he had last played.

Ieuan, picked up on my open mouth disbelief and whispered, "Never underestimate what can be achieved when sufficient encouragement and support is given!" More quietly, out of Cookie's earshot he continued, "Cookie certainly has a gift, but so has every other child you come across – the secret of teaching is finding and developing it."

"Cookie, have you calculated this week's attendance and done the dinner money reconciliation?"

The answer was a nodded yes from the distracted Cookie.

"Then be a scout and take it over to the Secretary's office for me then – see if we can be the first to hand them in – again! And don't let on that you've been doing them will you – or I'll be shot and then where will you be? I'll tell you – with a normal teacher – telling you to complete exercises 13 to 24 from page 60 onwards – and you wouldn't want that would you!"

"No sir I wouldn't!" said the smiling Cookie as he gathered up the register and the large envelope containing the dinner money and the calculations of which pupil had paid what. "I sorted Julie from the tontine," added the disappearing Cookie.

"Good lad Cookie, that's the ticket, not a word mind you!"

I looked at Ieuan at the mention of the word *tontine,* as I hadn't reckoned the word or the concept of a community social fund had travelled beyond Wales. Ieuan picked up on my quizzical stare.

"We've a scam going on the dinner money. It can be awkward and embarrassing when a family sometimes hit lean times. There are some proud people here and Cookie and I make sure that everyone can count on a cooked dinner without too much administration." He spat out the last word with some venom.

"But can't people apply for Free School Meals if their income falls below a certain level?"

"Yes indeed. But let me ask you this…did you receive a full grant for your three years at university?"

I reddened at the thought of the paperwork I'd filled in on my parents' behalf outlining their income and having official confirmation that it constituted so small a sum that I qualified for a full grant. I remembered my parents' relief that I was guaranteed that my education was not going to be compromised by their financial circumstances, like theirs had been by the Great Depression and Second World War. But there had also been embarrassment that a lifetime of hard work had not lifted them, in their late fifties, out of the clutches of a state handout.

I nodded yes.

"Well what you've just been playing out in your head is exactly the mixture of embarrassment and shame that the parents applying for Free

School Meals go through - not nice is it," he said, capturing my embarrassment precisely.

"So, whilst we can't stave off the inevitable for some people, we can make sure that they are not disadvantaged in the short term and it takes a while to process FSM paperwork anyway. So we even things up a bit – I put in some of my wages and we cream off a small amount from the takings of the Annual Fayre. It's a journey *mun*, everyone gets on the charabanc, and no-one…no-one is left behind."

It was the most eloquent exposition of Socialist values in action I'd heard and seen in a long time.

"With you!" I replied, meaning not only that I understood what had been said, but also I was with the enterprise on a philosophical level.

"*Non Pasaran*! They Shall Not Pass! Not Thatcher and not one of her bloody minions!" winked Ieuan, his voice betraying a steely determination in the wake of a few months of Tory rule.

Ieuan rooted out some documents about the work we would be doing in the next fortnight and I took the time to shuffle uncomfortably on the chair.

"So where did Cookie learn to play like that?"

"I'm not sure, he hasn't access to a piano at home, but his dad was a big NUR man, worked at York Station, and I think he started playing at the local Workingmen's Club. Either his dad was an inordinately heavy drinker or he learnt very quickly because he has been playing and composing like that from the time I've taught him. Light the fire Davy *bach* – in them rather than under them, that's the secret. Music's not my strongpoint, played trumpet at school, but haven't had call to reveal my *embrouchure* in many a year, if you get my drift."

I didn't as I was not familiar with the term *embouchure* nor the workings of the trumpet. *Embrouchure* had the sound of a sun tan lotion to it though, but that hardly fitted the context.

"I just make sure he gets as much piano time as I can so that the lad can get on with it. You'll meet his mam later. She's a cleaner here, works well really as he can play for an hour and a half after school and then head off for tea with his mam. I'm a bit worried about how he will fair in the 'Big School' next year though, doubt that they will be as accommodating, which would be a pity, still he can always pop back here after school."

Ieuan talked me through what was planned for the next fortnight. My idea of him as a chaotic influence was laid to rest by the military precision of his planning. Every child had an individual pathway through the work, with key points to draw out highlighted in different coloured pens. The main themes were highlighted as well as excursions into individual topics which would appeal to what he knew of each pupil's interests, and he knew a lot. Under mathematics, geometry, he had written navigation exercise. I'd asked how that was going to work and he outlined a complete theory for the teaching of mathematics.

It appeared that as a child he, and me as it turned out, had found maths difficult when there wasn't a context and easy when we could capture a problem in our heads.

"Area, see, that was always easy, it was always a garden that needed lawning or a room that needed carpeting – simple once you had the picture. But Algebra – incredibly difficult because I didn't know what x and y were see – had they been eggs or counters, I'm sure I could do it, but no-one could tell me what they were, see so I couldn't get my head around the problem. So I try and make everything visual to start off with so that they always have an image to work from. So next week we take the models of the lighthouse, the harbour, the headland and the oil tanker, which has now turned into an aircraft carrier, we made in art last week and we place them at carefully marked spots in the Hall. We've made theodolites out of a protractor and some string and paper and we should be able to make an accurate scale model of the Hall with all these features. They can mark out the angles between the features and we can check them with the master protractor in the centre of the Hall. Every team will produce a scale map and can convince themselves of its accuracy by measuring with the tape measure. What do you think?"

I was amazed that he had such confidence in the children to engage with a problem of this complexity.

"Nonsense!" he replied. "We've been working on changing attitudes for two years – I'd be insulted if they weren't up to it and actually this is just the taster for the main course…which is a scale map of our playing fields and buildings. I've blagged the use of a proper theodolite for a week from a parent who is a surveyor, it'll be brilliant! Better still, after school I'll work with a volunteer team of pupils and we'll map the whole York skyline from the centre of our playing field – it'll be a work of historical importance *mun* – something they can tell their grandchildren about, we can link it to photographs and have it properly printed so each one of them can have it presented to them when they leave the school – but they don't know that yet so keep stum!"

I was overwhelmed by his enthusiasm, the intricate planning and major scrounging which was underpinning the enterprise and the understanding for making the difficult conceptual elements real and visual.

"Brilliant!" was all I could muster.

"Glad you like it. So which piece are you going to teach? I'll launch with you on Monday and you can teach Tuesday then."

I looked at him for a hint of a smile but he appeared deadly serious. He handed me a copy of his master plan and asked to see my annotations for what I was doing on Tuesday by close of play on Monday. I sensed my weekend ebbing away in indeterminate planning for children I had not even met yet, to a standard that I considered to be close to Nobel Prize winning.

The bell sounded and I heard the avalanche of small feet crossing the yard noisily as the class returned from the Assembly. The chatter subsided as they lined up in the vestibule. Ieuan made a hushing gesture and from outside the room there was a loud ululation, a stamping of feet and, after five seconds, a cry of "Learning!" the door opened and a cascade of children lit up the room as they made their way to their desks and settled themselves for work.

Children, even of this age, were quite intimidating on mass and I momentarily reviewed career options, believing I had neither the skill nor the patience to achieve what Ieuan had achieved so seemingly effortlessly.

When they had settled down, Ieuan launched into his lesson.

"You see before you a happy and contented man. Proud I am, that apart from Phillip's visit to the dentist, never much fun at the best of times, (Phillip nodded in agreement at this point) we have achieved 100% attendance for the third week. Our esteemed Headteacher has asked if we can make it four weeks in a row. To be honest, I said that I didn't think we could, that it would be pushing you too hard. Four weeks in a row – that would be next door to impossible - what do you think?"

The children rose as one to declare their commitment to a fourth week of full attendance. Ieuan turned to me and winked conspiratorially.

"Well, if you insist, I'll let the Headteacher know that 6M are up for it!"

There was a quick cheer which was subsided with the raising of an outstretched left hand.

"The sun is shining, the week's heavy work is done, and I've arranged Art and PE on the field for this afternoon, followed by the award of certificates for this great week. Jane have you counted the nominations, and do you have the results?"

A pig-tailed girl in a floral dress, white socks and black shoes affirmed that she had done the required calculations.

"Good lass Jane – keep them guessing over lunch. So, all in all, we all have a wonderful weekend ahead of us."

There was a murmur of satisfaction of a hard week's work rewarded and then an air of anticipation fell on the class.

"So, that leaves us half an hour before lunchtime. How to fill it, that is the question. See, what we have here is a hiatus."

Ieuan wrote the word very deliberately on the board, and unprompted the children all reached into their desks and consulted their dictionaries. I was hoping he would not turn to me for a definition at this point as I'd probably have given myself a hernia trying to come up with a form of words to describe the word in a way that ten year olds would understand.

"Hiatus is our word for the weekend and you must aspire *frantically* to use it in a conversation with the folks at home and report back their reaction on Monday."

The children had whooshed with delight on Ieuan's heavy pronunciation of frantically – he explained later that he was on a mission to restore the colour to life and that involved the liberal use of adjectives to seed sentences with colour and vibrancy. The use of the adjective was the mark of the person at one with the world, as was despising the universal adjective, the one used when nothing better could be though of and that word, that terrible word was 'nice'.

"But wait, how remiss of me, I've forgotten the most important job of the day and that is to introduce Mr Hughes, a teacher of some repute, who will be joining us for a fortnight beginning on Monday. You have three minutes to ask Mr Hughes twenty questions to ascertain what measure of man he is. Starting now!"

I was so pleased Ieuan had not used the word 'student teacher' to describe me as I thought that based on my own proclivities at their age, I'd have believed open season had been declared on the hapless buffoon standing in front of them and trying not to twitch too nervously.

There was an initial silence as the children formulated their questions and I steeled myself for the inevitable "What is your favourite colour, which football team you support, what type of car do you drive?"

Sophie ventured forward first, "If your house was on fire what would be the three precious things you'd be determined to save?"

Having constructed a less than coherent answer to that question Mark asked, "What do you think about the Beeching cuts to the railways in the sixties?"

In a railway town, this was a question of some importance, and I was able to put together a more spirited response of opposition to the work of Dr Richard Beeching which was well received.

The questions were unrelenting and rivalled the grilling a politician might suffer on *Question Time*. I was pleased when question 20 was finally answered.

In this time, Ieuan had moved imperceptibly to the armchair at the opposite side of the room to his desk and the pupils were now baying like Labradors to be released from their desks to sit on the red carpet at his feet. With a gesture he beckoned them over.-

"This is no hiatus, this is the highlight of the week, *Question Time* with Mr Hughes followed by the latest instalment of *Tales of the Mabinogi*, so proud am I of your achievements this week!"

I couldn't believe that of all the books, this was the one he was sharing with his class – a classic book of Welsh folk lore, as read to me by the venerable Mr Ambrose a decade before. I sat as rapt as any of the pupils as Mr Morgan's voice galloped and pirouetted through the tales of Celtic derring-do and intrigue.

The chapter ended with the abrupt closure of the tome to a cry of disappointment from the children as they imagined the fate of Pryderi. All further conversation was lost to the insistent sound of the lunch bell and Ieuan bade them tidy up quickly before heading out to lunch.

"Carol and Jackie, remember what we said about young Anna – spend some time with her over lunch time and make sure she is OK and has plenty to eat."

It transpired that young Anna had her father in hospital at the moment with a heart problem and she was consumed by worry and was skipping meals. Carol and Jackie were the task force assigned to ensure she had a hearty lunch today, and as it was fish, chips and mushy peas, served family style, with the elder pupils serving the younger ones, I was confident that Anna would receive more than her just desserts today.

"Right, lunch duty, let's get cracking!"

We moved briskly into the playground. Ieuan stepped into and out of hopscotch, football and skipping games. I became a rather awkward spectator. I was happy to join in the games, indeed I had a very good reputation with my younger cousins as a fun sort of older cousin, but I found it difficult to square this with my new developing role as a professional teacher. I was conscious that Ieuan was a one-off. I knew I could not simply mimic his easy relationship with the kids; that would take more effort than the two weeks 'observation' afforded.

I drifted away from Ieuan, reckoning he would not want me as his shadow and that I would have to make my own way forward with the pupils. I felt as awkward as the Prince of Wales looking for a meaningful question to ask any youngsters who might listen "What do you do?" crossed my mind and was dismissed. "Who are you?" seemed too intrusive asked by an adult they did not know so I just tried to look in control, walking round in no specific direction and stopping at certain points to survey the domain. A morning of transformation from amateur student to professional teacher was proving too much for me.

Currently I seemed to be looking like a professional bollard standing in my dark trousers and light grey sports jacket in the middle of a writhing mass of ball-playing, hula-hoop toteing, screaming humanity. I'd spent the last five minutes practising where to put my hands. In my pockets? Too slovenly. Behind my back? Too austere and military, too Prince Phillip. I'd settled for by my sides and was now working this into a causal yet affirmative stance which said, avuncular with clear boundaries.

I was suddenly aware that a small and rather grubby hand had slipped into mine. I froze for a second unsure of what the protocol was in such situations. My first thought was to withdraw immediately but the little hand was now pulsating, willing me to engage hers and offer some security. Despite the inner uneasiness, I tightened my grasp and looked down to see who was so desperate for such reassurance. I expected the little girl to look up but she didn't. She clutched a rag doll to her chest with her left hand, the thumb of which she was sucking incessantly. She was latched on my hand with her other. Looking down on her I saw that her hair was black and matted. Her grey faded dress had an iron burn on the shoulder and looked as if it had seen previous ownership. She looked pathetically thin and abandoned.

I realised that it was not me personally she had fixed on, any adult would do. She simply wanted reassurance. She was flotsam and jetsam in this world and I was the first buoy with which she had made contact.

I wondered what had made her so indiscriminate in her need for reassurance that she would clasp the hand of a stranger in a crowded playground, but realised that this was a desperate track along which I did not want to tread.

I began to walk slowly around the playground and my partner promenaded with me right up until the bell sounded to announce the afternoon session. At which point she clasped my hand tighter for a second and disappeared off to her class without so much as a backwards glance.

"Well done," said Ieuan "Susie found you then? See that's the thing that kids and dogs have in common – they can spot a phoney – you can't fool Susie. If Susie has decided you are OK with all her problems, then you are OK with me! Right, go and get some lunch and bugger off back to your ivory tower for a weekend of sin and debauchery, you lucky sod! To get the fish and chips, tell them Ieuan sent you, and play the hungry student look for all it's worth!"

"Actually, could I join your class for the afternoon to see them in action?" I asked, not wishing to sound too Uriah Heep, but keen to see Ieuan handle the afternoon session and pick up further tips for the following week.

"Good man, no problem if you are sure I measure up to the alternative, which is an afternoon of idle student loafing – not mocking it mind, miss it dreadfully really! Get your fish and chips down you and I'll see you on the field in half an hour."

So started my two week introduction to teaching.

Chapter Ten
SCREEN

From the heady fortnight of observation, we were thrown headlong into our PGCE course. Having a reputation as a pioneering Education department, and the home of the Centre for the Study of the Comprehensive School, York was innovative in its approaches to preparing us students for life in the classroom.

One new experiment had been in the use of television as a way to capture the performance of teaching. The idea of this so called 'Micro teaching', the dissection of a prepared talk through the medium of television, sounded horrendous to me, particularly as it took place in a fully fledged television studio on campus.

The assignment seemed simple enough. Meet in the television studio in the science block at 1 p.m. and be prepared to be filmed telling a story or demonstrating a skill for approximately three minutes.

This was week one of a unit called Micro-teaching where, we had been told, we would take a microscope to the teaching process and try to establish what constituted 'good' teaching. Tremendous, I thought. I'd never been in a television studio before so that will be a novelty and, I'd prided myself on coming from a Welsh storytelling tradition, so the task would be easy. And that's were the trouble started.

What sort of story should I tell? I'd aim to make them laugh I thought. A funny story. I censored out all the stories I knew which were too risky and was left with a limited choice. I thought the talking dog story might fit the bill so set about editing it to fit within the time constraints.

When you dissect what is supposed to be a funny story and edit it to a time constraint, it is amazing how the fun in the story wilts. Trying to shoehorn the art of storytelling into the science of the demands of the television studio proved almost impossible and I was not totally convinced by my final effort.

A businessman was walking home from work one day and decided to take a different route than his normal one, by way of a change. His new route took him through a council estate and as he turned a corner in the maze of roads he saw stuck up in the garden on the back of an estate agent's board a sign that said, *Talking dog for sale. Three quid.*

He thought that this would be another of those dogs, much beloved of Esther Rantzen, who, when it's throat was manipulated could be made to say an approximation of 'Sausages' .

As he was not pressed for time, he knocked on the door and a man in a string vest and a bad haircut answered it.

"I've come about the talking dog – does he say more than sausages?"

"Yeah," replied the man, "you can't shut the mutt up. Come round the back and you can have a chat with him – he'll like you."

Intrigued, the businessman walked along the side entry, through the gate and into an unkempt back garden with overgrown grass, bare patches of compacted earth and abandoned bicycles and car tyres.

The dog owner shouted out, "Killer, come. Killer, heel!"

From amongst the long grass at the end of the garden a clipped accent replied, "We've been over this so many times – my name is Stuart, S-T-U-A-R-T as in the dynasty of Scottish kings, as opposed to Stewart, S-T-E-W-A-R-T as in the clan or the fifties matinee idol Stewart Grainger. My name never has, nor ever will be KILLER!"

"There's a bloke here wants to chat to you," shouted a patronised and chastised owner.

Until now the businessman thought that he was part of an elaborate practical joke. At that moment, the face of a collie cum mongrel appeared from the long grass and clearly spoke the words, "Why ever didn't you say so, at last the chance of some decent conversation!"

"You CAN talk!" said the businessman, "really talk!"

"Jolly nice to make your acquaintance," said the dog, offering his paw by way of a handshake. "Yes, indeed. I found I had a facility for languages when I was a young pup. You might say I have an ear for it!" said the dog, scratching his large ears and laughing.

"But you can talk English with a beautiful accent."

"Thank you most kindly, but if one is going to master a language, one might as well endeavour to speak the purest form of it. I also speak French, Spanish and Portuguese, Russian and Mandarin and Cantonese Chinese – the choice of languages was determined by my previous work."

"Work?" enquired the businessman, "You are a working dog?"

"Don't particularly like the term 'working dog' – saw myself as more of a professional really. I had a career in the Diplomatic Corps."

"Doing what exactly?" asked the businessman incredulously.

"Espionage and counter-intelligence mostly. I'd be taken by politicians and diplomats to international conferences and left in the conference room in recesses. I'd eavesdrop on what the foreign delegations were saying and report back their unguarded thoughts to my superiors. Jolly sneaky really, never felt very comfortable doing it to be honest, but one's sense of patriotism overrides the niceties of etiquette. No-one ever expected such faculties from a dog so I was exceptionally successful in this role for many years.

Previous to that I'd been involved in marketing, but I found the commercial pressures there rather vulgar. Of course, what I'm most proud of is having sired seven litters of pups, so hopefully my genes and my linguistic talent will be transferred to a new generation."

"This is truly unbelievable!" said the businessman, "A unique talking dog – a polyglot, what a conversationalist. I'll take him – how much do you want for him?"

"He's yours for three quid, mate, to be honest you'd be doing me a favour taking him off my hands, I'm totally sick of him, for one thing he talks like a nancy boy, and for another he's such a bloody liar – he hasn't done any of those things!"

So that was the story I was supposed to tell. I'd timed it to two minutes and forty seconds and had practised it until the words seemed drained of any meaning and then practised it some more to get the key parts sharp and the delivery tight with intonation and pauses. The problem was that the more I practised it the more difficult it became to sound spontaneous.

When we entered the film studio in the Physics block the difficulties of delivering this short joke multiplied. The room was vast and cluttered with the equipment of a professional recording studio. There were lights and boxes, sound systems and some officious students milling around adjusting things. Our session followed the York Television (YTV) broadcast of the *Daily News* so the studio had had two hours to build up a sweltering atmosphere in which tension, and the heat from the innumerable lights which flooded the area, conspired to make the room as hot as the Arizona Desert on a particularly sunny day.

We were sat on the benches in front of the main camera stage and what appeared to be a science lab table was rolled on in front of us and secured. Our lecturer drew lots to decide the order in which we would appear. I was last but one slot which meant I would have to sit through the presentations of eight others before mine. I reasoned that it was probably the best slot in that I'd have time to hone my performance based on the presentations of the seven who preceded me. To be honest, I'd have preferred the first slot, to get it over with and then relax.

Linda was first up and we had to wait an interminable five minutes whilst she was wired for sound and given a video check. We could see this all happening on a series of monitors and it was more than a little unnerving, like being spectators at a medical procedure as she stood stock still and ash white whilst people attached her to contraptions. Doubtless Linda felt similarly, as the stress and the heat combined to bring on a dead faint and the last we saw of Linda was her limp and lifeless body dropping out of the bottom of the monitor screen, her face finally relaxed. As we had witnessed it on TV, we were slow to react to this occurrence as a real event.

One of the technicians, showing all the social clumsiness associated with such staff muttered, "Bugger, bet she has broken the mike!" which was picked up across the sound system in the studio which echoed with feedback.

I was one of the first on the scene and was able to put Linda in the recovery position quickly 'using quiet words of reassurance' as recommended by my St John's Ambulance trainer the week before in the voluntary lessons I was attending in Heslington Hall. Linda was unceremoniously wheeled out of the hot studio on an equipment trolley once she had come round. On reflection, I think the polo-necked angora sweater she was wearing was a contributory factor in the debacle. It was fine for the cold east wind outside, but somewhat inappropriate for conditions inside the studio.

Tim was next up and having gone through the same wiring up palaver as Linda, managed to stumble incoherently through a demonstration of some scientific process. He started well but within a couple of sentences his delivery had speeded to a gallop and his volume level had decreased to not much more than a whisper. Tim was usually a confident and outgoing lad but the TV studio was getting to him. He finished abruptly and, sweating profusely, was so determined to get out of the glare of the lights and camera, immediately walked off the set, pulling out a vital lead in the process. This caused further delay.

The ensuing presentations were no better and it became clear that if the objective of this exercise had been to completely demoralise us, it was a resounding success. The only lesson I picked up from presentations was the value of props. Kath had demonstrated how to bake a cake and she had a prop illustrating all the stages, there were baking tools and laminated photographs of the various stages of the preparation. The presentation was not much improved, but whenever her thoughts deserted her she picked up a prop and found fresh energy until, inevitably, she again ran out of steam and reached desperately for another photograph or baking tray. Things weren't helped when she dropped her visual aids and her commentary went out of synch with her pictures. We all gestured to her and she looked aghast and tried to re-order the pictures. The scene did not look out of place from a Tommy Cooper trick, except it was no laughing matter for Cath who also ended abruptly. The tears filling her eyes showed up really clearly on the monitors as she stood there being uncoupled from the mike leads. The camera operator and director didn't have the wit, presence of mind or discretion to turn the camera away from her dissolving face. We watched mesmerised as our friend's humiliation was complete.

Visual aids, props, that was what I needed but with me next but one up, I thought it improbable that I'd have time to rustle up any combination of a talking dog, a businessman or a council estate, vest wearing moron. I forced myself to rehearse the joke but it seemed increasingly stilted on each running.

Charlie had finished now and I was ushered forward to be miked up. I'd no idea how Charlie had performed as I was too busy rehearsing the joke again and again in my head. I tried not to look at the monitors either side of me as they appeared to show someone, superficially like me, but certainly not as good looking, standing nervously, staring into space with beads of perspiration running down his brow and silent words being mouthed.

"Action!" called the director and I summoned up a smile and launched headlong into the joke. I was ten seconds in and finding my feet when the director called,

"Cut! Cut! Cut! What the hell is that noise in the background – check the door to the corridor please."

I was left high and dry, with only the plaintive faces of my fellow PGCE students sympathising, their heads slightly tilted to one side.

On the word action I started again, adrenalin levels high and determined to finish the exercise. I was thirty seconds in this time and beginning to relax into the flow when the decisive word "Cut! Cut!" brought me to a stop once again.

"Are you getting a strange reverb on the sound track?" asked the producer to which all his technician minions shook their heads in unison.

"Silly me, that should fix it," declared the director, adjusting a couple of knobs on his console.

"Good, good aaaannnnnnd Action!" he directed me like some performing seal.

By now the adrenaline and spontaneity had left me and I was left shambling through a series of words until, without change in intonation I delivered the punch line. I wasn't expecting rapturous applause but some measure of appreciation might have been warranted. I got two nods from my fellow students indicating that the ordeal was over, whilst the rest looked anywhere in the studio rather than meet my stare. I took this as proof positive that my future did not lie on the stage or television. I was also beginning to have grave doubts, if this was what was expected, about my future in the teaching profession.

Chapter Eleven
TOUR

I was exhausted and disheartened that Christmas. Four and a half years seemed a long time to have been a student and now, with the economic crisis deepening and the prospect of an election in May, which Labour might well lose the way things were going, the prospects of a job by September seemed slight.

I think I shocked my Dad as he dropped me off at the railway station and helped me out with the same battered suitcase that had provided a shuttle service to and from York for the last 13 terms when I said that the way I felt, I'd throw in this student lark for two pins.

This wasn't like me, but to be honest, I was probably heading for a cold and had overdone things a little over Christmas and New Year, although what precisely I had done, was not particularly clear. It was all a blur and the cold weather and leaden skies were certainly not helping either.

As always, my dad offered me a £10 note. We went through the normal rigmarole:

"No, it's all right dad, I've got enough to get by."

"Don't be soft lad."

"No really. I'm OK."

"Well take this and then you'll be flush and you can buy your mates a round."

I could see now that he was getting slightly irritated to be standing there in the cold with a ten pound note in his hand so, as always, I took it. I reminded him of the time he had handed over £16 to buy tickets here when we went on holiday in 1967.

"Handing that money over, that really hurt. I got a pain in my chest!"

Whereas previously, I'd always been happy for my dad's tenner, though always a little guilty about taking it, it no longer felt right that I, who was now over twenty one, was taking money from my dad, who was now almost a pensioner, and had taken a few financial knocks himself in the last few years with short time working. I resolved that this was definitely the last time I'd accept the money…just as I did last time.

We laughed and said goodbye and I lurched off with my bag full of clean clothes, this week's *Rhyl Journal and Visitor*, assorted food, including Welsh Cakes for Adam (I didn't have the heart to tell my mum Adam had graduated the year before, still I'd have no problem polishing them off) and a series of little notes my mum had taken to hiding in my clean clothes.

The notes dated back to the previous autumn when my mum had come over to York for a weekend just after term had started. This had been the first visit she had made alone in all the time I'd been in York. I'd cleared the decks of all other things so that I could give her my undivided attention. Her request to come over had been quite urgent and at short notice, I'd asked her if there was a particular reason for coming over now and she said not.

My mum had been a regular visitor to York since my arrival at university. She adored the city and would stare lovingly at the Minster from any viewing point in the city and declare "It's a landmark!" which was a statement of the absolute obvious really. Usually, she took every excuse to accompany any party of aunties and cousins who wanted to come across to see the city and university.

She was genuinely fascinated by History and Clifford's Tower and the local museums took good revenue whenever my mother was in town.

One of the reasons I chose York was that it was far enough from Rhyl that you had to make an effort to get there. That suited me, and it meant that nobody would be turning up unannounced to see me.

The pattern of Criddie's tours was that I'd get notice at least two weeks in advance that a visit was due and which itinerary I was to follow.

Itinerary 1 was the short tour, particularly good when young children were included. This involved me meeting the party at the railway station, usually the 11.20 train from Llandudno which meant that my mum would not get flustered having to change trains in Manchester. Straight onto the Number 5 bus to Badger Hill and my mum giving a commentary on all the places of interest we passed on the way. She had picked up on just about everything I had ever told her about York from the various periods of occupation from Romans, through Vikings and the current archaeological digs associated with them, to the years when the river flooded and the height of the flood marks on the King's Arms on the quayside.

The guests would be craning their necks as my mum pointed out the fleeting views of the Minster to left and right as the bus followed its sinuous route. "It's such a landmark, you know!" she'd repeat at each viewing, a cut price Lord Clark of *Civilisation* fame, who just happened to be the Chancellor of the University. My mum's opinions on the Minster had even been shared at home. My Auntie Glad, who was now stone deaf and suffering from Bell's palsy regularly quoted my mum with one of her Malapropisms.

"York Minstrel, it's such a landmark you know."

Auntie Glad had never even seen it, but was happy to rely on my mum's cultural and historic insights.

Once at the university, we'd dismount for a tour of the campus and I was grateful that Badger Hill obscured views of the Minster for the rest of the afternoon.

My mum, and my aunties, wanted to take advantage of the fact that they had this opportunity to show their children around a university. I thought there might have been a subtext here of, "If David can manage to get to university, then so can you!"

I never had a problem with this as the prospect of a railway journey and a tour around a city and university would have been right up my street when I was their age, which was usually between 6 and 12.

In fairness, the university was worth a visit in itself with the massive lake, tremendous fountain and, if they came when the nights were drawing in, the prospect of me scaring them witless by getting them to stand on the stepping stones under PX001 and throwing bread crumbs to the little fishes only to have monster carp emerge out of the darkness. How their screams would echo off the concrete and ricochet across the lake!

My mum would always enquire after Eric at the Porter's lodge, almost as if he was an old family retainer. Eric would always be most solicitous and make a point of saying that he could do with more like me who were polite and tidy and could hold a conversation. My mum would fill with pride and I'd move the party on quickly to avoid further embarrassment.

We'd then process around the campus. In Rhyl no public building had public access to more than two storeys, so climbing the staircase to the balcony of Central Hall was a particular treat for the younger ones. My mum was never very good with stairs, and didn't like even moderate heights, so she would often miss this treat out and I'd warn all who did make the climb not to mention, on pain of death, that there was a tremendous view of the Minster from up there. There wasn't actually, but I thought that shard of information might encourage my mum up there to consider the landmark that was the Minster from a different angle.

We'd take in the wildlife at the margins of the lake, the college notice boards, Heslington Hall, 'It's extremely historical you know!' and, if time permitted, Heslington Village. Nothing ever diminished the excitement for my mum as she announced that, "this is where David sometimes buys vegetables and that is his local bank branch." to whoever was still listening at this point. It made me sound like some minor local celebrity.

The direction of the tour was always determined by which college was open for food that weekend, as sitting in a cafeteria setting, even if it was Vanbrugh, with its dire catering arrangements, was a highlight of the tour. The choice of meals, drinks and salad vegetables was almost overwhelming at times. The catering staff were patient and polite with the visiting country bumpkins, as were the students, who either ignored us or gave me a sympathetic smile, (for next week it might be their turn to entertain family) both responses were entirely acceptable.

As dusk drew in, I'd shepherd them back to the bus stop at Heslington Hall and wave them off, knowing that my mum would do her York commentary in reverse. The party would depart tired, to either sleep, or be fractious all the way home on the train.

Itinerary 2 was the wet weather version of the tour which involved moving between colleges under the covered walkways, and Itinerary 3 was for those who had successfully completed Itinerary 1 or / and 2 and were desirous of the City tour, which was circular, involved all the usual streets, museums and views as well as a short hop along the city wall at the point which involved least climbing up stairs, as demanded by my mum as she didn't do stairs, thank you very much.

Against this background, my Mum's request to visit a few days after I had left to start the new term and before even the new term had begun, was unusual. I thought Auntie Beryl and Uncle Harry might be up from South Wales, or perhaps one of the New York branch of the family had visited at short notice and she wanted to let them see the original York.

She would be coming alone she said and I felt that this was a little ominous. Not wishing to hasten bad news, I had not pressed her. She said she would be arriving on Friday so I suggested that perhaps she would like to go to Leeds for the day on the Saturday. She said yes without enthusiasm, which heightened my sense of foreboding.

Watching my mum step gingerly down from the train on platform 10 made me realise that she was getting old. I seldom saw my mum from a distance of about one hundred yards, where she was just another person in a crowd. She looked slightly flustered as if something was preying on her mind. She peered up and down the platform but did not spot me moving towards her amongst the crowd of detraining passengers. Clearly she wanted to walk as little as possible with her luggage.

For this visit my mum was clearly travelling light as her luggage consisted of a very small vanity case and a Marks and Spencer carrier bag full of home made food. This time I would have to come clean about Adam and admit that he'd graduated last year and I'd been eating his rations for the last twelve months.

She was looking particularly thin and drawn I thought, as if she had not been sleeping. Although it was a bright October day she was dressed for the middle of winter. She smiled when she finally saw me, no more than ten feet away and we did the rapid kiss and cuddle that she always insisted on in public. She seemed to relax a little and drew up her best smile for the occasion.

"Good journey?" I enquired, and was regaled across the station concourse and onto the bus and almost to the point of the bus stop at the university with tales of people she'd spoken to and where they were going and who also had a son at university and how they were dressed and what their accents sounded like and the funny things that they'd said. All this interaction was meat and drink to my mum. She would have made a brilliant Victorian traveller

Since graduation I had been accommodated in Bleachfield. This was a series of linked houses, each with five students rooms and a communal kitchen. It felt like, as graduates, we had been moved to 'low risk accommodation' from the high density of the colleges. I liked my Bleachfield room. It was a little bigger than standard college rooms but with the same facilities. I'd arranged to borrow a friend's room for the weekend and house my mum in my room. My mum seemed delighted by this arrangement and I guessed it was because it would give her a taste of authentic student living of a sort she would have loved to have had in her own youth.

I quickly introduced her to two of my fellow graduates in the kitchen. The plan had been to quickly show her where the tea, coffee and milk were kept so that she could make a cup of tea should I not be around. Unusually, Avi, a psychology student from Israel and Ross a Physics doctoral student from Canada were in the kitchen as we arrived.

I introduced my mum to them as informally as possible and made to whisk her away before she started asking them questions. Unfortunately, she had her food parcel under her arm and quickly broke out the Welsh cakes for what she considered to be two undernourished students.

"Excellent Mrs Hughes, simply excellent, you settle yourself down at the table and I'll fix you a nice cup of tea. Here's a plate for the Welsh cakes," announced Ross with a knowing gleam in his eye. He was going to milk this for all it was worth and get me back for the recent drubbing at Darts he had endured at my hand when I had made some throw away comment or other about colonial cousins and an unhealthy interest in bears.

Avi too was settling in for a session with my mum.

"Are you the Avi who brought David a scarf back from Jerusalem?"

"Yes I am Mrs Hughes."

"Call me Crid boys, it stands for Ceridwen."

"That's a lovely Welsh name," added Ross solicitously and my mum proffered him the plastic margarine catering pack full of Welsh cakes. I could see that this was going to be a long weekend.

Having drunk our tea and consumed a couple of Welsh cakes each, I suggested that my mum and I shuffle off to the library, where I had to return a book.

"You press on David, don't let me stop you, I'll stay and finish my chat with the boys."

I'd forgotten that in the last year, the new hospital had opened up at Bodelwyddan and that my mum was no longer an auxiliary nurse in the small casualty unit of the Prince Edward hospital on Grange Road but now caught the bus to the massive regional hospital beyond Rhuddlan. I hadn't realised that my mum's suspicion of all foreigners had been overcome by mixing with doctors and nurses from all over the world. Like me, who had slowly learned the beauty of food other than meat and two veg, my mum was now anxious to hear about different and exotic worlds. It was good that my mum had turned all cosmopolitan in her tastes after so many years being a 'little Cambrian'. Despite this I felt uneasy that Ross was to be one of her guides to these exotic shores.

I arrived back twenty minutes later to catch "…and that is how we have the north and south Wales branches of the family."

My heart sank at what had been said in my absence and how Ross would be using this ammunition in our verbal exchanges in coming weeks.

"Fascinating stuff Crid, and that would be the same Tonypandy where Churchill used troops against striking miners?"

Ross clearly knew enough to be dangerous.

"Don't get me going about Churchill!" her voice rising to the challenge, and I took the opportunity to intervene.

"No mum, let's not get going about Churchill and I whisked her out of the kitchen and to my room, in order to take her out for a meal.

"Don't forget Crid, fresh pancakes with lashings of maple syrup for breakfast tomorrow."

"Can't wait," replied my mum as I ushered her through the door, "*Shalom!* Avi!"

"*Shalom* Crid!" gestured a smiling Avi.

I wondered if my mum had been as solicitous of the American soldiers stationed at Bodelwyddan Camp during the war… I had a feeling she had been, given the tales of stockings, ham and chewing gum she's once shared with me. The only consolation I could find in this was that I could tell Ross that my mum thought he was American, which always wound him up. He'd go off on a list of the things that culturally separated Americans from Canadians. I'd simply state, "Yeah, but same difference really," which would always infuriate him. It was the one weak point in his armour, one bone he couldn't leave alone and I exploited it mercilessly.

It was on the platform back at York Station before my mum finally came clean about what was troubling her. We'd had an enjoyable day in Leeds, although the walking between shops had troubled her. We were now standing on the platform watching *Flying Scotsman* at the head of a number of catering coaches. Like me my mum was drinking in the atmosphere and talking in an animated way of rail journeys from Rhyl to Tonypandy.

Her mood was in marked contrast to what I can only describe as an 'incident' in Marks and Spencer's in Leeds. We were cutting through the store to buy some cakes for us and Avi and Ross when her eyes alighted on a maroon coat. My mum went through all the stages of buying it, with me egging her on. She felt the material, tried it on and saw that it fitted well, looked in the mirror in that way that women do and caressed the material again. I was reaching that point, as I had previously done with girlfriends, when my initial enthusiasm was about to wane. Like said girlfriends, she asked if it suited her. I affirmed that it did. She said it was expensive though. I said that it was Marks and Spencer and that it would last her for years, which was a homily that had been used on me on more than one occasion.

It was at that point, with a tear in her eye, she replaced the coat on the hanger and moved off to the food hall. I tried to bring her back and teased her that another lady was about to make off with her coat, all to no avail. She walked unusually purposefully for my mum to the fresh cakes without so much as a glance back. I was unsure what was troubling her but I reasoned she would tell me when she had a minute in a not so crowded place.

In the midst of the hissing steam as *Flying Scotsman* departed into the night I thought the time might be right to ask her what was troubling her as she had stared fixedly out of the carriage window in the half hour on the way back from Leeds. As the red tail lights disappeared under the Holgate Road bridge and the station fell silent I asked her why she hadn't bought the coat. She sank onto the uncomfortable station seat and sighed, trying to form the explanation.

"I didn't think I'd get much wear out of it," was her starting point.

I assumed she meant that she would have few opportunities to wear it for social occasions, as it was a bit better quality than required for the dash onto Vale Road to catch the bus to work.

"Well you need to go out more."

"I don't think I have time for that," she said, without looking at me, "I think I've not got long left."

I finally grasped her point wondering what terrible medical news she was about to share with me. It turned out that she had been feeling unwell for a number of weeks and that she had convinced herself that she was terminally ill with cancer or the 'Big C' as she called it in hushed tones, as if to say it was to breathe life into the idea.

"What has the doctor said?"

"I've not been to him yet," came the unexpected reply.

We got into an animated conversation about how she could say what she had without any medical evidence. She claimed that being a nurse, she knew the tell-tale signs. I reminded her she was an auxiliary nurse with no medical training, a point that she indicated that she resented.

We left things with my insistence that she went to the doctor's immediately she returned home to Rhyl on the Monday, which she promised to do.

It transpired that she had come over to spend the weekend away in the thought that this might be the last quality time we would spend together before her impending demise.

I never did get to the bottom of what had spooked my mum, and she phoned a couple of days later to say that the doctor had given her a clean bill of health. I was glad however, that whatever the reason, we had been able to have that weekend together and I'd shown her a good time at the university.

On the bus back to the station on the Monday morning she had craned her head yet again to grasp any fleeting view of the Minster. I waited, and as sure as rain on a Bank Holiday it came.

"York Minster, it's a landmark you know."

I was pleased that over the weekend I'd been able to organise a meal in a restaurant opposite the Minster so that she could gaze on the floodlit vista to her heart's content.

It was a very disquieting time having my mum confronting her own mortality like this. I'd never had cause to consider a time when my parents might not be around. I'd taken home, family and occasions like Christmas and Easter as constants and this was the first inclination that I'd have to revise my view of a never ending series of unchanging family occasions. I realised that I shouldn't take such things for granted because among my university friends, some came from homes where a parent had died. I wondered how they could ever recover from that loss and the truth was that they didn't, they were forced to accommodate the new circumstances, no matter how difficult.

Such, I suppose, was the process of growing up.

Chapter Twelve
PRACTISE

Epistemological is a long and very complicated word. If you look up the definition in the dictionary and read it for several minutes, for a fleeting instant you think you understand it but when you come to use it in the inevitable essay, or more rarely in speech, you realise that you don't understand it at all and you are conscious that you've probably used it incorrectly.

All this makes epistemological a very useful word for academics. Backed into a corner, when they find themselves not knowing the answer to a student's question, beginning a sentence with epistemological is the academic equivalent of engaging warp drive to leave the Klingon dullards reeling in their ignorance.

If epistemological is in the first part of the sentence, then what follows will be increasingly unintelligible.

I quickly learned to recognise the tell tale signs of an academic in trouble when replies to an earnest question began:

"Well, epistemologically speaking…"

"The epistemological research would suggest…"

I found that the question that most frequently led to the engagement of epistemological warp drive in the Education Department was, 'How do I deal with bad behaviour in the classroom?'

Our education department lecturers had many admirable qualities and experiences to impart to us, but how to cope in the mean corridors of comprehensive schools was not an experience they were able to share.

"What might be the context for the behaviour?" they might ask, buying time to assemble a set of propositions, or to press the epistemological button. "What might be the contributory factors to the aberrant behaviour?"

"Probably genetics," I replied unhelpfully, but I thought truthfully. It was a mistake, as now the topic had been nicely generalised from my original query about a specific event to a broader sociological debate about the nature of deviance in society. I quickly realised that I needed to develop my own strategies if I was going to survive my school placements.

"It was so cold and so *very dark* in the orphanage when the matron put the lights out!"

It was five minutes into the lesson and my attempts to make a clear start to the day's proceedings had faltered and my setting the scene for the lesson had been consumed by the rising tide of apathetic kids and their idle conversations. I knew I had to do something or the work I'd completed half past midnight last night and committed to the Banda machine at seven thirty this morning would be wasted.

I was standing, back to the class, (a dangerous position in itself – 'never turn your back on them!') leaning, propped up by an outstretched hand against a laminated periodic table. My other hand was placed over my eyes in mock horror, although I was peeping between the gaps in my fingers checking for the effect.

Without me saying a thing, the room had by now drained of noise as the teenagers wondered if they had driven me to the edge of a nervous breakdown. If they had, there would be Hell to pay they would calculate. That meant they needed to plan a tactical position now.

The morning had not started well. Late night planning and early morning Bandas were a heady combination and a final twist was added by a sequence of complicated room changes necessitated by a previously unannounced examination explained in the teacher briefing. Bugger. That meant that not only would I be late out of the briefing but that I would have to escort a complaining class of youths from the class they were expecting to be taught history in to the new class in the science block. A block in which I was not familiar with the classrooms. Different room and facilities, complaining teenagers – it was no surprise that the lesson started badly.

This was how I came to be leaning on the periodic table poster in a now silent room.

"So very cold, and so very, very *dark*…" I added for effect.

The class was totally silent now – part wonderment, part the impact of the words, part frantic dissembling so that when the blame for breaking the student teacher was apportioned, it would not rest too heavily on them.

I was desperate to turn round and get the lesson underway, but I realised I had to play a long game now. What seemed like minutes passed, it was in fact seconds, before there was a sound in the room.

"Are you all right Sir?" enquired Amanda, an overly buxom girl for a fourteen year old with a penchant for high luminosity lip gloss which she was constantly having to remove and re-apply as she ran into teachers who demanded she conform to the school rules. It was always either the lip gloss, the length of skirt, the jewellery or the footwear with Amanda. Every day she set herself up as the fashionable alternative to school uniform, and every day she would be rebuked. But now she spoke with genuine concern in her voice. I recognised that it had taken courage for her to speak up above the official class code of studied indifference to the plight of others.

The class code was a difficult thing to breach. It was a strange beast. Individually, every young person in the room had a reasonably well developed sense of right and wrong, of 'fair play'or *Chwarae Teg*. Some didn't apply it that often, but they had it. Yet collectively there was an underlying attitude, a default position within the school, and perhaps all schools, which was malcontented and disruptive.

It was not like that in my day I thought, reaching back the eight years to the point when I was their age. We were compliant, easy going and studious as I recall. Polite as well I seemed to remember. Then the penny dropped and I realised that I'd hastily edited the memories.

There was the incident in Ma Bonnington's room when the new technology of the portable audio cassette player was used to deadly effect. Four cassette players, secreted about the room playing *My Ding a Ling*, interrupting Ma Bonnington's earnest efforts to deliver a treatise on the Feast of the Passover. The august lady with a nun's demeanour and hair tied in a bun, moved around the room trying to locate the source of the sound like an arthritic pinball, her poor hearing not helping her fevered pursuit of Chuck Berry.

Then there was Mr Trotman, a permanent teacher with the attitude and presence of a temporary supply one. Haunted, hollow eyes, a nervous disposition and a tendency to stutter when under pressure characterised his every lesson. He taught German in what my mum would call a 'sport's jacket and slacks' and the jacket really did have leather patches on the elbows. The nervous way he rubbed his head and furrowed his brow always indicated he was on the edge. He'd raise his voice and the class noise would rise above it. He would then shout and his voice would become reedy and weak and children would snigger and he'd be close to tears and he'd whine a lament as plaintive as any song of the whales. It was a lament against the cruelties of life really, and how his talents and his life force had been reduced to being held captive by Philistines in an airless second floor classroom with people who had no love of learning. Luckily for him it was the second floor room with the high windows, otherwise I don't doubt he would have clambered out of the window and jumped to the inviting crazy paving below, all pain, all humiliation and all life gone.

I realised I had been as bad as them when I was their age and it was going to take something subtle and ingenious to win them round to learning.

When I'd first entered the staff room of the school one, more mature woman, in a twin set and pearls, opined that I was just what the school needed, a "strapping young man" (I was initially flattered to have made such a positive impression on a middle aged lady) she continued "to knock the little buggers and ne'er-do- wells into shape!"

I moved very quickly to dispel the notion that I was going to be using physical force in any circumstances. So I wasn't going to be baited, I wasn't going to shout or use physical violence. That only left brute cunning and humour. I reasoned that if I could be unpredictable, then they would never have a stable platform on which to be able to mount an assault on me.

"Please sir, are you alright?" repeated Amanda with real genuine concern in her voice now, "do you feel ill sir, should I go and get another teacher?"

I left the poor girl's words hanging and turned round slowly.

"No Amanda, thank you for your concern but I think I would feel better if we just got on quietly with the lesson…"

"Was you in an orphanage sir?" asked one of the surly boys with curly, sandy hair. Amanda and Lorraine glowered at him and his lack of tact.

"I don't like to talk about it," I replied stealing a great line from Clement and Le Frenais' *Whatever Happened to the Likely Lads* script.

"But was you sir, in an orphanage like?"

"We've work to do now," I replied to the mass of faces now focussed on me. "Perhaps we can return to this question at the end of the lesson, if all has gone well."

To my surprise, they accepted this and having had the disruptive energy vacuumed from them, sank into work without a murmur. I could almost hear the internal dialogue going on in some heads: either this is an elaborate ploy on his part and he is lying, or he really was in an orphanage. I need to think this through. If he is telling the truth and I make fun of him, I'm in big trouble. If he is lying then he is in big trouble but I can't decide if he is lying or not so I need to wait and get more information.

Some were clearly eying me with suspicion, but Tina and Amanda, like matching adorable Labradors were looking directly at me with large sad eyes, heads slightly tilted as if to mime, 'Poor you!'

I'd bluffed it and without threats and put downs I'd got the lesson back on track and we had managed to cover everything I'd intended in the lesson. As the class left at the end of the lesson, Amanda even offered me some of her chewing gum by way of consolation for me potentially having spent my formative years in an orphanage.

This was all in great contrast to the events of the previous week when I'd had a stinker of a lesson with a usually affable group of third years. I'd choreographed what I was going to cover with them within the hour long lesson down to the minute and second. It formed on my planning sheet an exquisite, beautiful learning opera in seventeen movements. I'd sat back in the gloom of my cold bedroom at midnight, drank the last of my hot milk and nibbled a custard cream while admiring the ingenuity of the seamless transitions between stages of the lesson, the exploration of different avenues of research and the culmination of the work in a plenary session. It was truly a work of art. For once, I slept soundly that night and awoke ready for the off.

The lesson started badly with me hastily shuffling my props and ensuring that the filmstrip, cassette player, worksheets and instructions were all working and in the right place. The start of the lesson therefore had less impact than I'd hoped and I was conscious that the clock was ticking and giving me less time than anticipated to cover all the material. I'd set the teams of students a task saying that they had five minutes to complete it and then give them three. The projector played up at the critical time, meaning I had to rethread the filmstrip whilst the class filled the vacuum with noise. More time was lost getting them back on track. It was rapidly turning into the sort of nightmare which all student teachers feared. Then Jack decided to play up.

Jack had clearly become increasingly confused by the series of commands, exhortations to hurry up and record all his answers. This latter request was particularly galling to him as he had gone out of his way in the first lesson to seek me out and explain, "My name's Jack and I 'ate writing' me, so it's best that you don't ask me to do some cos I won't."

On Jack's part this was an honest summation of the writing situation. I thought it was challenging behaviour and determined that Jack would be doing quite a lot of writing. I'd show him who was boss. This attitude persisted only for the first week when the realisation slowly dawned on me that I could either try to bend Jack to my will or change Jack's attitude, but I couldn't do both. It was only much later that it dawned on me that this had been a heartfelt plea from Jack rather than a disciplinary challenge. Jack was so lacking in confidence in writing, so scared of making errors, that it was so much easier to play up and never be found out than risk writing and be publicly humiliated in front of his peers by the result.

Jack was a rotund lad with a red face and the irksome habit of having no social understanding of situations. He compensated for his lack of writing by stating the obvious when nothing needed saying. When a girl had asked discreetly to go to the toilet in an earlier lesson and I'd quietly nodded Jack, had piped in with, "Why is she going to the loo sir, does she need a wee or is she having a period?"

Jack might have been asking what a number of the boys were thinking, as they were of an age when the rude mechanicals of a girl's anatomy were of increasing interest, but even they winced at Jack's candour and loud voice.

Helen chipped in, "You're a twat Jack and I'm going to twat you at lunchtime!"

Twat as a noun and a verb in one sentence I noted, and I was going to share this thought with the class when I thought better of it. Neither did I step in to dissuade Helen from committing an act of intense violence against Jack. I was even thinking she would have a better chance at modifying his behaviour than I. Momentarily I pictured the aftermath of the severe beating Jack would get and me being interviewed by the Head afterwards with the words, "So Mr Hughes, a child threatened another in your class and in front of witnesses and you did nothing?"

I could plead mitigation and Jack's inflammatory attitude to the poor girl who needed the loo. I could explain how I intended to deal with it at the end of the lesson as my plan was falling further behind, but in truth I thought it best, given that we were in a science room, that Jack learn the relationship between action and reaction.

The lesson limped to an ending and the thought I took from it, in a vague unformulated way, was that teaching the subject was not enough, you had to teach the learners you had in front of you. My best prepared lesson had been one of my worst classroom experiences to date – for me and the students.

I didn't take much convincing that Friday evening when Mick, who taught Technology which he always suffixed by the words woodwork and metalwork, invited me on one of his legendary benders.

"The Grapes at seven!" he declared much like a Musketeer summoning up the spirit of "All for one and one for all!"

I arrived late and drenched, having had to make two bus connections from my digs up the valley.

"All hail the student teacher!" exclaimed Mick as I entered. "Another week survived, and no children killed!"

I smiled weakly as he gestured to the two pints already stacked up for me due to my late arrival. All the usual suspects were there, six guys, between five and ten years into the teaching profession with houses, wives and mortgages in place. I envied them the certainty in their lives, the end of the period of provisional this and temporary that. Indeed this was a circular conversation we entered into after twenty minutes of talking bollocks in the way that only a group of men can do in a pub.

"The thing is," said Geoff through bleary eyes and a faltering voice, "the thing is is that you say you envy us, but really we envy you. This is it. This is it for us, we've made our house, no our bed, and there is nothing more for us. I should be in Tithati, no Tahiti, not here, I could be studying volcanoes now rather than showing filmstrips about them. Give it up before it is too late, choose a different life, not teaching."

Geoff sunk into his pint and followed up with the remainder of the salt and vinegar crisps that were in an open bag on the table.

"I've said my piece I have, said it. I'm now going home to my lovely wife and an enjoyable weekend before the horror starts again next week. Four more weeks 'til Easter, four more weeks," he whined as he got up unsteadily to leave, having four goes to get his arm into the sleeve of his coat. John and Eric decided to leave with him. That left Mick and I and two pints of Robinson's deceptive falling over water.

"Drink up, drink up, let's go and get something to eat."

The fact that I had not had something to eat between finishing school, playing our staff game of five-a-side, scooting to my digs and back again, might have something to do with the reason I now felt unsteady on my feet. I was torn between food and finding my bus home, but it suddenly dawned on me that we had been involved in a lock in, and that any eateries, be they chip shop or Chinese, had long since finished serving.

To compound things, that meant that the buses had finished running also, and I was faced with an eight mile walk home along dimly lit country roads in drizzle and limited visibility.

I though that I could be the new Mark Pullen, the University of Kent at Canterbury student found dead at the side of the roadside with only his wallet on him. This was a reconstruction exercise developed by the Schools' History Project team in which students were asked to use the limited evidence available to reconstruct the scene and come up with possible theories of what had happened, whilst realising the provisional nature of conclusions, and the gaps in the evidence record.

"I could end up being the new Mark Pullen!" I stated rather too loudly on the deserted rain swept streets under the harsh glow of the sodium lamp street lighting.

"Never heard of him." replied Mick as he strode quite purposefully on in his bedraggled Hush Puppies.

We walked for some time along frayed pavements and from the major road to minor ones and finally through a small play area and onto a relatively new housing estate.

Clearly we were not heading for some eatery now; Mick was on home ground. He made a sharp right on to a driveway that had yet to be tarmaced. Under small tarpaulins stood a number of uncompleted projects, what looked like a motorcycle with sidecar and a pile of bricks which had been delivered on a pallet. We pushed past them and through the front door.

"I'm home love!" shouted Mick up the stairs where a landing light remained on. A baby awoke and started crying. Mick seemed unperturbed.

"The baby's awake love, see to him will you," he continued absently.

We moved into the large rectangular living room which had been divided into a dining area at one end and a living room at the other. The living room space was dominated by what I first thought was a very large colour television which had been left on. It turned out to be a massive tropical fish tank back lit and with a host of darting and ambling fish inside. I recognised the electric blue neon tetras and the black fighting fish but the others were lost on me. A clown fish, I thought one was a clown fish, and my mind was taken back to Sunday afternoons with Jacques Cousteau and the voyages of the *Calypso* over the reefs and archipelagos of the Caribbean, the Indian Ocean or the Great Barrier Reef. Mick's fish tank was that vibrant with life. I was having difficulty focussing both my sight and my brain by now. For an innocuous looking drink, that Robinson's bitter really packed a punch. I thought of the disappointment if Jacques had turned up to plumb the mysterious depths of the coast off Rhyl.

"'Ere, in all its beauty, brilliantly camouflaged to match its surroundings, is a flounder and there, a shrimp, past master of feeding in the nutrient rich environment of the sewage outlet pipe. In the distance an ancient form comes into view, amorphous and mysterious. It is a jellyfish, spineless blob of the ocean."

It wouldn't make for edifying viewing – poor visibility, marauding holidaymakers skimming stones at the divers and the occasional flash of inert gold as a goldfish, won at the fair, is flushed out to sea from a boarding house toilet.

"Rustle us up some food love, me and the student are famished!"

I though this request was well out of order but was happy to sit still, out of the rain at least, as the room and the fish slowly rotated.

Mick fiddled with the remote control of his state of the art stereo system. The speakers he had constructed himself, and they still showed the raw plywood waiting to be varnished. He had now put on some jazz, a pet hate of mine, and was waxing lyrical about the sound quality as some saxophonist meandered irregularly up and down some scales. I heard some slippers padding slowly down the stairs behind me.

Within what seemed like a few minutes Linda appeared at the door with two plates of food. I suddenly realised I was hungry after all.

I was shocked to realise that Linda was heavily pregnant, swathed in a pink dressing gown and slip on floral slippers. She was a good looking woman but her blonde hair was bedraggled and her eyes were ringed with tiredness. She shambled over to Mick and handed him a plate and knife and fork.

Without looking up he asked, "Did you have a lovely night in love, good stuff on the telly?"

"Yes," she said rather ironically, too tired to argue, which I thought they might have done had I not been there as a guest.

"This is David, the poor student." continued Mick.

I got up to shake her hand but it all got lost in the handing over of the plate of food and the knife and fork.

"Thank you very much for the food, it is really kind of you, especially considering the time."

I looked down to see what had been cooked in so short a time and it was a Vesta chicken curry. My stomach churned as the smell hit my nostrils and I was transported back to the good ship *Nevasa*, heaving through churning seas off the north coast of Scotland with only the smell of the British India Line's Indian crew cooking curry to mask the smell of vomit.

I distracted the almost comatose Linda with the aside, "I love these undersea documentary films on BBC2."

"That's a fish tank," she replied, beyond humour.

I looked closely at the tank and replied, "Good lord, so it is. I thought the picture quality was suspiciously good!" hoping to rescue what was turning into an awkward situation.

Linda and Mick at this point got into a low energy argument about a new part for the broken washing machine and the purchase of a new tumble drier, which had clearly been on the arguing agenda for some months.

I was left to stare in horror at the plate sitting on my knee. I couldn't just leave it saying I didn't like curry, nor could I hide it anywhere. There was a Yucca plant present but it was on the other side of the room beyond the arguing partners. The fish tank was not really an option, there was too much in terms of volume and although the rice could be argued to be a tropical product, wherever the reconstituted chicken came from, it certainly wasn't tropical in origin. It was a pity the tank did not stretch to holding a shark, of any variety – then we might have been in with a chance. It was looking like I was going to have to eat the curry after all.

We cannot be sure what the human mind is capable of until confronted by an extreme situation; cannibalism following a plane crash in the high Andes; lopping off one's own limbs when faced with life threatening frostbite in the Arctic; peeing on someone covered in jellyfish stings, or even sucking the venom from a bite wound from a venomous snake on the backside of a companion on an Amazonian expedition. On that particular evening, in those particular circumstances, I resorted to a desperate measure.

Furtively, so that I could present a clean plate at the end of the exercise I nibbled at the untainted rice and forked the body of the curry into the pocket of my coat. I say coat, it was more a quilted anorak sort of affair. It was quite old and not particularly effective against wind and rain and I reckoned I could call on it to make the supreme sacrifice. Slowly but surely without dropping any tell tale evidence I made my way through the meal feigning to be eating it and then at the last moment diverting the forkfuls into my pocket. At one horrible point I had to tamp it down in the pocket so as to complete the loading. It was an unpleasant sensation all round and, thinking carefully to the last, I was finally able to slowly zip up the pocket securely. I proffered my plate to my host with a 'yum–yum' of appreciation.

"Would you like some more?" the exhausted Linda enquired.

"No, no thank you!" I replied rather too eagerly.

"What about pudding? We've some coconut and almond cake. Or maybe a fig roll – I'm sure we've got some in the biscuit barrel."

"I'd love some pudding," I lied, "but I have a nut allergy which means I can't go near almonds or coconut."

It was ironic that she was coming up with all my pet hates. Fig Rolls – such a nasty little confection which not only tasted horrible and served as a laxative, but also tainted every honest biscuit in the barrel. She'd only have to mention rhubarb now and she'd have covered the unholy trinity. Rhubarb, a pudding so vile it looked like phlegm and was poisonous to boot – surely God was telling us something there.

Linda finally relented and determined to return to bed.

Mick promised to be, "Up in a minute, love!" and fell asleep on his chair.

I curled up on the other chair, having hidden my coat by the far side of the chair, placing it in such a way that the curry, congealing in the pocket all the time, would need to soak through four layers of anorak before staining the carpet. I could be really thoughtful like that when I put my mind to it.

I woke up with a start the next morning as someone opened the curtains and broke my dream of drowning in tropical seas. The fish in the tank all seemed to be congregating at the glass at the front and looking knowingly at me. I'd thought fish did not have a memory measured in more than seconds, but these knew of my foul deed from the night before.

"Bacon butty?" asked Mick, remarkably bright eyed from the session the night, or early morning before.

"Eh, no thank you," I managed to get out once my dry tongue released itself from where it had been spot welded to the roof of my mouth. "What's the time?" I asked nonchalantly, for it was a Saturday morning and the whole day was hopefully ahead of me, and it was a bright sunny late winter's day if the sun streaming through the windows was to be believed.

"Ten to nine," called Mick from the kitchen and I closed my eyes and relaxed. I was bounced awake again instantly by the remembrance that my girlfriend Jane was coming up from London today and we were due to meet in Derby bus station at 10 a.m.

"Glad to see you made an effort, sartorially speaking!" said Jane as she hung around her car, anxious not to incur the wrath of the prowling traffic warden. I was still trying to get my hair to lie flat, so I smiled weakly and looked for sympathy, which was not noticeably forthcoming.

"Sorry, I had some unexpected occurrences last night," I said, being as vague as possible.

We drove off out of the city and settled for a walk along the river and a meal at the riverside pub.

Jane was looking elegant. Six months into a job in London, she had moved on from student days and the relaxed code of dress. She matched a brown skirt with a white blouse and rust cardigan and was wearing her new Chinese style coat in a quilted style and tan boots. She could have come out of the pages of one of the catalogues entitled 'This Spring's key colour combinations'.

I, on the other hand, might have been described in the newspaper under the headline 'Student Spends Night in Custody' accompanied by a wild man haircut, a dishevelled green anorak with both pockets zipped up, and scruffy jeans. My ensemble was finished off by my blue suede shoes which had seen better days.

The walk along the river began to clear my head and the mood generally picked up. I looked around me a couple of times to seek out the source of the terrible smell that seemed to be accompanying us, to no avail. Surreptitiously, I checked the soles of my shoes to make sure I hadn't walked in some dog mess. I even checked the soles of Jane's new boots as she delicately crossed over the stile in front of me. Nothing there either. Walking up and down the river bank, I ensured as my mother had taught me, to keep on the outside of the girl to avoid oncoming traffic, or in this case, to ensure that I fell in the river before her. This piece of etiquette had first served me well when I'd walked Susie home from school when I was twelve. She'd asked me why I was switching sides every time we crossed the road and I had said that my mum had told me to. I'm sure she's been heartily impressed, although I don't recall a second date after that.

"Have you got any sweets on you?" asked Jane, knowing that whenever possible I'd have some wine gums or similar sweets on my person.

"I'm not sure, check my pockets," which she did.

It was the second pocket that revealed its abominable surprise. Her little woollen gloved hand snook into it and feeling what she assumed was a bag of sweets, grabbed at the mass. It took less than a second for something glutinous and damp to soak through her gloves.

Her initial reaction was of shock but when she withdrew her hand and saw the full horror of the congealed curry she started to gag. She continued to gag for some significant time. I'd completely forgotten my deadly cargo in my rush to get into Derby and even the smell emanating from me had failed to jog my memory about the sordid events of the night before.

I toyed with the idea of saying that someone must have planted it on me in favour of telling the full truth. Knowing my hatred of curry, she'd have to believe me. She did, and insisted I discard the anorak in the next bin together with her woollen gloves. I took the line that both the gloves and the anorak would come up as good as new with a good wash. Jane was of a different opinion and would have set fire to both garments on the spot had there been petrol available.

We did visit the pub but only to wash our hands thoroughly and to imbibe a quick tonic water to clear away the physical and mental distaste of the incident.

"I can still smell it – I can still smell it!" Jane repeated when we got back to the car and for a considerable time after that. I didn't reply as without a coat on, on this brisk cloudless February day, my whole body was anaesthetised to sensation.

"As long as I live, I will never, ever, forget this incident." It sounded ominously like a threat.

After what was to become known as 'the curry incident' the teaching practice passed less eventfully. I stopped trying to plan lessons to death and listened more for feedback from the students. I never went out drinking with Mick again though; one night of mayhem was more than enough.

A few weeks later I decided to take a bold line with my troubling class. My tutor was due down from York for my final observation and, being taken ill at the last moment, Professor Lister substituted for him. This might not be good news as Professor Lister was a wily and perceptive guy and I did not know him as well my tutor. I thought I'd hedge my bets by planning the lesson particularly boldly with students leading part of the session and me acting as a mentor rather than simply teaching didactically. This was a higher risk strategy so I took measures to ensure that I had the students onside.

"You asked me before about my past and in the last lesson of term in three weeks time, which will be our last lesson together, I am prepared to answer questions you might want to ask me. But before then I have an ordeal to overcome. In the lesson before that, a man in a suit will enter the room. He will sit quietly at the back for most of the lesson writing on a clipboard, but then he might get up and ask you questions about what you have learned and what I am like as a teacher. This man has my future in his hands."

I looked up to see the effect and I had rapt attention across the room. I surprised myself to see that I could summon up such dramatic effect, never being comfortable on the stage since the split tights incident whilst playing the King of Hearts aged five when I 'came out' on the final night when we all had to fall down at the end of the atishoo, atishoo scene.

"I come from very humble beginnings. There were some who said that people like me shouldn't get the opportunity to go to university as I grew up on a council estate."

There was a muttering of shared resentment here as most of the class came from a similar background.

"Never believe that!" I continued. "Everyone has the ability inside them to achieve university – it is whether it is important enough to you that will decide whether you are good enough."

"However, I cannot control the next bit of the puzzle. That will depend on you. What Professor Ian Lister writes on those sheets will decide whether I pass the course. Whether I pass the course will determine if I can get a job for September. Whether I can get a job for September will determine if I can get engaged and married. Still, I shouldn't be sharing and burdening you with this. There is nothing you can do to help, and it would be wrong of me to ask."

I left a heavily pregnant pause, and, as anticipated, Amanda filled it.

"We'll help you sir. You've been fair with us so we'll give you a good lesson, won't we?"

Amanda turned on the class and I, for one, expected some dissent from the boys, who might have sensed that they had me at their mercy, as I had admitted as much. To my surprise all were nodding with some gravitas, it appeared that class solidarity trumped the opportunity to torment the student teacher.

"I really appreciate your support, honestly, but it is not that simple because I want to try some quite difficult things to impress the Professor and we'd need to practice them in every lesson to get to the point that we all feel confident."

"We can do that sir," volunteered one of the hard core lads and even Tom, this class' version of Jack, was nodding, feeling part of the wider sense of purpose.

The last three weeks of the final teaching practice were a dream. Knowing that we had a common deadline to make for our performance, focussed all the learning beautifully. There was no backchat and surliness, as everyone was depending on the others to get it right. Not having constant interruptions to deal with over discipline meant that I could relax and aim at quality learning over volume of information imparted. This meant that we could evaluate our work in class which gave me less marking to turn round at home.

I tried the 'ask two before me' strategy to see if the students could work out answers before needing to ask me. To my surprise it worked and they were increasingly presenting me with solutions rather than questions which they had already tested on their peers. I thought back to the beginning of the academic year and thought Ieuan would be proud of me for picking up on his techniques and extending them in a secondary setting.

It got to the point where some of the permanent staff were noticing the difference in the group and three came to observe me to see what I was doing, one of which was the Deputy Head. The way I'd enticed the students into this form of working might not have been ethical, but the results were consistently good and I wondered if the ends do justify the means?

The observation lesson went to plan and the good professor was duly impressed by the lesson, the student and staff feedback. It appeared that some of the students, included Tom had laid it on a little thick, stating that I was the best teacher they'd ever had and that I made all the learning wonderful. I winced at the thought, but liked the level of support.

True to my word, we had a celebration on the last lesson which included cakes, sweets and twenty questions, only one of which I politely deflected. At the end of the lesson I told them some rather risqué jokes, on the understanding that they didn't repeat them to anyone until after Easter when I would be long gone.

We'd finished the business of the lesson and I was gathering my things together, having given the students free chat time for the last minute of the lesson, when it suddenly fell ominously quiet. I looked up to see Amanda and Tom clearing their throats and standing self consciously at the front of the class.

"What's going on?" I asked suspiciously.

"We'd just like to say that we have enjoyed you teaching us sir," spoke Amanda with some emotion.

"Yeah, I though you were a posh dick when you first came, but you are like us really aren't you," added Tom, to the annoyance of Amanda.

"Anyway," she continued, "we've had a whip round and have bought you something for your first job in teaching."

I was genuinely touched and uncharacteristically lost for words. I thought back to our torrid first meeting and my concerns that either the class or me wouldn't survive the term. The smart money would have been on me buckling first. I could feel tears welling up, for the first time in all my school career. It looked like I would blub in school.

Amanda passed over a neatly wrapped small parcel. I recognised the copperplate writing as Lorraine's and said as much as she smiled.

"Do I take it with me or do I open it now?"

"Open it now!" came the chorus.

The wrapping paper gave way to reveal tissue paper and then a box containing a fountain pen. I inhaled and exhaled a couple of times before I could speak.

"This is a really beautiful present. I'll always think of you all when I use it. I can't believe how much I've learnt from you. You were all pretty scary when I first met you but you came up trumps when it mattered. I meant what I said about what you can achieve. Whether it's your beauty parlour

Amanda, or your garage Phil or university – be the best you can be and surprise yourself."

I trailed off at this point, emotion and the sound of my own voice sounding old and pompous prevented me saying more. I was relieved to hear the bell and made my way to the door to thank them each individually and to shake their hands.

Amanda and Tina hung at the end of the queue, Amanda pursing her lips as if making for a kiss. I was sure that many of her classmates would be only too happy, if a tad nervous, to make landfall on those bow-like fluorescent lips, but I was pretty sure the protocol was very clear on this point. Whereas with most of the girls, my height advantage would have meant I could have avoided contact, Amanda was tall enough and bold enough not to be bluffing. Feeling embarrassed I smiled, stepped backwards and took her hand to shake.

"Spoilsport!" she said, winking conspiratorially and I smiled again, partly with relief.

It was left to Tom to have the last word, as it usually was.

"Do you know why we bought you that pen sir? It's because you are cack-handed and shit at writing!" he said with truthful sincerity as he ran out through the door and down the corridor, laughing. I decided not to pursue it, safe in the knowledge that I had survived teaching practice and now had a long relaxing summer term ahead of me. Only one task remained for my time at university – securing a job.

Chapter Thirteen
INTELLIGENCE

In the last weeks of the last year of my university life I should have been relaxing like all the other undergraduates. The sun was shining, the campus looked at its best, all greenery and ducklings, and I was busy in my room with my inherited typewriter knocking out letters of application to just about every post to which I might be considered qualified advertised in the *Times Educational Supplement*.

I might have preferences for where in the country I would prefer to teach but such preferences were cast aside for the greater economic good and everywhere from Eccles to Beccles and from Cramlington to Cambourne was to receive a typed letter of application from me.

My typing had improved, but there was no denying that the typewriter ribbon was past its best and bled into red at increasingly regular intervals. I thought a typewritten letter might give me an edge over handwritten ones. On average it took me five times longer to type a letter than hand write one so I was finding that I had very little spare time on my hands.

I mused about whether the confident prediction made on *Tomorrow's World* about us all having a computer in our homes within a generation was any more feasible than the hover cars and the silver lamé suits which had been promised so earnestly in the early seventies and were still conspicuous by their absence. Certainly my experience of computers, large clunking things which occupied whole rooms, like the Dec 10 tended by the bespectacled spotty youths in autumnal coloured jeans and polo necked sweaters in the new computer block, gave me little confidence.

They needed a week to process any information and you had to enter your query through a mechanical typewriter which clunked away knocking chads out of punch cards in a laborious process which seemed to be as time consuming as the work of the stonemasons constantly repairing the fabric of York Minster. The punch cards then passed to the aforementioned spotty acolytes of the Dec 10 and they whisked them away to their voracious Oracle who mused on the answer to your question and produced a semblance of an answer 'a week next Tuesday'.

The answer, when it came, was in the form of pages and pages of computer paper on which you searched for anything meaningful. Line ten had a sequence of forty eight numbers and letters, as did line twenty, thirty and forty. Line 240 was more forthcoming, containing the number 48.7

which was the average of all the answers submitted in my questionnaire. I longed for one of the new but expensive Casio calculators, or even a slide rule which would have saved me a number of days and trees in arriving at this answer.

Things did not improve when we were first presented with a computer screen and were trusted to put in our own data and use the manual to write the appropriate code for the computer to digest our information. Coding each line took so long and the research from the closely typed manual so induced eye-strain that most abandoned the cutting edge 'Computer Programming/Beginner's' course within a couple of weeks. I could not see a practical application for this technology in my lifetime and, had I had the time, I would have knocked off a well drafted letter to the guru of all things futuristic, James Burke, to inform him of what I thought of this technology. Yet James and the rest of the *Tomorrow's World* ensemble were assuring the nation that a computer in every home was possibly no more than 'three years away.'

I was entering the job market in the teeth of a recession and the tenacious brutality of one Mrs Margaret Thatcher gave me little hope that my circumstances would improve in the short term. I waited on every reply from a school, hoping that one would hold out the promise of an interview, of the prospect of a job and the chance to earn some money and avoid impending penury.

So it was, that in my best, and if truth be told, my only suit, I made my way on a rattling Diesel Multiple Unit across the fens through the delights of March, Manea and Ely to Cambridge, summoned to a school in the Cambridgeshire Fens, summoned by an official looking letter and the promise of gainful employment.

It was a roaring hot mid May day and I was anxious not to arrive in a dishevelled state, all sweaty armpits and shiny forehead. I'd placed myself in the path of the rush of wind from the open carriage door window and opened all the top windows beyond the point indicated by an arrow and a metal sign stating 'Do not open beyond this point'. I'd looked pretty fair in the mirror when I'd set out a few minutes before seven a.m. that morning in my pearl grey shirt, black polished shoes and light grey suit. If I squinted at the image in the mirror I might even believe that I'd employ me as a teacher with all the responsibilities that that entailed. The suit had been purchased in the winter however and was heavy in cut and fabric and I'd a recurring concern that I'd melt under questioning during the interview.

I was taking this seriously, as I had forsaken my seat behind the driver's cab where I could enjoy an uninterrupted view of the track ahead of the DMU. This would be my usual perch when exploring some new railway route, but today I was trying, in the sway of the train on the track and the whistle of breeze in my hair, to read two of the books the JB Morrell library at the university had on the Village College system in Cambridgeshire.

I was hoping to drop in a nugget of my new found knowledge at the appropriate point in the interview to clinch the post. Which nugget though? Each page swam with information and I could not see gold for iron pyrites. I tried to recall some vital gobbet of information from the informational films shown when there was 'a technical fault' on the telly but could not remember any feature of Cambridgeshire specifically, or East Anglia in general coming to mind, other than the fact that *Survival* was made by Anglia Television.

I had, as planned, arrived in Cambridge ridiculously early for my afternoon appointment. I'd considered every possible source of delay: leaves on line, water buffalo on track, industrial action, industrial inaction, act of God, civil disturbance, mechanical breakdown, nervous breakdown of the driver or guard, missed connections, no connections, surfeit of lampreys, inappropriately inserted hot pokers and the full and bizarre causes of demise of the English kings as outlined in *1066 And All That*. Clearly by this stage I was rambling and I made a mental note not to do this in the interview.

All potential causes of delay were carefully factored in and assigned a value in minutes and I was now standing on the seemingly endless platform of Cambridge railway station four hours earlier than my appointment at the Village College. To arrive this ridiculously early I considered to be a result.

I'd visited the City only once before and then briefly to stay overnight with Andy as he completed his PGCE here. I'd been mightily impressed by the place, the colleges, the river and the general cleanliness and friendliness of the place.

Perhaps the first view you have of a new place is the one that is forever captured in your mind's eye. I'd arrived in Cambridge to see Andy on a sunny autumn day and sunny and autumnal is the way I have always subsequently remembered Cambridge: a stiff breeze rustling fallen leaves at Parker's Piece and the daunting sight of the New Zealand All Blacks limbering up on the expanse of grass outside their hotel, no doubt anxious to humiliate the Home nations in the course of their tour.

I spent some time sitting in the shade of an avenue of lime trees in the park that penetrated deep into the heart of the city, surveying a skyline of churches and colleges whilst assaulted by the noise and exhausted diesel fumes from the buses and coaches of the nearby, and wholly inappropriately sited bus station.

At five minutes past eleven my thoughts turned to lunch and I made my way back through the town and the market place, turning right into a broad pedestrianised street with highly individualised, and outrageously expensive fashion shops and delicatessens. Amongst this retail wonderland I spotted a pub advertising delicious fare and adorned with floral hanging baskets and decided to try my luck with a request for food and the ridiculously early hour of eleven thirty.

The middle aged man at the bar suggested I make myself comfortable, offered me his copy of *The Sun* to seal the bargain and promised that he would take my order as soon as cheffy arrived. Asking me what I wanted to drink he seemed genuinely repulsed when I suggested a tonic water. I mouthed that I was on my way to a job interview by way of explanation but the damage had already been done.

With a lip curling sneer he asked me, "Will you be wanting ice and lemon with that sir?"

Thinking practically on this exceptionally hot day, I said yes. I realised immediately that I had now compounded my first offence.

Despite the earliness of the hour I was not alone in the pub. All the oil cloth covered tables with seats were free but at the bar was an assortment of the kind of humanity who congregate at such times in such places out of circumstance or habitual need.

There were two delivery men in blue overalls, who may have been draymen about their deliveries, drinking ice cold lager and talking and laughing loudly. A lady, ample in proportions, but elegantly dressed and made up, was looking like she was waiting for a partner, or possibly a customer. Two older men stood at the far end of the bar, one with a chronic skin complaint which reminded me of a joke Barry had told me in passing a few months before "You could tell that he came from 'Ackney...it was written all over his face!" (the joke sounded like it outdated Barry by a couple of generations, but it made us chuckle). Anyway, the two men were deep in conversation over the runners and riders at Newmarket and were oblivious to anything else in the vicinity.

Nestled on a high stool at the far end of the bar was a rather bedraggled man in tired suit and a pea soup coloured tie secured very loosely around a creased check shirt. He sat in a strategic position, able to survey the whole pub, the entrances and the exits and nobody could move behind him. His positioning reminded me of something that had been said in *The Godfather* films about where a mobster should sit in a restaurant to ensure that he was never taken by surprise. He nursed a pint of Guinness and looked like he should have been studying a copy of the *Sporting Life* or *Racing Times* like the other pair, but instead he surveyed me with a smile on his lips and darting eyes. I smiled back and he allowed me time to find a seat, place my veteran school briefcase, that had been given to me on the day I entered secondary school, on the plush bench seating and settle myself.

He smiled and nodded and I smiled and nodded back, thinking, wrongly as it turned out, what a hospitable place Cambridge was. He smiled a little longer and I turned away to engross myself in searching through the briefcase, to find the letter inviting me to the interview, which now had sweaty paw prints along each edge where I had inspected it every fifteen minutes on the train, adjusting my itinerary accordingly. This was not going to be a repeat of the hospital medical debacle.

I now had one hour to eat my lunch, probably be able to pare that down, thirty minutes to find a taxi, which was extravagant in the extreme given that there was a taxi rank in the market square no more than fifty yards away, and one hour twenty minutes to travel the eight miles I calculated to the Village College. All was in order.

As I replaced the letter I felt the reassuring distressed leather of the inside of the case, a constant companion in the journey from the first day of secondary school to this day and read, in what had once been my best joined up writing, my name and address, continued beyond Great Britain to include the World, the Solar System and the Universe but with no postcode added. The Quink Ink had advertised itself as permanent but age had seen it spread and fade and my once reasonably neat writing was now bloated and imprecise. From childhood to my first job this briefcase had been a constant witness and I determined to use it in my new professional capacity, should I be successful in this afternoon's interview.

Despite being engrossed in these ramblings I was conscious of an intrusion into my personal space. Sure enough I looked up to find the man at the corner of the bar still looking at me and smiling. He nodded slightly and I felt strangely compelled to nod back.

He looked unflinchingly at me, smiling, but without warmth in his eyes. I tried to look away first as this was becoming uncomfortable. After an interminable few seconds he spoke.

"Would you look at yerself sitting there!"

I thought about this and considered that without a mirror it would be difficult to comply.

"I know who y'are," he continued, running the last two words together in an unmistakably Irish brogue, "and I know what you've come for."

I quickly looked around the pub, hoping to find some other passing punter who might be the object of this interrogation. Unfortunately for me there was no-one else seated in the body of the bar. I toyed with the idea that he might have been talking to the person who wasn't there, who was standing eclipsing me like the poor souls I'd seen in the psychiatric hospital but his eyes remained focussed on me directly and with purpose.

"British Army!" he said loudly. "Yer bastard!" And he punctuated these words by slapping the bar with his fist in as loud an exclamation mark as I'd ever heard.

I had a terrible urge to explain. To explain that I was a student on his way to an interview who had happened on this pub for an early lunch and that I indeed appreciated that an Irish Republican viewpoint might, with some cause, have misgivings about the British Army. In fact being Welsh, although not inclined to nationalism, which I saw as one of the greatest and most scurrilous causes of war and misery in the twentieth century, I might even sympathise with his viewpoint.

"Easy, Pat," said the barman to the intense Irish man, as if this tirade was a daily occurrence.

In that second's intermission I decided to do something different, something that reflected how different my life could be by the end of this day. I looked back, smiled and held him fixed in my gaze. I reached down to my briefcase and secured the one remaining serviceable clasp with an engaging click.

"There you go, there you go, surveillance is it, that's the game is it?" ventured the animated Irishman.

"Don't think I don't know what's in the bag, you've a little persuader in there have you not, a Webley persuader perhaps or one of Mr Browning's?"

I was about to give him guidance on the use of the double negative in his sentence, but thought that might be better employed if I was called upon to take a lesson as part of this afternoon's interview process.

"Know this boy, know this, I was stripping and assembling them before you were a glint in your father's trousers."

As I remember it, my father's trousers had creases and often turn ups, but I didn't ever recall a glint in them, nevertheless I caught his meaning and continued to smile fixedly at him. He was ambitious in stating he knew the contents of my bag and I considered that, with the two betting men present I could have got decent odds on him failing to correctly name the contents of my bag. Not even I, who had assembled them, would have guessed an interview letter; a second tie, some underarm deodorant and a small bottle of Christmas gift aftershave; one University of York book on school improvement strategies and two on the Cambridgeshire Village College system; some Panadol high strength pain relief tablets, in case I got a headache; a half eaten tube of Rowntree's Pastilles and a travel pack of tissues as recommended endlessly as an essential travel accessory by my mum. No Army service issue revolvers or automatic pistols in the list as far as I remembered, still I might have included them by oversight.

My inane smiling seemed to be doing the trick, and he relaxed knowing that my cover was now blown and that he had outwitted the best of the British Army Intelligence system. To signal the fact that I had been well and truly rumbled, he touched the end of his nose with his left index finger and pointed at me in a way I had last seen demonstrated by Paul Newman as Henry Gondorff in *The Sting*.

When he broke his stare, I looked away as well, content in our strange encounter. As promised I was the first and only customer served by Cheffy and the meal of pie and chips with an apology for a salad passed the next twenty minutes uneventfully, without so much as me dropping a segment of tomato down my shirt front.

When I went to pay at the bar I ended our encounter using a gambit I had practiced in my head for the last half hour. Summoning my best Northern Ireland accent, the one I had used to convince the gullible Colleen that not only did I came from her home town of Coleraine, but that I was born and grew up down the road and round the corner from her, I ventured, "You take care, Pat." in a manner that went beyond social niceties, and added a note of threat.

He winced and smiled and reached out his hand and I shook it, enemies with mutual respect. I wondered which of us would have the better story to tell that night.

Chapter Fourteen
INTERVIEW

Six pounds! Six whole pounds! That was how much the taxi driver had charged me to take me the eight miles into the countryside and to the school. That was as much as I'd paid for my return train ticket with my student railcard!

The Village College was a solid affair in the light coloured brick which characterised this part of the country. The taxi dropped me outside the main doors, having negotiated a short driveway lined on one side with what looked suspiciously like staff houses and on the other by the staff car park with an adjacent area set aside for the school buses which brought, no doubt reluctant learners, in from the outlying villages.

Six pounds for the taxi was hideously steep but it would have been unseemly to be seen arguing with the driver as to whether I was paying for the journey or making a takeover bid for his business. I let it go and hoped that there would be a kind teacher at the end of the day heading from the village back into Cambridge.

The main doors of the college were glass and, I believed, light oak. The wood was substantial and there was the worn graininess of two generations of pupils and staff pressing hands on the wood rather than the polished brass fingerplates.

I entered a sizeable and quiet entrance hall with displays and artwork plaques and sporting cups displayed in cabinets. All was calm and order, except for an errant chip left on the floor from when lunch had been served. The entrance hall felt polished and the air was still in there. It might have been the entrance to a great municipal building and already, I felt dangerously at home here.

Looking to my left I saw a glass-framed hatch marked reception and, retrieving my sweaty edged letter, I made for this opening and mustered what I hoped was my best winning smile.

The lady behind the glass smiled back from under big hair.

"Hughes, David," I said in that bizarre way that I always managed to reverse my name when confronted with any officialdom. "Here for the interview?" I noticed that my tone had raised at the end of the sentence. Why did I do that? Was I suggesting that I harboured some suspicion that I was not at the right time, or in the right place or even on the right day.

The school secretary, who I was later to find out was in fact the Principal's Secretary (a fine, but significant distinction not immediately apparent to me) did not pick up on my strange inflection but instead reached across to pick up a pack of materials held within an illustrated folder fronted by the school crest and pictures of students in meticulous school uniform. She ticked my name off the list of six and I remember thinking that, as it stands, I currently have a six to one chance of landing this job.

To be honest, I would have said yes to any job at present. The clock was ticking down to the end of May and that meant Whitsun Bank Holiday. We had been warned that the pick of the teaching jobs for the coming September would have been filled by then. We were a week away from the end of the half term and, although I had two further interviews organised for the following week, one in Towcester and another in Grimsby, neither appealed to me as much as the post for which I was now on the starting line.

All the people on the PGCE course were now suffering from application fatigue with long and expensive trips across the country punctuating their lives. I'd visited Exeter and had had a thoroughly excellent railway journey and introduction to the West Country but had missed out narrowly to a girl with long hair and a frightening intensity who had been a former pupil at the school.

I'd visited Worcester and a rather austere school on the edge of what would have been a delightful city to live. A random group of eight fresh faced applicants had crowded into a musty staffroom, making awkward conversation and even discussing our A level grades, as at the ice-breaking social at the first evening of university.

Beneath the pleasantries and conversation we were all conducting a ruthless appraisal of the strength of the field. He's too cocky and will overplay his hand in the interview, she is a timid mouse and won't get beyond explaining her love of the subject in muted tones and a breathless whisper. His hair is too long, the black painted nails would probably be an affectation too far for the governors and the large golden earning and sandals would probably seal his fate. Is crumpled linen ever a good look for anything other than a Middle Eastern war correspondent?

I always dressed conservatively, suit and tie being a must and a special cloth for the last minute buff up of my shoes. I'd bought a number of interview ties, well two if we are being precise. One a traditional understated dark blue and silver stripe which smacked of the Guards Armoured Division and one plain blue one with patterned stitching forming a series of blue squares with the weave running alternatively horizontally and vertically. I always wore one and had the other neatly folded in my suit breast pocket. I hadn't picked up on the fact that this made me appear that I was in the process of some hideous lop-sided breast enhancement surgery.

Sussing out the opposition at interviews, and indeed discomforting them by claiming after your interview that the questions were a nightmare or misleading them as to content was seen as part of the game to arrive at that golden place of a job for September. When the formal process had been concluded, you would be asked, amongst all the other assembled interviewees, if you would care to accompany the headteacher back to their office to be given the offer of paid employment. I noticed that at that point they never officially told you that the job was yours and it was only later that I understood that they always kept all the other applicants waiting, ostensibly for an essential debrief on the process and individual performance, but actually to have a backup plan should the 'anointed one' decide to turn down the job offer.

All the psychological warfare and jostling for position counted for nothing if you were not able to read the collective mind of the interview panel. What was it they were looking for in their ideal candidate? Perhaps they sought a mousey female bluestocking, in which case I'd have to work exceptionally hard to conform to their requirements.

The interview board usually comprised the headteacher, a governor or two, possibly a local authority representative, and the department or faculty head into whose department you would be arriving. In Worcester all the furious internal calculating about the place, the job, and people was truncated within ten minutes of arrival at the school.

We were sitting awkwardly in the untidy and care worn staffroom making banal conversation when a dispute erupted on the corridor outside the door. Among the scuffing of the feet of students making their way from registration to first lesson, there rose a voice of frightening intensity.

"Tie!" it declared with considerable intensity.

"On. Now. No excuses!" This was not a woman given to the luxury of verbs in sentences.

The calm and polite voice of a boy was heard explaining why he was not wearing his tie that morning and adding that he had a 'chit' from his mother countersigned by his form tutor confirming these circumstances.

"Detention. One hour. Tomorrow. Dismissed!" continued the harridan.

The door of the staff room was opened fiercely and in strode the very same lady.

In telephone conversations one often formed a picture of what the speaker looked like. I was usually wrong and voice and image diverged considerably on first meeting. In this case the lady striding towards our assembled and astonished group perfectly captured the shrill voice we had just heard in the corridor.

All yellow and light green tweed, she closed the distance between us in small deliberate steps of her dark brown brogues. Her pinched nostrils flared as she breathed and her round glasses glinted as she passed through a sunbeam which had unwisely penetrated the staffroom.

She came to a clipped halt and I expected to hear the click of her heels in the manner of some Prussian officer. So suddenly did she stop that her pearl twinset jumped from her chest before resettling itself on her beige high necked blouse. She quickly consulted her clipboard before placing it on an adjacent coffee table. Resting her hands on her hips in the manner of a strident sergeant major, she drew herself up to her full five feet four height and announced, "My name is Mrs Blunt. Blunt by name and blunt by nature."

I immediately felt the need to leave the interview. I'd seen enough to know that I could not work with this woman. There was no hint of irony or humour in her statement. What you saw, would indeed be what you would be getting, day in and day out, term in and term out for the next academic years until you made your escape. Then you would be reliant on this woman for a reference.

Curbing my initial inclination to walk away at this point I managed to endure the tour of the school that was the first element of most interviews. Those not put off by their potential Head of Department were already making the carefully rehearsed 'spontaneous' observations or questions designed to demonstrate the depth of their research about the school. It was a relief not to have to compete like chicks in the nest to catch the beaky Mrs Blunt's attention.

At the end of the tour we were returned to the staff room and I disappeared to make quiet representations to the Headteacher's secretary, explaining that I felt that I would not quite fit in with the dominant philosophy of the school. She looked askance at me and my temerity. Catching her mood I added that I had concerns that the proximity of the school to the river might have a negative impact on my sinusitis. The Headteacher's secretary became very sympathetic, particularly as she too was a sinusitis sufferer and my prediction, had indeed been correct. We lingered for a few seconds in talk of mucous and headaches before she winked at me and handed me the coveted 'Expense Claim Form'. This had been a considerable result. I could now spend an hour wandering the streets of Worcester before returning to the station and a connecting train to York.

The Expense Claim Form was a vital part of the interview process. Like most of my fellow students, our search for employment was taking us in ever expanding and expensive circles from York. Even with the student railcard, costs were mounting up and everyone was relieved to be handed an Expense Claim Form at the end of the interview process. Such was the need for the funds that most filled in the form and returned it before leaving the school. Only the successful candidate was beyond worry regarding the form as they had the satisfaction of knowing that their expenses would be paid in their first pay cheque at the end of September. And there was the rub, the expected protocol was that the form would be distributed at the **end** of the interview process.

Time-wasting individuals who absented themselves from the interview process at any other point during the day forfeited their right to have their expenses paid. There was always the secondary concern that the school would contact the university and make a complaint against you. Luckily at York, we had been briefed by our tutors that the choice of school in which to begin our careers was a major decision and that a negative impression we gathered on interview day was less than likely to soften when we took up our posts causing us misery and the school the abiding concern that they had made a mistaken appointment. It was better to withdraw than risk two parties feeling disgruntled.

The nightmare scenario was to go through the whole interview process knowing that there was a significant mismatch between you and the school, only to turn down the job when offered it. This would immediately entail the withdrawal of the Expense Claim Form in retribution.

Andy had recounted how he had travelled from his PGCE course in Cambridge to a town in the middle of the Lake District to endure an interview in a school for which he immediately realised he was unsuited both by temperament and geographical proximity to all the things he held dear. He had tried unsuccessfully to appear lacklustre in the interview but had made the cut for the afternoon session. Either they were setting appallingly low standards for the person they would recruit, or they were simply desperate. On either count Andy was now down to the last three and, with one person having withdrawn in the morning session, he knew that the Head was taking a hard line on claim forms.

No matter what he did to ration his performance it gave the wrong result. He did not believe in a pastoral system he boldly announced, believing it to be a structure designed to make excuses for poor performance and waited for the tidal wave of disapproval to strike. Instead they thought him radical and results focussed. He realised that his gambit that 'homework was a meaningless waste of time' was not going to work when the Head nodding sagely in agreement and it was only the last question that offered the opportunity to disqualify himself permanently.

"And finally," began the Chair of Governors, "you will have gathered that the school places considerable store on the extra curricular and sporting programme we offer students here. What role do you see for yourself in extending this programme through your own expertise?"

Andy recounted how he had taken a deep breath and, knowing that in every other educational situation his reply would be to risk professional suicide, he replied with unshakable confidence, "Extra-curricular programme? I'm sorry, my intention is to work to the very best of my ability within the hours of the school day, but to be frank with you, once that school bell goes you won't see me for exhaust fumes as I leave the school car park. I intend to have a life beyond school which extends to evenings and weekends."

There was a stunned silence as the interview board waited for their chosen one to qualify this outrageous statement, as if his statement had ended with a comma rather than a full stop. As the seconds mounted up and Andy sat uncomfortable and motionless with fixed expression, the Head broke first and asked if he had anything to add or clarify the statement.

"I don't think so, only to thank you for the opportunity to attend the interview."

Andy had his expense claim form and also a quiet word from a representative of the Local Education Authority, the PE Adviser no less, who had grasped him by the elbow rather harder than was professionally necessary and had warned him never to present himself for interview in Cumbria while he was still in post!

In the short walk down the corridor from the Warden's Secretary to the Community Room I had already decided I wanted this job. The Community Room was a sunlit filled expanse with windows on two sides. Student pictures filled one wall together with cups, shields and certificates. On the opposite wall was a series of wooden display partitions and each one contained an exquisite piece of pottery sculpture and the name of the student responsible for it.

There were tired, but comfortable chairs arranged in sixes around coffee tables and at one was a jug of water and glasses arranged on a tray and a series of brochures was arranged in a fan. Here I was ushered to sit.

"You are very early," said the Warden's secretary and she pleasingly qualified her remark with, "It always pays to plan ahead. You've some time to compose yourself and focus. Now, tea or coffee? I'll try and rustle up some biscuits whilst I'm about it, are you a custard cream fan? "

Like some character in a Victorian novel I confirmed that tea and custard creams would suit me well. I resisted the temptation to add, 'at this hour of the clock.' The secretary clip clopped away across the parquet floor and out of the door. I surveyed the room and, even on this short acquaintance, knew I wished to be part of this.

I had quality time to rehearse all my stock answers to the most asked questions, cross reference my library books with the school prospectus and, with eyes closed, picture the Warden shaking my hand profusely whilst offering me the job. After half an hour, and before everyone else arrived, I had time to saunter up the corridor to enquire where the toilet was located so as to ensure that my tie was straight, my hair was neat and I was ready for the off. My timing was rather unfortunate though, as I heard the Warden's secretary on the phone as I approached,

"Yes, arrived an hour early from York – Yes I though that was a good sign as well – very tall, very, very dark hair. Ummm. Yes, and a woollen suit in this weather – nicely polished shoes though! Likes custard creams and no sugar in his tea."

I realised that it was me being described and this was confirmed by the flustered way that the secretary spun round in her chair when my squeaking shoes announced my arrival at her window.

The interview format for the afternoon consisted of an informal interview with the Head of Integrated Humanities and a panel interview with the Warden and the Chair of Governors all proceeded by a tour of the school with one of the Deputy Heads.

The tour proceeded well. It was a neat school with some hidden gems like a swimming pool and the prospect of a new gymnasium in the offing. The staff that we saw seemed relaxed and inviting.

There was a tremendous Art and Design block, where the pottery sculptures had been designed and fired, and a Humanities department situated on the second, or top floor, of the main building that afforded views over the fens for miles. This was particularly useful as in the hour in which I had been in the Community Room there had been a regular roar of military jets and each time I ran to the window to see either F4 Phantoms or C131 Starlifters pass overhead in an easterly direction. I realised that we were on the flight path to RAF Alconbury and this was confirmed when a slender, quiet, single engined jet with thin, elongated wings passed overhead. This was a legendary U2 spyplane back from a mission somewhere deep in Eastern Europe. A job and a grandstand view of what the best of the United States Air Force in Europe could muster were on offer!

One candidate had arrived late and never really recovered her composure and I reasoned that she now had no more than an outside chance of landing the job. A guy with a beard had made a series of strident and, I thought, inappropriate comments about bringing civilisation to the yokels out in the fens and had laughed too heartily at his own jokes to be taken seriously.

I thought, or rather hoped, it was down to me and the lad from Liverpool who had engaged me in conversation about things other than our views on education.

The informal interview with Doreen, the Head of Humanities had, I thought, gone particularly well. She was approachable and realistic and when I told her my story of woe about the cost of the taxi journey said she would sort out a lift back to the station with one of the departmental team.

She spoke of my room, the classes I would be teaching and the resources on offer as if I had already secured the job. We sat in a small stock cupboard of a departmental team room, a table, six chairs and innumerable boxes of reading books, text books and packs of new exercise books, pristine and eager for those first careful words, those titles and dates neatly underlined, those shaded diagrams and graphs and maps. There were folders and treasury tags for the older students and reams and reams of punched file paper, lined, plain and graphed, just waiting for new flights of imagination. I dearly wanted to be part of this.

"How about a cup of tea? Or would you prefer coffee?" asked Doreen rising from her seat and flicking on the switch of the kettle two paces from her. She checked the small fridge that had been humming hesitantly in the corner and confirmed there was a carton of fresh milk in there.

A pen portrait of the team followed. As the department operated as an Integrated Humanities team everyone pitched in to ensure that the English, History, Geography and R.E. were delivered in Years 1 to 3. This suited me fine and I said as much. Taking a holistic view of the curriculum was what had attracted me to this particular job and now everything seemed to be coming together nicely. It would be harder not to get this job than any other that I'd applied to and the prospect of Towcester and Grimsby did little to console me should I be unsuccessful today.

R.E. was the responsibility of Mary and the tune *Lying in the Arms of Mary"* came to mind. Roberta and Janice led on English, each in a distinctive way, but two more different characters could not be imagined. Roberta was petite and studious with an encyclopaedic knowledge of English and even more obscure literature. Janice was tall, loud, and full of fun with a booming voice and an inexhaustible supply of literary one liners with which to taunt her students. Doreen, Caroline and I would lead on the development of the History and Geography elements of the course. They were looking for some fresh ideas to engage the students as they were all established teachers at the school and needed some fresh blood.

We drank our tea, some biscuits were produced from a hidey hole, custard creams, as luck would have it, and Doreen smiled whilst looking at the packet and asked if I had any questions as she seemed to have been talking rather a lot. I had prepared a whole list of clever questions for this point in the interview, but Doreen had been so disarming that all I managed to say was, "I really hope I get the chance to be a part of this team." and I truly meant it.

"Look at the time!" said Doreen as we talked a little more about the local area and its history, our families, my home town and her upbringing in war-torn Coventry.

"I must get you back down for your interview with the Warden!"

Which was the best order in which to be interviewed? Going first meant that both you and the interviewers would be fresh, which must be a good thing. But what if the tedium of those that went after you prevented them remembering the sheer brilliance of your answers. Similarly going last could mean a turbocharged you casting pearls of wisdom to the exhausted.

I arrived in the Warden's office fourth in line and passed through his secretary's office to get there. She smiled as I passed, which was encouraging.

The warden was a tall man with an ecclesiastical edge to him, very polite and friendly, but slightly other-worldly. He introduced me to the Chair of governors, Mrs Dale, a redoubtable lady in a powder blue two piece suit that my mother would have admired. Pinned to her lapel was some form of honour and I tried to identify it without paying inordinate attention to the bosom of a seventy year old lady.

Mrs Dale relinquished the black leather handbag that sat across her lap and by way of apology said, "Do forgive me young man, I've just been powdering my nose."

I moved forward to shake her hand and she appeared to recoil backwards against her armchair.

"My, my, you are very tall!" she exclaimed.

I couldn't think of anything to say, but managed to confirm her observation.

"Yes, I suppose I am!"

She then offered her hand, which I shook.

"A good firm handshake – it is so very important don't you think? We had someone in here earlier – handshake like a wet lettuce. Do sit down dearie."

I replied that my father always made the same observation and she asked if he had fought in the war, to which I replied that he had been in the Royal Artillery on anti aircraft guns.

"Bofors, 3.7 or 4.5?" she had enquired showing a remarkable knowledge of Royal Artillery Ordnance.

"3.7," said I, "on the predictor."

"Clearly a clever and sensible man," she concluded.

This was a promising if unorthodox start, for which I had clearly not rehearsed. It seemed my father's army record was going to be of particular importance at the interview stages of my life as this was the second time it had cropped up.

Mr Felstead, the Warden, then interjected with a series of more educationally focussed questions and I was able to answer, without any artifice, about my general educational philosophy, specific organisational aspects and how I'd work with parents. I even managed to weave in the key elements of the Village College system that had encouraged me to apply.

My only concern was that in my enthusiasm I'd rambled and perhaps given too much detail. Only once did I find myself at that embarrassing point when the words were still pouring out of your mouth but I had no recollection what the original question had been. This interview was a dream in that I was being allowed to talk about things that really mattered.

No sooner had I finished the fifth answer though than Mrs Dale interjected, "Enough, young man. I think we've heard enough."

I was dumbstruck, thinking that I'd outstayed my welcome with my ramblings.

"I think we've seen enough Warden. This young man clearly looks like the sort of teacher we want and sounds like him as well."

Mr Felstead thanked me and escorted me to the door without giving any indication as to whether he concurred with Mrs Dale.

Back in the community room there was much excitement among the candidates. It transpired that whilst I was being grilled, or rather lightly toasted, like a muffin, one of the Deputy Head teachers had entered and explained that the houses we could see opposite were indeed staff houses and that one would be available for the successful candidate. This had considerably increased the attractiveness of the job. I cursed that I had not been able to pitch for the house whilst in the interview room. Then again, neither had the three other candidates. Only Colin, the lad from Liverpool, and the late arriving girl, who had spent most of the time in the toilet, were left to be interviewed.

I eyed the houses. They were substantial three bedroomed houses in light yellow brick and clad on the upper storey in a wood façade. I imagined the excitement of landing both a job and a house in one day and then sat disconsolate and not inclined to make polite conversation as the pattern of my future was presently being decided and I was powerless to do anything more to promote myself as the ideal candidate. I had to hope that being tall, a firm handshake and a father who had served in the Royal Artillery on 3.7inch anti-aircraft guns were enough to swing it my way.

It was torture sitting through the last interviews, they seemed to have an inordinate amount of time to expand on their philosophy and practice! I excused myself and went to the toilet at one stage simply to have a space where I was not required to engage in social chit chat. I was surprised to find Izal, mildly medicated toilet paper, as absorbent as polished diamond in the toilet! It made good tracing paper though, providing you didn't want to trace anything bigger than 6 x 4 inches! For a second I was back at my Nain's outside toilet a decade before and I was pleased that the toilet paper had provided such a pleasant and unexpected distraction.

Finally we were all assembled in the community room and twenty minutes of further deliberation took place.

The last time I had wanted something so much it had been Victoria and that had been seven long years ago, and then there had been the day of the A level results. Those had been nebulous things. This was something concrete; a job and a house and the chance to get my life on the road. I analysed everything that had been said and left unsaid. I suddenly remembered pithy and succinct answers to the questions I had been asked. I even rehearsed the disappointment of failure and the prospect of Towcester and Grimsby the following week, hawking my tired body to school after school with the clock ticking in the background.

Finally Mr Felstead and Mrs Dale arrived at the door of the community room. Mr Felstead had a sheet of A4 with the names of all the candidates written on it and unhelpfully, each had some summary comments written against the name.

He thanked us all for coming and explained that it had been a difficult task as it had been a strong field. Every candidate was a credible one who could have fulfilled the role advertised.

The Warden had been careful to share his gaze equally with all the candidates so as not to give any hint of the selection. This was the measure of a scrupulously fair man. My spirits rose as he looked directly at me and fell as they moved on. We must have stood like puppies at an RSPCA rescue shelter begging to be chosen.

He'd moved to the far end of the line when, speech completed, he added, "Mr Hughes, would you like to come to my office please."

I had to be cautious now, I could not assume that he was following the normal convention, this might be a de-brief for the losing candidate!

I squeaked down the corridor in painfully noisy shoes accompanied by Mrs Dale. Doreen was waiting in the Warden's office with a broad grin on her face. We entered and Mr Felstead closed the door.

"David, I'd like to formally offer you the post of Assistant Teacher in the Department of Humanities at Longstanton Village College. Are you willing to accept?"

"Yes. Yes please!" I gushed, perhaps too enthusiastically.

"Will you be requiring a staff house?" he asked.

"Yes. Yes please!" I gushed again, certainly too enthusiastically.

"I'll see what I can do to arrange it."

"Well done young man, make us proud," added Mrs Dale with a firm handshake.

"I'm really looking forward to you joining the team," said Doreen warmly.

"I can't believe this and I can't wait," said I, my voice trembling more than a little with emotion.

"Now," said Mr Felstead, "I've secured one excellent appointment, let's see if I can secure another. We've decide to make two appointments and Mr Colin Plessey will also be joining us in September if he accepts."

"That's brilliant news, we really hit it off in conversation," replied the College's newest teacher.

Doreen was as good as her word and I was given a lift back to the station by Roberta and the New Zealand exchange teacher. In the lulls in the conversation, which were not many, I kept hearing a voice in my head repeating, 'David Hughes – teacher.'

Chapter Fifteen
STAFF

Despite my genuine joy at being appointed, the time between May and September disappeared very quickly. Knowing that there was the prospect of regular money coming in from the end of September I'd eaten in to the remains of my grant that I had carefully eked out in my final year to indulge myself on a foreign holiday.

A number of official letters arrived for me at home in Rhyl confirming my contract and these were duly passed around the family like some medieval religious relics. My BA Hons, MA, and PGCE certificates which I'd left on the mantelpiece of my bedroom for safe keeping while I gadded about that summer, had mysteriously been framed and placed in line on the longest wall of the living room, where other homes might have three plaster ducks. The house was quickly turning into a shrine to my academic success but, I suppose I'd always know where to find my certificates if I needed them in a hurry.

It was only later that I felt a pang of guilt at my studied indifference to my mum and dad's pride. To have displayed the certificates, above all else in pride of place in the living room was a measure of how highly they valued my educational achievements and I remembered how both had had their educational dreams shattered by the Depression and the war.

What was conspicuous by its absence in all the documentation was any mention of the staff house. Having tried and failed to contact the Warden by phone, I received a well crafted letter in elegant blue fountain pen script which apologised for there not being a house available for the September, except for the one that he had deemed most equitable to give to two new female members of staff. I was assured that I was next on the list for a house but that he thought it unlikely that one would become available before Christmas. This was definitely a blow and I was forced to try to organise some temporary digs to see me through to Christmas. This problem was made doubly difficult by it now being the last week of the school summer term and in a turn of phrase that was to become one of my trade marks, 'Time was of the Essence!'

Despite the house debacle, I arrived in Over, the late Sunday afternoon before school started, in considerable trepidation. We wandered around the village green on a beautiful balmy September evening at the end of the village fete. Happy families were heading for home having taken part in the

Tug-O-War and other assorted entertainments. There had been coconut shies and darts stalls, a gypsy fortune teller and a beer tent.

It struck me that I could have witnessed such a fete on the village green in any of the last two hundred years and some of the faces would have been from the same families, with the same measured local drawl. However a newer phenomena was probably the more clipped tones of the new generation of economic immigrants, people who had settled in the villages in commutable distance of either Cambridge or Huntingdon Railway Station, from which they could be in London within an hour. They came like a tide, and now I was one of them, admiring everything quaint about village life, but we could so easily turn into a tsunami, denuding the village of all its soul, and magical afternoons like this, with the village fete.

I watched the sun go down over the fens casting a giant sunburst before dropping over the far horizon. It all seemed idyllic, apart from the prospect of starting my teaching career on the following morning feeling more than a little like a fraud.

I slept fitfully in my new digs that night. Although I'd endured some chaotic house moves in the course of the last few years, this was different. I was now embarking on a proper life rather than fannying about in student houses with their gloriously temporary nature and ability to reconstruct living spaces at a moment's notice. This was real, and insofar as anything was permanent, this was.

I endured a night of checking the alarm clock and calculating how much more time I had left in bed and then twitching and cursing the fact that I couldn't disengage my brain long enough to relax into sleep.

The Staff Room was entered by a door like any other along the long corridor. Unlike the other doors on the corridor, the window had been part frosted and the prying eyes of the local scholars had been further excluded by some strategically placed sugar paper and aged Sellotape which had worked its way into the wooden fabric of the door, being indistinguishable from the varnish.

Being ridiculously early for my first day, the room was deserted but a water boiler of the type I had been used to at university was busily reaching the humming, boiling stage. Someone had clearly preceded me into the room as a sign next to the boiler announced in a scholastic script 'First In – Switch me on – Last out Switch me off!'

The room smelt of floor polish and old coffee and it was clear that a fair proportion of the latter, spilt liberally on the parquet flooring, had prompted a fair application of the former. The room was, in truth, a mess, as I was to find that most staffrooms were. The collective sanctuaries of all teachers, and I suppose any large group of people working under pressure and to a constant ringing of a bell, are untidy in the extreme. This was always a problem where there was a collective responsibility to keep a room tidy, as I had found out in some of the shared kitchens on the university campus.

The furniture was of no common age. There were tubular steel chairs with stretched canvas that I remembered from primary school, chairs that would not look out of place in an old people's home with high sides to prevent the incumbent's head lolling limp while they dreamt of their favourite soup and Christmases past. There were wooden framed chairs with the lacquer faded and peeling, upholstered in elaborate floral design fabrics that the sun had reduced to subtle shades of beige, terracotta and grey. There was a broken wooden chair with a hastily scribbled note exhorting no-one to sit on it.

The chairs were dotted around coffee tables that looked like they had been assembled by someone from a manic day at an auction for house clearance furniture. Dark wood and pine as well as more avant garde plastic coffee tables vied for space, all covered in sheets of yellowed A4 paper marked, as if cherished by octopuses, with circular coffee and tea stains from a thousand discarded mugs. Some tables had a lower shelf, and on these the yellowed paper, having reached the point of being stacked so high on the table as to be unsafe to perch a mug of any description, had merely been decanted en masse to the lower shelf for someone else to ultimately dispose of when the aesthetics or the fire hazard of the mess became intolerable.

On more careful examination, each sheet in the pile seemed to hold some information of fleeting importance, critical on the day they were produced, less so now. Memos, circulars and meeting agendas that, on the day of their production, were of infinite significance, but now were like all thoughts and pronouncements, reduced in their stature to fading mementoes.

There was the familiar smell of roneoed paper, the carbony, chemical whiff of official administration, with *o's* and *a's* saturated with ink. In the damp air of the early September morning I could also smell a second distinctive odour, of strong and vaporous industrial strength alcohol, heady and aromatic.

This was a smell I had first become familiar with at university – the Banda machine – standby of the harassed teacher.

The Banda machine worked on a simple principle. You wrote on the upper of two sheets of affixed paper and your scribblings picked up a layer of colour from the lower carbonised sheet. Torn from the backing paper, the upper sheet was now attached to a circular steel drum and the mirror image writing was rotated on the drum through a bath of alcohol. An invisible arm picked up a sheet of crisp A4 paper from a magazine and impregnating it with boozy indistinct writing, before depositing it limply in a second magazine, or if this was missing or broken, depositing them like Gatling gun spent ammunition cases on the floor.

In the coming months I was to see teachers in the closeted reprographics room, I may have been one myself, stood trance-like turning the handle of the Banda machine, generating countless copies of worksheets whilst held in thrall to the heady mist of industrial alcohol. Less absinthe, more educationally induced mental absence. It reminded me of the treadmill I'd once seen in Beaumaris Gaol on which prisoners pointlessly shuffled out time to no purpose.

My fondness for the Banda Machine was to lead me to an early and unfortunate encounter with the senior female deputy head. I'd only been in the school for a couple of days when I ascertained that to avail myself of the full range of audio- visual aids, the OHP acetates and 'pens OHP for the exclusive use of, permanent and non permanent', coloured chalks and banda stencils of many colours, I needed to present myself to the senior deputy in her office to fill in a 'chit'. It was explained to me that I had had to report to the school secretary no less, to apply for a chit that would then need to be completed and presented to the deputy head.

I'd filled the chit in using my best teaching practice fountain pen, trying to create an air of unwarranted gravitas, like a doctor filling in a prescription scrip, and probably as illegible. I felt my request was appropriate and modest, but it was pointed out to me that that was for the deputy head to decide.

I'd knocked jauntily on the deputy head's door at the end of the school day and had not been bade to enter. There was the sound of laughter within so I knocked harder, straightening my brown tweed tie which had adopted a jaunty angle through the exertions of a full teaching day. I also took the opportunity to straighten my hair which was annoyingly sticking up at the crown, the result of too much rush in the shower this morning.

Again I was not bidden to enter. This was perplexing as I had knocked hard enough to be heard over the laughter within. What should I do now? I could walk away, but if someone came to the door to open it they would think me, the only figure in sight, an idiot for knocking and walking away. I decided to enter, with a Labrador flourish of enthusiasm.

My foot was hardly over the threshold when I realised I had made a mistake. The room went suddenly quiet and none of the three women in the room gave me a clue as to which was the deputy that I had yet to meet. They eyed me with suspicion and the Scottish play came to mind. The elder of the three women looked me up and down whilst dunking a digestive biscuit deliberately.

"Yes?" she said, irritated at being interrupted.

"I understand I need to hand my chit in here," I replied apologetically.

She reached slowly for the lit cigarette in the ashtray, inhaled and exhaled in my general direction (it was all I could do to stifle a cough as the smoke assaulted me) and gestured dismissively, to a set of wooden filing trays behind me.

"Put it in there – in the one marked CHIT. I'm far too busy to deal with it now."

I turned and located the tray marked CHIT from the twenty filing trays arranged on the wooden bench behind me and turned again to give her a thankful smile. Her attention was now deep in some paperwork which required the use of the ornate tortoiseshell glasses, which had hung until now, by an intricate necklace around her bosom, and which were now perched on the end of her nose. It struck me that my life was increasingly taken up with the tortoiseshell glasses ladies. She merely waved her cigarette dismissively towards the door, spilling ash over the desk as she did so. The two other women, having taken their cue from the deputy were also deep in paperwork now, one reading the typing she was completing to join the pile of urgent waste paper in the staffroom.

Not wishing to overstay my welcome, if indeed welcome was the appropriate term for this encounter, I made to make the three steps to the door. I had executed only two when the deputy rejoined the conversation.

"On second thoughts, let me peruse your outrageous stationery demands now."

I swivelled overenthusiastically and retrieved the chit. I was about to place it in her hand but both were occupied, one by her cigarette and the other by the next digestive, so I placed it in eyeshot, facing her on top of her pile of paperwork.

She completed a flawless dunking operation and consumed the digestive in two bites. Putting the cigarette to her crumb laden lips she studied my chit with some care.

She exhaled noisily and demanded of me why I should require chalk of several different colours. I explained that I wanted to use a colour code on the blackboard so that, for example, in sentence construction red could be used for verbs to emphasise action and animation, blue for nouns and green for adjecti—

I didn't get to complete the sentence. Her eye had moved down for the same multicoloured request for Banda paper.

"And how long have you been teaching, to have placed such profligate demands on the resources of this school?"

"Two days," we both managed to say at the same time, me by way of explanation and her by way of exclamation.

I was beginning to think that she would ask for my mother to come in for a parental interview when I remembered, with some embarrassment, that I was in fact a teacher employed in a professional capacity in the school.

"You do realise that I will need to make a special requisition order to obtain these resources?"

"I'm sorry," I replied, although I wasn't, nor was I prepared to rescind my chit.

She looked me up and down from my hastily rearranged brown tie to my brown brogues and ventured "A bit flash aren't you?"

I wasn't sure if she was referring to my educationally philosophy or my sartorial taste so I just smiled inanely until she looked away to her paperwork and beat a hasty retreat from the room and the torment.

"Just a minute!" she recalled me as I crossed the door again. "You'd better take this for now…"

She swivelled on her office chair and reached into her handbag as she did so to retrieve a key. She opened the cupboard behind her as if it was a safe and the full length door yielded to reveal hundreds of boxes of white school chalk. I'd never seen so much chalk. Large boxes, small boxes, dozens of boxes clamped together under cellophane. I had definitely never seen so much chalk. I didn't think there was so much chalk outside the environs of Dover. She reached in to a middle shelf and took out one box of twelve white chalks, only the third one to be removed from the whole cupboard.

"And don't waste it!"

I thanked her for her beneficence like some Dickensian urchin and finally left the room. I was so taken aback by the encounter that I slunk to the staffroom and recounted the incident to an older member of staff trying to complete *The Times* crossword. He smiled and reassured me that she'd mellow once I'd proved myself, as indeed she did over the coming months. He then recounted the story of how, having misread the ordering code in the stationery catalogue, the deputy had ordered twenty gross of boxes of chalk rather than twenty boxes and that there were another four cupboards stacked as full of the first one. If ever there were a world school chalk shortage, he stated, we'd all be able to retire on the profits from selling the chalk mountain.

But that was two days in the future and I had to negotiate my first morning first…

The staff room was now filling up with weary older teachers and more energetic early risers. I didn't know where to sit in the room as there was obviously some unwritten seating plan. I finally settled for one of the high back chairs and perched my cup of coffee on the top of the memo mountain. I looked around and waited for a face I knew to arrive. I looked for potential allies and remembered that the Warden had said that a number of other staff, direct from university were due to start this term. Perhaps this would be the start of a number of beautiful friendships, especially as the Village College felt a lot further from the metropolis of Cambridge than I remembered on the day of my interview.

I refocused on the present and was aware of a man now sitting in the seat next to mine.

"I wouldn't drink that coffee, son!" exclaimed the red faced middle aged gent in the kind of brown overall usually worn by sales assistants in traditional hardware stores. "It'll make your nose bleed!"

"Why's that?" I answered, trying to work out what properties of the coffee might bring on a nose bleed.

"Because it's mine!" came the reply from the man who looked like he belonged in a livestock market perusing sheep.

"New boy eh?" he said to his cronies in the high backed chairs lingering over their early morning drinks. Clearly he intended to hold court over the room and I braced myself for what was the inevitable good advice.

"Let me give you some good advice as you start your career all fresh faced and idealistic," he said predictably. "Basically, kids are malevolent bastards, and the one's that don't appear to be are simply sly with it."

Two of the cronies, a short man in a smart suit that screamed Maths teacher and a taller well set man who had the look of a scientist about him nodded in mute agreement.

"When you've been in the business as long as I have, lad, you'll realise that what comes around goes around. There's nothing new under the sun, just the same crap that keeps resurfacing. So we don't need you spouting any new ideas here son – just look and learn, lad, look and learn."

"Thanks for the advice," I replied and smiled. I hope he picked up the note of sarcasm in my voice, but it was very subtle and probably passed him by unrecognised. This was day one and I didn't want to go burning my bridges before I'd established myself.

He tapped the arms of the chair, satisfied with his sermon and effectively dismissing me.

This put me in mind of a conversation I'd had with my tutor at university after an almost identical altercation in the staffroom on my teaching practice.

"What you have to remember David, is that some people in every staffroom have up to forty year's experience in the craft of teaching and others manage to exist in ekeing out one year's experience for a forty year career. You need to decide to which group you want to belong. You can be sure though that the latter group generally despise children and may be prepared to sacrifice happiness and fulfilment on a daily basis for a pension and a six-week summer holiday."

I had been surprised how strident my tutor had been on this point, given his reticence to go beyond the philosophy and sociology of classroom discipline into practicalities. This had been a real flash of insight and was immutably true of any staffroom I've been in subsequently.

It came as no surprise on the following day that I found the small Maths teacher, for such he was, berating an unkempt girl on the crowded corridor at break time by announcing in as loud a voice as possible, "Janet Moody, the good Lord put people on this world to be either useful or decorative. You are neither."

There was a phrase used in the army, or in the artillery to be precise, 'Fire for Effect' and this Maths teacher would probably have been familiar with it from his military service. This is precisely what he was trying to achieve.

Certainly, the effect was lost on the aforementioned Miss Moody who furrowed her brow, and, for a second at least, stopped chewing like a ruminating cow, before deciding that she couldn't be arsed to work out precisely how she had just been insulted. Those students around her in the corridor caught the shrapnel of this stinging rebuke and cowered slightly until the diminutive Maths teacher disappeared down the corridor and into the staff room, pleased with his barrage.

I decided I'd made a mistake in positioning myself with this group of ne'er do wells on my first morning.

Chapter Sixteen
SLUGS

It was the first time I was to hear the words in my teaching career...but it certainly would not be the last. The fateful words were to be the preface for whenever somebody, usually the Head or Deputies, but sometimes the Head of Department, wanted you to do something that was either mindlessly, skull numbingly boring, required much work and no recognition, or involved some risky innovation that they wanted to be able to plausibly deny in the future when things had gone horribly, terribly wrong.

The words might be dressed up as an opportunity to be at the cutting edge of innovation, to take a personal responsibility for a new and exciting project or as playing a critical role in moving the school forward, but three words would always form part of the appeal...professional development opportunity.

Professional development opportunity was a very, very clever use of words. To have a professional development opportunity outlined to you, to be mesmerised by the explanation of why you, exclusively, had the precise skills (or required them developed and honed through this experience) attitude and values to pull off this project and then, to apply your own common sense, to reject such an offer was tantamount to professional suicide.

To reject a professional development opportunity was to demonstrate questionable professionalism, to ignore the concept of personal development and to lack the judgment to recognise an opportunity when it was thrust before you.

The staffrooms of the land were always populated by at least one teacher who had rejected a professional development opportunity early in their employment and who now sat isolated in the corner seat of the staffroom, their career becalmed in a Sargasso Sea of mindless paperwork and concern over who had used their personal mug at break time and had omitted to wash it and return it to its nominated cup hook.

Most new teachers reacted like Labrador puppies to the prospect of a PDO in the early stages of their career. I was no exception. In fact I was really rather flattered that my first PDO was presented to me within twenty minutes of arriving for the administration day which preceded the first day of term that September.

My new head of department took me up to the departmental office with a mug of strong tea and went through the pattern of the first day and week which included first view of my timetable. It was explained what the code for each subject and group meant. Much of this was largely self explanatory: IH for Integrated Humanities, Hi for History, Gg for Geography, Ss for Social Studies. I was beginning to relax into my comfort zone as, being a new teacher I saw I was not down to take a tutor group in my first term and also there were some blank periods which I was advised never to refer to as Free Periods but as Preparation Periods.

We both arrived at Friday with something of a jolt. I saw a free period, sorry preparation period, followed by three lessons labelled SLG extending from the period after break to lunch and from lunch through the two afternoon periods to the end of the school day. I could not think of any subject, or combination of subjects that would conjure up the initials SLG and began to speculate as to whether this was some private contemplation time when I would be left alone in some darkened room to reflect on the week just past and contemplate the one to come. Silent Learning Generation perhaps or maybe Sit, Looking Glazed? Neither acronym sounded plausible. It was left to Doreen, my new and kindly Head of Department (HoD), to reveal my first PDO.

She was most apologetic in her manner, which should have given me cause for concern. She explained that the SLG group had previously been the responsibility of the Deputy Head and that it was with great reluctance that he was even prepared to contemplate handing over his pet project to me, a probationary teacher. She did not sound particularly convincing when she outlined what a mark of esteem it was to have been allocated this group in my first week of teaching, how the Deputy Head had spoken extensively about me since my appointment in May to assess if I was indeed worthy of the role that was now being thrust upon me. It was, apparently, a professional risk on his behalf to surrender all the work he had put into the group to a novice, but he had seen signs in my CV and what my HoD had told him of a young teacher with 'bottom' with 'professional presence'.

I must have looked particularly blank at this point as Doreen felt the need to say, "He wants you to teach the SLG group."

"Oh," I replied, less than decisively.

It was amazing how quickly Friday came around.

I'd spent a lot of time preparing for the lesson – with two thirds of a school day to play with it could clearly go one of two ways. If my planning was up to scratch then a well crafted series of activities would see the time fly by. If not, this could be a very long and bumpy ride.

One of the things Anthony, the Deputy, bequeathed to me was a sheaf of neatly written notes outlining the choreography of the term's lesson development. It was an extremely worthy document, detailed and with references to resources, audio cassettes and, at one point, a TV programme. He had also gone to the trouble of including a short pen portrait of each of the characters that made up the Slow Learners Group or SLGs.

I'd a real problem with this compendium of information though, as it was really a reflection of the Deputy's approach to learning and his perception of the students. I'd found on teaching practice (that now felt a lifetime away!) that the same students behaved differently with different members of staff. If that were the case then there must be an element of how the staff reacted with them which determined how they behaved. What I would look to do was try, over a number of uncomfortable lessons, to build a relationship with each of the seven students so that we could all relax and get on with some learning.

I couldn't do that if I was to rely solely on the Deputy's notes. In fact I would have preferred a blank piece of paper to start from and to tease out for myself what worked with each of the characters. Similarly, in trying to be helpful in supplying detailed lesson plans, I'd been offered a straight jacket, complete with timings for each individual activity. Putting the character sketches and the lesson plans together I reckoned would mean that I'd have to be a *ushabti* of Anthony to deliver them successfully. (*ushabti* were funerary figurines placed in the tombs of pharaohs among the grave goods and were intended to act as substitutes for the deceased, should he/she be called upon to do manual labour in the afterlife. This about summed this PDO situation up.) *Ushabti* was one of my words for that week which I contrived to work into my lessons, whether it was relevant or not, to try and develop vocabulary and to have as a conversation piece at the end of the lesson.

Theme: The Five Senses, Lesson One: *The Caged Skylark* by Gerard Manley Hopkins. Poetry Analysis.

I read the poem at first with some satisfaction. The fact that Mr. Hopkins had written it a few miles from my home town in the Clwyd Valley, and had indeed visited Rhyl in the year of its composition seemed a good omen.

Adam was a thick set boy who, at the age of fourteen already had the build and demeanour of a farm labourer. His face and arms were berry brown and he clearly was not one for spending time indoors if there was light and fun to be had outside. His hair was so close cropped that the pattern of scars from previous adventures could clearly be seen etched beneath the millimetric length hairs. He had intensely dark eyes, which showed no emotion and he had an unnerving habit of fixing you in his dark gaze and turning his head without his eyes shifting their focus from you, like an owl. *Difficult to engage!!!* Anthony's notes said ominously and the three exclamation marks emphasised the point.

Milly's notes were prefaced by a remark about having a quiet word with the school welfare officer to understand the context for her withdrawn behaviour.

There was no chance of mistaking her when I first entered the room. She was staring with a blank expression at the desk and Karen, an extremely animated girl with a shock of frizzy blonde hair was talking to her as if she were her interpreter. Every so often a slight movement of the head indicated a Yes or No to the endless propositions that Karen was putting to her, but her eyes never moved from the desk and not a sound did she utter. What was her favourite colour brought no response, did she like *Coronation Street* last night the faintest nod of the head. Had she heard the Adam Ant single? Was she going to youth club this week? Both were answered with the merest shake of the head. In between this interrogation Karen had managed to clock me and give me the biggest of beaming smiles through yellow teeth.

"Hiya sir!" she said with puppy dog affection.

Karen had been summed up as *helpful but extremely volatile – keep her away from Adam and Adrian!* in Anthony's notes.

Doreen had accompanied me in and proceeded to introduce me to the class. How lucky they were to have me was made abundantly clear as were a number of veiled threats about their conduct. The threats became even less veiled when Jeffs burst through the door, seemingly determined to recount some incident that had just happened in the playground involving a slug and a catapult. (Jeffs had warranted *unreliable and deceitful* in the notes as well as *prone to exaggeration and overreaction*). Robert and Stuart were particularly keen to have a full report of the incident. But Doreen pressed on to subdue the room and have them ready for the lesson.

The room was only about 20 feet by 15 feet and it reminded me of the Remove in Emmanuel School, a room for containment as much as anything. The eight desks were arranged in a horseshoe shape and each student had a full desk to him or herself. This was unusual as students in all the other classes sat two to a desk, but long experience had shown that with the SLGs, the niggling and bad temper of too close proximity had led to this spacious solution.

Doreen worked the room like a lion tamer worked his animals. Scanning them hawk-like, she looked for any sign of muscle movement which indicated an imminent snarl or jibe against a fellow student. Only Milly escaped attention, her eyes still intent on the spotted pattern on the light blue formica of her desk top.

Doreen took the millisecond when all seemed calm to hand over control of the class to me.

"Right, I'll let Mr. Hughes get on, I know he has some exciting things for you."

She put down the cup of tea she was holding on my desk and whispered, "Made you this to keep you going."

I'd assumed that the cup of tea was her own, and thought it a little ominous that she had gone to that trouble. I sat into the wooden slatted chair and produced the register.

Doreen squeezed my shoulder by way of encouragement and backed away to the door. She stood in the doorway for a few seconds to hear me read out the first names on the register and was gone, the door shutting silently behind her, a little like an air-lock being closed, I thought.

I'd anticipated the first trial from my time on teaching practice. Apart from the three girls, apparently none of the boys on the register was present.

"That register's out of date said Adrian!" who was now claiming to be Mickey and I knew he was struggling to contain himself at the thought of me asking him to confirm his surname.

Trying to outwit him I ventured, "Well, if it is, Mister Mouse, you need to remember that if I add your name to it you will be permanently added! If it turns out that an Adrian turns up, I'll be expecting homework from both Adrian and Mickey – and I won't be expecting it to be copied!"

Adrian was momentarily dumbfounded at being beaten to his punch line and considered admitting his real name. You could see in the contortions of his face that his brain was working overtime at a plan B.

"OK sir, only joking. My name's Stuart."

Picking up the joke too quickly for it to be reality, Stuart immediately claimed to be Adrian. The rest piled in with swapped names. This was getting wearisome but it was nothing that I hadn't met before. I wondered if Ieuan Morgan, far away in York, had had to put up with this before designing his fiendish methods of engaging children.

"No bother, I'd prefer to do the register at the beginning but it might be more fun for me to have Mrs. Ginn come in at the end of the lesson and we can do it properly then. Not sure how Mrs. Ginn will react though – Fish and Chips on the menu today – her favourite she was telling me. She likes to get down early for lunch before the queues form. Not sure how she will react if she is here, having to do a register because you lot have been messing about."

"We've not been messing about!" said Karen indicating with her index finger both herself and Milly. She was clearly already brewing up with the injustice of the possibility of having to stay behind.

"Quite right, and I think that it will be only fair that you two get to lunch on time," trying to placate her and set the tone for the room.

"Yeah well, you would be Miss Goody Two shoes wouldn't you – you should have played along with us!" chimed in Adam, and my best efforts were undone as Karen flew at him in a Harpie rage.

Obscenities were exchanged and that lowest jibe, saying something about your opponent's mother quickly came into play.

I'd found that this was a universal incitement. Anything could be justified in retaliation once something had been said about someone else's mother. The majority of fights that I'd seen in the schools I'd visited could usually be pinned down to the trigger point of, 'He called my mother a...' and then it all went off.

I always thought it was less about familial honour at that point and more about crossing a line in terms of intent to move from words to fists. Some children I'd come across were truly indifferent to their parents but would still react to this jibe.

"Ah couldn't let it go sir, not once he's brought me Ma into it!" had been the response of one really good student when I'd quizzed him about a fight in which he had been uncharacteristically drawn into during my teaching practice. I didn't remember this pretext for a fight in my own schools days, which seemed to be rapidly receding into the mists of time. I felt very old, or rather mature, amongst all these shenanigans.

There was a part of me that was also proud to have seen off this kerfuffle without recourse to the standard rebuke: "It's your time you are wasting not mine!"

On teaching practice I'd refined this to "The strange thing is I get paid by the hour, so whether you learn anything or not shouldn't really matter to me – I'm still going to get paid!"

It was, like all things when dealing with adolescents, all in the manner of the delivery, slow and deliberate, with a hint of a smile and completely unflustered. Deliberately leaving the sentence hanging, like a grenade with the pin out, without over-elaborating, meant that they had to react to it. It was amazing how well it reduced what appeared to be a well organised frontal attack on your classroom discipline to a routed and despondent mob looking desperately for leadership.

If you knew who the influencers were in the class you could then deliver the *coup de grace*. Focussing on them and addressing them directly, I'd developed this follow up line…

"Stuart, my preference is that I deliver this one hour of learning within the time allocated for it on the timetable, but if you wish to continue to muck about I'll be forced to extend it all the way into lunchtime until I'm sure that we have all had one hour of learning. Of course, that's your choice not mine, but I think it is only fair to warn you that everyone will be having one hour of learning in lessons – I'd feel really bad about picking up my wages otherwise. Fair play though, or as we say in Wales *Chwarae Teg!,* I'll be really sympathetic to those students who are keen to demonstrate to me that they will learn within the lesson time. They will not have to wait here salivating for their fish and chips."

On this morning this left three camps now thinking feverishly. Stuart and the other disruptives were calculating whether I meant what I said, as my retribution was delayed rather than delivered instantly, they could not know if I was bluffing or not. A second group was, like the dog of Pavlov, salivating at the thought of Fish and Chips for lunch and I'm not ashamed to be numbered in this group. A group of girls took a different tack.

"Can you speak Welsh sir?"

"Enough to get by," stretching the point like an elastic band to the point that it could easily twang and take my eye out.

"Can you say that long place name?"

"What, *Llanfairpwllgwyngyllgogerychwyrndrobwllllantysiliogogogoch,* er, no, no, I can't say that."

To my surprise, there was a spontaneous cheer in the classroom.

"Say it again, sir!" bellowed Karen excitedly.

"Say what again?"

"The Welsh word!"

"But I told you I can't say it. Tell you what, I'll have a go at the end of the lesson, but only for those people who get on task and stay there for the whole lesson."

Most people now settled to work, a couple looked to Stuart for guidance and were met by a shrug of the shoulders. It seemed like I had stifled revolt for now.

I was finally able to distribute the highly coloured text books and had drawn their attention to the Gerard Manley Hopkins poem on page 48.

"Jeffs and Adam don't like poetry, cos they don't like reading, cos they can't read!"

"I ain't reading nuffink," said Adam defensively.

"So you are reading something?" said I, seeing the opportunity to explore the use of the double negative.

"No, I just said, I ain't reading nuffink!" insisted Adam.

"But think it through, if you aren't reading nothing, you are actually saying you are reading something – you've used a double negative which is the same as saying a positive."

Adam considered the nuances of this proposition for a second. It clearly did not register.

"But, like I said, I ain't reading nothing," repeated Adam.

Jeffs came to my aid unexpectedly. "Don't you see Adam, not doing nothing equals must be doing something."

Stuart saw the possibility, "I've never not liked Cambridge United!"

"Brilliant! Who is next up?"

We went around the room making up our double negatives.

Even Milly was brought into the fun; she mumbled something into the frizzy hair near Karen's ear. Karen turned and whispered something back into Milly's ear for clarification and announced, "Milly says she is not not going to watch *Doctor Who* tomorrow."

The class clapped, sympathetic to the trouble Milly had taken to be a part of this exercise. Milly merely stared at the desk top but her mouth widened slightly into what I imagined was the beginning of a smile of satisfaction.

This was all well and good, everyone involved in an exercise and sharing ideas reasonably patiently, but this was a million miles away from the set text we were meant to be studying.

We laboured on with studying the Skylark but most people's concentration fell away very quickly. No one after the first two lines wanted to volunteer to read a line to the class. Some put up the standard response of it was boring, but I could tell when I scanned the room for the next reader, that there was real fear of being asked to do the task, and failing in front of everyone. It was the same fear that I would have if I'd been asked to sing so I understood only too well their discomfort. This was clearly something I'd have to work on, but it was pointless spending time setting students up for failure in their first lesson.

The Banda sheets I'd laboriously prepared the night before were generally appreciated, particularly by the girls, who liked the different colour of text but were stumped by the reason why some words were red, blue or green. I asked them to sort out what was the rule for the colour and, by making it a quiz, which they could win, another fifteen minutes were filled with people thinking. Not always purposefully, thinking though…

"Those are your favourite colours?" said Jeffs to sniggers from the usual quarter, a prosaic and not very elegant answer which just about summed up Jeffs really.

"Those were the only colours left and I bet Mrs. Shawcross put up a fight to stop you having all those!" said Stuart.

He clearly knew Mrs Shawcross very well. This answer summed Stuart up equally well, he was very perceptive and had a keen sense of humour. I had the feeling that Stuart might be the key to keeping everyone in the class onside.

I was loathe to do the thinking for them but after five such replies I buckled and explained that the blue words were naming words or nouns.

"So what do you think the red words are then?"

"Words on fire," said Adrian from nowhere.

"Do you know Adrian, you are spot on, they are all words to do with movement and doing."

"Verbs, doing words are verbs!" said Karen.

"Absolutely right Karen!" and I punched the air in genuine enthusiasm. Karen did likewise and as she turned to Milly, the girl who had said nothing for the last fifty nine minutes nodded slightly in what approached uncontained excitement.

The bell was suddenly upon us and I dismissed those who had performed best first. That included Karen and Milly. Karen, despite her good work in lesson, did not help my case by giving the boys left behind two fingers as she exited the room.

A couple protested, Adam was sat up really straight, arms folded, as he might have done in primary school to demonstrate compliance to the teacher. Fish and Chips were clearly closer to Adam's heart than arguing. Ominously, Stuart was shuffling the papers he had been working on like a barrister preparing his brief.

I decided, on balance, to be magnanimous.

"I wasn't happy about your behaviour at times today, gentlemen, but I think you managed to turn round a poor start and work the way I want from you by the middle of the lesson. On the basis of the improvement, I'm not going to keep anyone behind."

Not waiting for a formal invitation, they jumped up and headed for the door. Hardly ideal, but the aroma of battered cod and chips was upon us all so I let them go.

Stuart was last to leave and as he exited the door, he turned as I was locking it and said, "That was all right."

And he was gone along the short corridor and down the stairs.

"How has the morning gone?" asked Doreen, poking her head out of the Humanities office door and showing more than expected concern.

"Not strictly as planned, I'd have to admit, but I think some progress was made."

"Better than generally expected then," she said beaming, "and by the way, what's the Welsh word Karen said I'd to ask you to pronounce?"

"Whoa! Whoa!" I protested over the baying requests to be heard from all but Milly. "There's only one of me, I haven't got an army of *Ushabtis* you know!"

It momentarily went quiet as they all looked at each other quickly and quizzically.

Lunch was now over and we were back in the small room for a two hour period leading up to the glorious bell that would announce the weekend. My attempt to carry on from the morning session had been deflected by refuelled students high on food and the rush of illicit sugar filled drinks.

It was left to Stuart, unsurprisingly, to speak on behalf of the group.

"What's that then, sir?"

"What's what?" I replied innocently, thankful for the lull in the noise which must have been travelling through the windows which had yet again been opened despite my express instruction that they be kept closed (as much to contain the boisterous noise of the group).

"That word, that word that you said?" ventured Adam with some suspicion.

"*Ushabti*?" I replied casually.

"Yeah. Right. Yeah that one!" they bayed again noisily.

"Shush, I could tell you..." I rejoined quietly and conspiratorially looking from side to side as if to confirm that no other adult was present, "but I'm not sure that you are supposed to know about *Ushabtis* at your age and it could go horribly wrong if you had this knowledge before you were mature enough to deal with it…"

I left that idea hanging, knowing that such a challenge could not go without reply. Collectively they were weighing it up and I saw a few nods directed in Stuart's direction.

Instinctively, they had picked up on the 'mature' comment, and instead of all shouting out they had nominated Stuart to speak for them. This was a very positive development as it showed that, when they wanted to, they could exercise individual self-control.

Stuart decided that he would play on my better nature.

"Go'on sir, you can trust us sir, we're good 'ole boys when we want to be. Well most of the time we are anyway. We won't tell anyone sir! Adam can be a rum 'un at times but we'll smack him if he mentions a word."

He claimed they were "good ole' boys" without any sense of irony, and without any reference to the behaviour of the morning session.

"I'd like to tell you all, but look at how this lesson has panned out? How much work have we achieved since lunch and how have we helped each other like I'd said to you at the beginning of the lesson – if this is the best we can do together you certainly aren't ready to learn about *Ushabti*, especially after the terrible things that happened when I shared this secret in my last school!"

I surprised myself how easily I'd worked in 'at my last school' rather than 'on my teaching practice' to bolster the idea that I had vast experience.

"What terrible things?" they were now asking.

Even Milly was looking at me quizzically and narrow-eyed, as close to demanding an explanation as Milly ever got.

"I don't like to talk about it." I said with an air of finality and visibly shuddered at the recollection. That would keep them guessing I thought.

Two things happened now. Half the class started what sounded like they were singing a round which consisted of a repetition of "Aw, please sir, please!"

While the others. Milly included, sat bolt upright and folded their arms, repeating an action they must have learnt in primary school signifying compliance and attention – it was not just Adam who played on this behaviour. We were clearly in a negotiation phase.

"Well, Sirring and sitting up straight is all well and good but I'd expect a little more than that. I'd want twenty minutes on the task and finished work ready for us to share…and…sufficient silence in that time that I can work quietly with people and hear myself think."

These suggestions were not very well received. Adrian went as far as to venture that I could stick it, as he was not working silently for twenty minutes to find out about a word that might not be worth the effort, and what was more, I was trying to con him to work and that he would be telling his Ma about me that very evening.

The situation was delicately balanced and I knew I had to intervene decisively. Some of the others were prepared to accept the proposition.

"The *Ushabti* involves death, disembowellment and the after-life!" I said in my best Vincent Price edge of madness voice, making what I hoped was perceived as a horrific face, as opposed to a 'man, having a stroke' face.

"What's disembowelment?" asked Adrian, now potentially intrigued.

"It involves, Adrian, making a cut here (I indicated my throat) and slicing downwards all the way to here (I slowly moved down to my tummy button) and spilling the contents of the body cavity, the gizzard, the stomach and the entrails out onto the desk!" (I mimicked the action onto the desk in front of him).

"Ugh!" they all exclaimed in unison.

"Said you weren't ready to handle it didn't I!"

"No, "they implored, "it sounds brilliant!"

"The twenty minutes start now then," said I, consulting the clock on the wall behind them.

To be honest the treaty did not last twenty minutes, more like fifteen with some sporadic interruptions breaking out after twelve minutes. It was better than what had gone before though, and demonstrated that the future might be better, if I did not break first.

The Friday sessions were peppered with these interruptions to learning in which I described something that I thought might capture their attention. They were quick to tell me if they thought my little gobbet of information was a worthy reward for work and they were very demanding in their quality control of my historical, geographical, religious or English references. Generally, at the beginning, if it did not involve death, gore or violence they were acutely disappointed, but over time their interests became more catholic.

It took me some time to work out that, as far as the class was concerned, these interruptions were the most valuable part of the learning that took place. This was when they were attentive and prepared to listen to the views of others and ask questions which really challenged each other as well as me. The rest was just stuff we had to get through to get to the reward of something interesting. I was even more surprised to find, over time, I started to think that they were probably right in this belief.

It was some weeks later, when I had regaled them with the sorry tale of my thigh bones being too long to fit into the cockpit of a fighter jet, thereby dashing my hopes of joining the RAF as a fighter pilot, that Adrian, in a slight lull in the conversation, announced that he was going to be a millionaire when he grew up.

"How are you going to achieve that then Adrian?" I asked keen to have him extend his reasoning by the use of open questions to which he could not grunt or nod.

"I've already started," he said with an earnest stare. "It began last summer. I found a fox that had been knocked down on the back road and I took it back to the coal hole at our house. There were all flies buzzing round it and some had climbed in where its eyeballs were and others were going in through its mouth and a wound on its side. Anyway its belly was all swelled up like a beach ball so I got a knife and did that disembowelling thing you told us about."

I wondered what else my little tales were responsible for in the local countryside, but said nothing and let him continue, so that he could have practice in storytelling and so that the others could listen intently to what they clearly regarded as a gripping tale, the equal of any of mine.

Adrian continued.

"When I cut it's belly all this gas came hissing out and it really stank. I was going to shout out, the smell was so bad but I knew my dad would go mad if he knew what I was up to so I just had to sit there in the coal hole waiting to breathe."

"What did it smell like?" asked Karen.

"Terrible!" replied Adrian, but that was clearly not graphic enough for the group. I resisted the temptation to say anything, which I had noticed myself doing all too frequently since I'd started this teaching lark. The shared expectation of the group pressurised Adrian to expand.

"You know the smell of burning rubber," he outlined

"Yes." they all said, hanging on his every word.

"Well it didn't exactly smell like that but it got in your nostrils and throat like that and didn't go away. Like the smell of gas from the cooker when the flame goes out...you can still smell it later. It was also like the smell of dead off milk and a long dead fish."

Everyone recoiled and screwed up their faces as they recalled such a potent smell. "It was like all these things together…but worse and I couldn't escape it in the coal hole."

"Anyway," continued Adrian, "there didn't seem to be much blood in the guts but all the tubes and pipes had turned greeny grey and it looked like all the guts were wriggling about."

"What's this got to do with you being a millionaire?" asked Jeffs, spoiling the effect once again.

"That's what I'm coming to!" retorted Adrian, "It was only when I looked really closely because of the dim light in the coal hole that I realised what the movement was."

We had all mimicked Adrian and craned forward as he had bent his head to the desk. With great presence he hesitated a second, holding us in thrall and announced, "Maggots!" and banged his fist on the desk.

"Uuurrgghh!" came the collective explosion of disgust.

"Adrian Bush you dirty bugger – you gave me a Polo mint last week and passed it to me with your fingers!" retched Karen. Milly screwed up her eyes.

Stuart sat back in his chair and exclaimed, "Cor, you're a rum 'un Adie!"

But Adrian wasn't nearly finished. "I got some jam jars and spent the next two hours trying to collect every maggot."

"What with yer hands?" gasped Karen, recalling the dubious taste of the Polo mint.

"Yeah, of course with me hands – it's really tricky trying to pick maggots out of a fox's guts with anything else – you should have a try. Anyway I managed to get seven jars full of maggots in that time, three jars the next day and another three the day after. By then there wasn't much left of the fox's insides so I threw it away. But the thing is, that fox must have been dead for a couple of days by the time I got to it so the best day's maggot picking had already gone. Anyway, if you can get that amount of maggots out of a fox I reckon you could get five to ten time more out of a dead sheep."

The girls and I were looking perplexed, not doubting Adrian's logic but wondering why you would want to collect maggots on such a scale? The boys were already ahead of the game and were sharing knowing looks.

I was glad that, as usual, Karen piped up to ask the question I wanted the answer to.

"Because, Karen, you can sell them to fishermen as bait."

"Yeah, but the maggots will turn into flies." said Stuart with an air of finality.

"Not if you put them in Tupperware boxes and put them in the freezer they won't!" countered Adrian triumphantly and Stuart had to concede the logic of this. The rest of us were making a mental note never, ever, to accept a sandwich from Adrian's Tupperware lunch box.

"I've tried this and have been able to keep them as maggots for over a week. But I only need to keep them as maggots for a couple of days because I then take them down to Taylor's on the High Street and he gives me twenty pence for a pound of maggots.

Adrian now reached into his inside pocket and produced his folded up and dog eared school diary. He carefully thumbed through to the section headed notes, licking his fingers to make the pages part, and placed it on the desk in front of him.

"I've done some calculations and I reckon if I had twenty dead sheep and could maggot harvest them for twenty days, possibly twenty five in the right conditions they would give me £20 each in maggot sales. I could harvest more from a dead cow of course and make more profit. All I need is a large barn and fridges, loads of fridges. My dad knows a farmer we could rent a barn off and I know where I can get three fridges. I worked out I could make a million pounds in twenty eight years. Of course that depends on the price of maggots staying the same, but that goes up and down. They are more expensive in winter so I could harvest in summer and sell in winter if I could keep them cold enough."

Although he had been a little sketchy on a few aspects of the plan, essentially Adrian had modelled a complete economic process and business plan in his account.

"But where are you going to get the dead animals from?" asked Stuart, clearly seeing the potential of a partnership.

"I'd pay people like me to collect animals that had been killed on the road – there's plenty of them and they all get maggots. I'd also take diseased animals off all the farms in Cambridgeshire – a problem for the farmers is a profit for me. Imagine if big animals die at Linton Zoo – think how many maggots could grow in a giraffe's neck? I'd get in touch with London Zoo – they might let me have their dead elephants!" and his eyes glazed over at the profit potential of a dead elephant and he quickly wrote *London Zoo, elephants, hippo, rhino* in the note section of the diary.

"Well" declared Karen as Adrian ran out of steam, "I wouldn't marry you, even if you were a millionaire, if you spent every day up to your armpits in maggoty, dead animals, would you Milly?"

Milly seemed less perturbed by the prospect, but then again Milly's family were farm workers and this prospect would not have been so alien to them. She smiled enigmatically and expressed no other opinion.

The last fifteen minutes brought home to me that I was now living and teaching in a rural area. The catchment of the school was split about one fifth local people and four fifths incomers. The incomers had largely settled in the village as it was an easy commute to Cambridge, or had resettled from London and Essex to the new village at Bar Hill. The SLG group was made up totally of local children, many of whose parents were manual or farm labourers and these were probably the last generation of children who were going to experience a living made up of manual labour.

Just then, Robert pointed at the window and called out with excitement, "Look at that!"

We all moved to the window and sat looking at a double rainbow. On the wide open Fens you could see the complete arc of both rainbows set off against the grey sky. We watched silent as a US Air Force Phantom trailing black exhaust, pierced the arc as it made its way onto the flightpath for a landing at RAF Alconbury. No-one made a sound for almost five minutes and as the rainbow began to fade Karen asked me if I had made a wish.

"I wished that we could all complete some written work on the Skylark before the end of the lesson." I retorted, thinking that would be a good way to refocus them.

"No chance sir!" rejoined Karen. "Not now you've told us your secret wish – you've jinxed it!"

When they departed in a more or less orderly manner when the bell finally went I was left clearing the room and considered how the day had panned out. It struck me that these were not slow learners at all, when pressed on something dear to their hearts, like Adrian's maggots, they could be as articulate as any child. There were gaps in their knowledge and literacy skills which they sometimes disguised in bad behaviour, but perhaps that was a rational approach to failing repeatedly to be able to read out loud or write fluently.

I tried to think of the examples of poor behaviour in the last few hours and most seemed related to me telling them that there would be writing and reading tasks ahead. Of course there were some spontaneous acts of hostility caused by long running animosities as well.

I'd not come across kids who could stare at a rainbow silently for ten minutes before either. I was sure that despite the limited progress on his poem, Gerard Manley Hopkins would have approved of their wonder of nature.

Over the coming weeks I got to understand them better. There were ups and downs, pencils were thrown, as were tantrums, but generally we got used to each other and learnt to appreciate where the line was drawn in terms of behaviour and expectations.

To be fair, I still found that I needed to prepare twice as much work as we might need for the Friday lessons, as the collective concentration of the group was sporadic and unpredictable. I don't know what happened on Friday morning break, but each week a different combination of students would come in either animated and belligerent or sullen and uncooperative. That required a settler before the lesson could proceed on its intended course.

I was looking for a way to have them co-operating and seeing that they could accomplish so much more when they stopped arguing and interrupting each other. Having exhausting the possibilities of Mr. Hopkins I came up with what I thought might either be a brilliant ruse or, potentially a dangerous disaster.

Each week we'd cover one of the five senses and I'd prepare a 'get up and move around the room' type exercise as well as a recording exercise. It wasn't strictly sticking with the script handed me by Anthony, but if it worked, it could be justified and anyway, the earnest list of written exercises was falling further and further behind schedule.

The first week I decided to go with Touch as it seemed manageable as a starting point.

"I've a surprise for you this week!" I announced confidently at the beginning of the lesson. "But it all depends on us getting the written work out of the way this morning."

"What's the surprise?" asked Robert wide eyed, whereas the others eyed me with a little more suspicion.

"Think it through, Robert, if I tell you it won't be a surprise will it?"

He gave me a look that said fair enough, which was typical of the gentle, even tempered Robert. The others were less than convinced and eyed me with suspicion. Clearly I didn't have much credit in the collective bank of the SLG.

Well, written work now and the surprise this afternoon; it seemed they were either too tired to argue or had high expectations of my ability to surprise them.

Come the afternoon there was an air of excitement which I had inadvertently fostered by slipping out of lunch and locking myself in our small room to set up the session. I knew I had to set up a quarantine area where I could hide my samples otherwise they would be all over them like a herd of marauding cats on chicken carcasses. I also needed to hide a washing up bowl with soapy water and a towel.

By now there were increasingly insistent bangs on the door. I hastily arranged my bags of goodies behind the desk in the alcove, checked that they could not be seen from the main body of the room and smartly opened the door. The tribe almost fell through the doorway into the room, keen to see what I had been up to. I winked at Stuart as he passed and he winked back.

Having ascertained that Stuart was indeed the critical person in this group I had gone out of my way to cultivate him as my lieutenant, or should that be barrack room sergeant. I'd made a point of including him in the afternoon's revels and he had promised not to tell anyone. It was now time to see if his loyalty to the group was greater than his desire to be in the know with me.

The afternoon started with me insistent that all written work from the morning must be complete before we started on the exploration of the sense of touch. To my surprise, they all complied, heads down, writing as feverishly as they could and then going to help others complete their assignments. All except Jeffs, who was muttering under his breath that whatever I'd thought up, it would probably be rubbish and not worth the effort. I was coming to the conclusion on the basis of a large hillock of evidence that Jeffs was the definition of a pain in the arse, never happier than when miserable and able to cast a cloud over anyone's silver lining.

Half an hour passed in what, to the casual observer, would appear to be an ideal class, students completing assignments independently and then packing away and going to help their peers. Clearly, we had come a long way in a month. That said, the casual observer did well not to witness what was almost a stand up fight this morning, again, immediately following break. I'd had to stand between the two rowing banshees but could not remember who exactly was involved now. To be honest it could be any combination of the eight, possibly not mild-mannered Robert, nor Milly who, despite living on a farm, had never had occasion to frighten even a goose. That left Adam, Adrian, Stuart, Jeffs, Karen or Sandford.

Anyway, a lunchtime is a long time in teaching, especially with this group and the afternoon, with a warm sun and the central heating radiator blasting out at full tilt left everyone mellow and relaxed.

"Right everyone, books to the side. It's time to reveal the surprise, don't push, everyone will get a go."

I hadn't loosened them from the habit of leaping over the desk when the fancy took them, but they were genuinely excited at the prospect of what was coming next and I hoped I hadn't over egged it.

I handed out sheets on which a table appeared labelled one to eight and with space to write a description.

"Today we are exploring the sense of touch so I'm going to deprive you of your other senses and ask you to put your hand in these black bags, have a feel of what is inside and then return to our seat and describe the feeling and then have a guess at what is in there."

I'd realised that I had to be incredibly precise with all my instructions and to anticipate all the known combinations of alternative things they might get up to as the refrain 'You didn't tell us we couldn't cheat and look at everyone else's work' would ring out.

I held the first bag up and invited Stuart to come and plunge his hand into it. Stuart winked as his hand sank into the bag and his face turned to one of horror as he recoiled at the artefact that he had touched, He withdrew his hand far enough for the others to see a blood red liquid on his hand. Falteringly he plunged his hand down into the bag and grasped at the shape hidden down there.

"Can you describe it to us Stuart?" I asked.

"It's disgusting, that's what it is, it's round and squelchy and it's full of something squashy!"

"Oh my god, it's an eyeball!" squealed Karen, "I'm not touching no eyeball, not for all the tea in China!"

But when Karen's turn came she couldn't resist, despite her better judgment, lowering her hand gingerly into the sack.

By now the routine had been established. A quick dunk in each of the eight sacks, then wash your hands in the soapy water, return to the desk and record your ideas whilst they were still fresh. I was pleased that the three hours it had taken me the night before to concoct these sensory delights had proven worthwhile and the room was not now covered in semolina, a boiled egg in theatrical blood, cornflakes, washing up liquid, sea shells and Lego bricks.

I'd hit on the idea that one person was in charge of each of the eight sacks, and handed it over to the person they felt had been most responsible in the round. This avoided them arguing over my choice. Stuart handed over to Robert who handed over to Milly who nodded at Adrian (possibly looking to curry favour and stake a claim as the wife of a maggot millionaire).

This was working better than I had hoped and for the first time, the students were taking charge of the lesson, which meant that I could move around the room and check on the written work.

"Now then Raymond Jeffs, what have you got planned for the weekend?" I asked innocently, trying to strike up a positive conversation with him.

Jeffs looked at me as if I was a police officer looking to make an arrest.

"Nuffink." he replied, now unwilling to look me in the eye.

"He's lying sir!" shouted Stuart. "He's going lamping with some good ole' boys up Fen Drayton!"

"Lamping, what's that?" I asked innocently, although I vaguely remembered kids on the Reso doing it on the marshes of the River Clwyd to provide extra food for the family.

"It's hunting rabbits with torchlights and guns at night. The daft buggers just stand there when you catch them in the light and you can blast them for the pot. Here Jeffs, tell him about what your dad saw on the fen!"

"Hang on!" I interjected, we've just about finished the touch exercise. Let's turn the lights off and sit around and hear about what Jeff's dad found on the Fen!"

The room tidied, we gathered in the gloom in a circle of chairs. Jeffs was initially reluctant to say anything, but Stuart egged him on declaring to one and all that what Jeffs had to say would make us all shit ourselves!

Stuart corrected himself from his overly exuberant description:

"Sorry sir, I meant crap ourselves."

I let it go, anxious not to let Jeffs off the hook.

"Well, me dad goes lamping most weeks on one or other of the Fens. It keeps the rabbits down and it's more for the pot so the farmers don't mind. Usually he and my uncle go out and they take turns on the gun and the lamp. A lot of people go out there with shotguns but my dad won't hear of that as he says there is no sport in it, and besides, you've a load of shot to remove before you can eat the bunny. So my dad takes his .22 rifle when they go. When you go out on the Fens without a moon it's as dark as Hell and you can't see your hand in front of your face. Sometimes from my bedroom, you can see lampers and they look like ghosts moving silently across the Fen and then you hear the gun go off and know a rabbit is dead. You need to be careful as well because there are pools of dead water out there that can suck you down and you'll never be seen again because the fen can swallow you. I only go out to places I know that there is no dead water. I was walking past some dead water at night once and it groaned at me and there was a gassy smell."

"Sure it wasn't you farting Jeffs!" asked Adam, totally predictably.

"Last year my dad and uncle were out on Fen Drayton, near the river. It was a good night and they'd already downed six bunnies when they heard some scuffling in the long grass to the right of them. My uncle turned the light on where the sound was coming from and he saw two red glowing eyes looking back at him. It wasn't no rabbit, and he reckoned it was somewhere between his knee and his goolies in height."

"Coypu," said Adam confidently. "Massive South American water rodents, some daft sod set some loose in the Fens years ago and there are still some out there now."

The mood of menace Jeffs was unknowingly building up was about to subside, punctured by Adam's matter of fact explanation, but Jeffs picked it up magnificently.

"That's what my dad thought as well and he sighted on the animal to get in his shot, but faster than anything he'd ever seen before on the Fen, the beast was running at him from no more than ten yards away and it was running on two feet and screaming and howling. It brushed by his legs before he could get a shot off and then it headed at my uncle, knocking him over so that he dropped the flashlight, and then it disappeared into the Fen. My dad goes out in a group of four now when he's lamping so that there are at least two guns if the beast turns up again. He still hasn't a clue what it was but he ain't taking no chances."

The room was transfixed, both because of the graphic nature of the description and the fact that they had never heard Jeffs extend himself beyond a single sentence.

The boys were all speculating on what the Fen Beast could be, whereas the girls were reaffirming what their mothers had told them about not wandering out on the Fen at night for fear of what Karen claimed were "Beasties, kiddy fiddlers and Jack O' Lanterns – spirits who lured people to their death in the dead water pits by giving them false lights!" Karen clearly thought each eventuality as likely as the next and it made me think there was much hidden in their imaginations that would be lost within a generation.

We were all in a moment of quiet contemplation of the Beast when Mrs. Ginn burst in and all the girls and most of boys screamed!

"Just checking that everything is alright in here Mr. Hughes, it has been awfully quiet, most unlike this group."

"We've been discussing the Beast of Fen Drayton," I reassured her.

"Have you indeed," she replied disbelievingly. "Have you indeed! Well, Mr. Close lives in Fen Drayton, I hope you don't mean him!"

"No!" said Karen, "Mr. Close is lovely, he's no beast, he's a cutie."

All the children nodded in agreement.

The following week, having marked and displayed both the student work for the senses quest and a number of stories and speculations about the Fen Drayton Beast on the Wall, we proceeded to explore sight.

The task was an old favourite of having to negotiate a partner over an obstacle course of chairs and desks using only spoken instructions. Stuart had rounded up two of his trusty classmates to organise the course and Adam drew first go to be blindfolded and Sue was chosen to lead him round. This was going to be a stern test of Adam's patience and Milly's almost silent verbal skills.

Adam, in his usual blustering way, in the absence of a spoken instruction blundered forward, skinning his shins against desk legs and tripping as the floor dropped down the step in the centre of the room.

"Stop Adam!" called out Milly holding out her hands in genuine and heartfelt concern to make sure Adam did not tumble headlong over the chair in front of him.

The room instantly went silent; No one had heard Milly's thin reedy voice out loud before. It was quite musical but sounded rusty from lack of use.

"Stop," she mouthed again, almost silently.

Adam pulled up his blindfold and looked at Milly with surprise, his eyes wide open.

"You spoke to me. That was the first time you spoke to me!"

Milly was back to looking at the floor now and the idea that this was the key that would unlock her voice for good quickly faded. A couple of the other lads joined in and said, with great sensitivity and sincerity, what a nice voice Milly had. Jeffs of course had to spoil it,

"See, told you all she could speak, she just likes showing off by being quiet all the time so everyone will make a fuss of her!"

But Jeffs could not have been more wrong. Everyone else could see what an effort it had been for Milly to utter a sound and it was only her concern for Adam's safety that had enabled her to overcome her terrible affliction. I'm not sure such learning is rewarded in any syllabus known to man, but for all those gathered in the little remove room, it was a great day's work.

I felt the SLGs, who I now referred to as the Super Learning Gophers (we'd come to the fanciful idea that the Beast of Fen Drayton was in fact an oversize, bipedal gopher) had earned their prize of Cadbury's Fudges at the end of the lesson.

Chapter Seventeen
MIRACLE

Colin, who had been appointed on the same day as me at the Village College, had been handed as his Professional Development Opportunity custody on the parallel group to the SLGs in the year below. We often had call to compare notes and ideas about what we could do to keep our charges occupied.

In this time before the National Curriculum, it was possible to build your own CSE, or Certificate of Secondary Education course, so long as it fulfilled essential criteria, and we both constructed one which met the needs, and extended the learning of our groups.

Colin shared a loathing of the use of offensive language aimed at people with disabilities with me and built this into his CSE course. In one module which he had named The Other Side he had gone out of his way to address this issue.

In the course of the module, students experienced what it was to be deaf, blind or, have a physical disability and to be pregnant. Although not a disability, a useful exploration of the real experience of pregnancy seemed well overdue. Using weighted pregnancy belts and an annoying doll which had a crying alarm and needed feeding and changing every couple of hours the students came face to face with the responsibility of looking after a young child. This experience probably did more to reduce the potential pregnancy rates in the school than any other measure.

Colin was really bold in inviting outside speakers to talk about the experience of blindness and deafness and the students reacted brilliantly to these illustrated talks, asking questions which showed perception and empathy.

The use of 'flid', 'Joey' and 'spastic' were commonplace as terms of abuse at the time and Colin was not prepared to let this abuse go without challenging it. He arranged for a party of twelve students from a school for the physically disabled to come to our school at the end of one school day and booked the Sports Hall for the occasion.

"What's the point of booking the Sports Hall? asked Trouty, the equivalent of Stuart in Colin's group, "that's the last place they'll want to be. They'll think you are taking the piss!"

Actually, Trouty's sentiments had shown a considerable move from his original outburst of not wanting to be seen out around a load of spazzers! He was now showing concern for the sensibilities of the students in wheelchairs.

"I don't think that will be a problem," countered Colin, pre-armed with some extensive research conducted over the phone with the teachers at the special school.

So it came to pass that on a Thursday afternoon, Colin's class sat moping in one corner of the Sports Hall, all crumpled school uniforms and bad attitude, waiting for the students for the special school to arrive.

"I don't see why we have to stay behind for them. It's like detention this is!" moaned Warrener, a wiry short lad with unruly jet black hair and buck teeth. Warry, being small was often the focus of bullying and morning break was seldom complete until Warry was seen legging it across the playground with a baying group of would be bullies pursuing him. Many was the time that I'd find him when on break duty with my cold cup of tea, cowering in the shrubbery at the back of the toilets hoping not to be discovered. Warry was a born victim it seemed, and, at present, he had few social skills to stop his life being a constant repeating pageant of bullying. "The spazzers must think they are in detention too!"

Colin and I winced at this last comment and we went through the mantra that had been developed about treating every person with respect. We were interrupted by the door opening and a couple of staff from the special school ushering forward twelve students in wheelchairs. The wheelchair bound students burst into the room and revelled in the space, ignoring our students who eyed them with suspicion. Colin clapped his hands and instructed our students to distribute the drinks and cakes that had been prepared by the group for the visitors. This ensured that every one of our students would need to break the ice, identify a visiting student and engage in the beginning of what we hoped would be a conversation. We four teachers retired to the far end of the Sports Hall, deep in what appeared to be a discussion. We had arranged to have this awkward social hiatus for the students as it would mean that they would come to the point where the silence was so uncomfortable that someone, and my money was on Warry, would break it.

It is very difficult to watch two groups of twelve students studious ignore each other for almost ten minutes, but we had determined not to intervene so that the students had to make the running.

Surprisingly it was Kevin, a swarthy boy with cropped hair who broke the silence by asking no one in particular, "Which team do you support?"

"Why? Which team do you support?" came the frosty reply.

"Arsenal," was Kevin's proud reply, thinking that he might have common ground here.

If Kevin had hoped he would be rewarded for his effort to break the ice, he was to be sadly disappointed.

"Then you know nothing about football then, you country muppet!"

Kevin had not considered that he might be patronised by someone in a wheelchair. Our group had assumed that being in a wheelchair robbed a person of having an attitude.

"So who do you support?" asked Trouty in a belligerent tone, which would usually be the preface to a fight.

"United." came the reply, which disarmed Trouty, as this was also his team. He was torn between hostility to outsiders, and the shared camaraderie of a fellow Manchester United supporter. Apparently football affiliations won out.

To the relief of us four apparently disinterested teachers in the far end of the hall, the students were suddenly mingling. Suddenly the lads from the two groups came together in footballing solidarity and even Kevin found a fellow Arsenal supporter who was pleased not to be in his usual position of isolation in his group because of his choice of team.

"Typical boys, football is the only thing they can talk about!" declared Jodie as she waded into the group now the ice had been broken, and struck up some equally stereotypical conversation about fashion, music and hunky boys with the wheelchair bound girls. The other girls followed her lead as they usually did. It looked like our girl students believed this would be a one way conversation and were surprised to find the wheelchair bound girls expressing the same likes and dislikes.

It was no more than ten minutes before it appeared that our students had forgotten about the disabilities that had confined one half of the group to wheelchairs. Animated conversations were taken place about all those subjects beloved of teenagers and I even overheard Jodie discussing how her and wheelchair bound Samantha could slip away when the teachers weren't watching to have a quick fag.

The one way street of awkward questions we anticipated our students might ask about life in a wheelchair had dissipated under the much more interesting topics of football and fishing, cars and fashion, tv and films.

Half an hour passed quickly, and we could have spent the rest of the time leaving the students to get to know each other. Colin however had arranged a sporting competition.

"Time for basketball!" Colin declared decisively.

"I don't think so!" replied Trouty, thinking, with some new found sensitivity that his new friend and fellow Man. U. supporter was going to be humiliated on the basketball court. "I don't think that would be very fair!"

"We'll see at the end of the game!" countered Colin as five additional wheelchairs were rolled into the Sports Hall. "The game is wheelie basketball!"

Our students really were overconfident at the beginning of the game. How could they, who were able-bodied, be defeated at basketball by a group of people in wheelchairs? It was certainly true that our students in the wheelchairs were quick in a straight line, but what they possessed in straight line speed; they lost out in maneuvering and the ability to propel the wheelchair and catch the ball at the same time. The students from St. Luke's had also developed a canny line in bending the rules, of 'off the ball' incidents and underhand tactics which would later on come to be known by the term 'sledging'.

"He called me a Twat! He called me a Twat!" complained Warry on the one occasion where our team looked like they might get a single shot in on the hoop. In truth, Warry didn't believe that his meek, wheelchair confined opposite could extend to such language and tactics. It was becoming clearer to Warry that this lad was just like him, as trying to put his opponent off was just what he would have done in the same circumstances.

After the first half, there were pleas from our kids to mix up the teams as it was an unfair competition. Had they hoped to preserve their dignity by suggesting that they were too robust for their new found wheelchair bound friends, the score, at 24–0 told a different story.

Our students were exhausted and red-faced at the end of the game, whereas the St Luke's students looked fresh. It was only then that someone let slip that two members of their team were England international wheelchair basketball players. This generated a flurry of interest among all the boys, who now entered into animated conversation. The girls had now gathered in smaller groups which intermittently erupted into raucous laughter which seemed to suggest that they had found some common ground, probably in comparing the boys.

A couple of students with cerebral palsy had not taken part in the basketball game and we were now setting up half of the Sports Hall for a game of 'boccia' or wheelchair bowls.

Warry and Paul were talking to Dan, and whereas the slurred pattern of Dan's speech was still causing them some difficulty, they now saw it was worth persevering, particularly as they had noticed on Dan's track suit top an understated Union Flag and inscription 'Great Britain Boccia Team'.

The boccia tournament proceeded well, except for the growing frustration of our students who could not master the technique required and marvelled at Dan and Diane's flowing technique which meant that they easily won every end.

"You're a bit of a stand up spakker at this, aren't you Warry!" joked Dan to a shocked Warry.

"Are you taking the piss?" asked a horrified Warry.

"Yeah, I am," countered Dan laughing, "so what are you going to do about it?"

It proved quite difficult to part the friends at the end of the session and some of the girls from both schools resented us breaking up their conversation but 7 p.m. had arrived and the local badminton league were keen to claim the Sports Hall for their booking.

A mixed group moved out across the playground to where the St Luke's minibus was parked and extended goodbyes were said. The teachers judged the evening a success and began talking about a reciprocal visit to St Lukes. The girls had in some cases exchanged telephone numbers, and the boys had swapped football cards, finding some cops in each others collections.

We were still waving the minibus off when one of the first arrivals for the Youth Club, Moffatt, surrounded by his usual crew, shouted over,

"Warry, you mongo, hanging round with your Spazzer friends again are you?"

Colin and I moved to intervene and to spoil Moffatt's planned Youth Club evening by having him sent home. This was typical of Moffatt, always bold in a group and always looking to cause trouble to enhance his poor reputation.

To our amazement we were overtaken by Warry, running as fast as his spindly legs could carry him, in the direction of Moffatt. This was a first, as he usually made a habit of running in the opposite direction.

Moffatt's crew parted to allow Moffatt to get a clear punch at the arriving Warry, no doubt they would all be supporting Moffatt's plea of self-defence at the ensuing enquiry of the incident.

Warry seemed to be accelerating, it was unclear whether he intended to punch or kick Moffatt for his insult. As it turned out he did neither and simply launched himself at the burly lad from the year above. Warry's hip impacted Moffatt's chest. Warry's slender frame must have been compensated for by the velocity of his impact and Moffatt, uncharacteristically, was winded and felled.

Warry gathered his wits first and sat over the prostrate and gasping Moffatt saying, "Don't you ever say that about my friends!"

All in all, and in some unexpected ways, the evening had been a very successful one.

Nothing succeeds like success, and Colin's students were allowed to develop a project for their CSE which explored the theme of disability. Working together, Warry and Tara came up with a project to look at how difficult it was to travel around Cambridge City Centre in a wheelchair. Other pairs had come up with similar projects and so the mini bus was booked and twelve students and the wheelchair that St Luke's had kindly left, were taken into Cambridge for the field work.

Armed with a tally sheet, a notebook and a tape measure, the first half of the afternoon, with Tara in the chair and Warry pushing, had gone surprisingly well. They'd measured the entrances to the main department stores. Recorded access to lifts and noted the names of shops which were impossible to enter with a wheelchair.

After an hour it was Warry's turn in the chair and the process continued.

Warry, being increasingly independently minded, asked Tara not to push him so that he could experience being alone in the wheelchair, and she had agreed to walk ten yards behind him.

Warry was getting a clear impression of the problems faced by people using wheelchairs as he seemed to disappear in crowds and rarely had a chance to steer for more than a few metres in a straight line. He found the wheelchair difficult to control and his arms were growing tired now. All proceeded well however until he reached the market square.

The market square at that time was under development, as there was growing awareness of accessibility issues, which would soon be enshrined in legislation. Unfortunately Warry arrived at the square when building work was in progress to improve access and pedestrian crossings were under construction.

An accident is an unhappy coalescence of a number of factors, and compounding the building work and uneven surfaces that day was a high wind that had blown wet plastic bags and some vegetable detritus into the road at the point of the crossing.

Keeping in role, Warry had arrived at the temporary pedestrian controlled light signals and pressed the wait sign, noting on his sheet that it was set too high on the post to be comfortable to reach from the wheelchair.

The traffic, in large volumes, continued to pass until at last the lights changed to red, halting them. Taking nothing for granted, Warry, from his wheelchair, looked left at the municipal dustbin lorry revving impatiently across the road and right to a German tour coach, carrying a large party of south German Catholics on a tour which would culminate at the shrine at Walsingham in Norfolk.

The green man was now flickering for him to cross and the sound beep was urging him forward. Taking a deep breath, and mindful of seconds passing, Warry bumped down unevenly from the pavement and onto the wet and litter strewn crossing. The size of the pavement at this point knocked him sideways onto the crossing and he furiously shuffled to regain the right direction. He stopped struggling and looked awkwardly behind him for Tara to come to intervene and help him across. Tara was nowhere to be seen, distracted some moments earlier by an absolute bargain in a nearby shop window.

Warry was now panicking. Shuffling his weight backwards and forwards in his seat, he had released the wheelchair from one crack in the road and had moved forward no more than a yard before a combination of another uneven surface and the slippiness of the surface, lubricated by waste tomatoes and cabbage leaves, had snared him again. The green man had disappeared, the crossing was empty apart from the struggling Warry and apart from the impatient German coach driver revving his diesel engine and gesticulating through the window in a very Teutonic way, and all was silent in Warry's world. Still he rocked and wriggled on the chair which stubbornly refused to move backwards or forwards.

Conscious of his slipping timetable the German coach driver, now sounded his horn, in the unlikely event that this would remedy the unfolding situation. Warry, exhausted from his exertions, and running on the sort of adrenalin that is only released when confronted by an impatient German coach driver, commanding several hundred horsepower of Vorsprung Durch Technik, suddenly leaped from the wheelchair as if released by divine intervention, flashed the V's at the driver and ran off, disappearing into the market, leaving only the wheelchair on its side on the crossing.

On the coach, the devout German ladies crossed themselves open-mouthed and clasped at their rosaries, convinced they had seen a miracle which had restored the waif-like lad with bulging eyes, jet black curly hair and buck teeth to full health. Not only could he walk, but he could now run! The Lord be Praised!

Chapter Eighteen
OPTIONS

You shouldn't have favourites as a teacher, but two other classes stood out from my time at the Village College. One was the very first class I had on the very first day. 2H they were known as then and I taught a fair proportion of them until they left four years later.

Given that much of my teaching until that date had been in difficult circumstances, 2H were a dream. They were affable and good humoured and comprised such a range of talent. 2H became my testbed; I realised that I could try things with them which I would prefer not to risk with other classes.

In 2H I had truly a truly comprehensive class of students. Both middle and working class children were represented and I was determined that their achievements should reflect their innate ability and not their social class. I tried to design learning so that everyone had a systematic view of what was to be learned. I developed ways to see the big picture stuff before concentrating on the detail, to have systems for organising information and little tricks to remember things. Some came from my own experience and others from things I'd read.

My vicious and virtuous circles which prefaced my 'big picture' review of a topic became a signature approach. I made the mistake once of drawing both the vicious circle and the virtuous circle and the small circle for the key headings at the same time and was surprised to turn and see my students smirking.

"Let's keep focussed!" I implored and went on to ask what was so funny?

"You've drawn a massive pair of boobies on the board!" explained Jason, barely able to contain himself.

I turned to find he was right and tried to rescue the situation by insisting that this would make whatever I wrote on them infinitely memorable.

Quite frankly 2H thought I was nuts, but good naturedly went along with me. I had a valuable insight into this when Kerry, a refugee from the East End of London who had resettled with her family in the new settlement of Barr Hill, ventured, "It must be very hard for you Mr Hughes, being a teacher an' all and teaching us English when you can't speak English proper like what we do."

"Well, thank you for your concern but how did you come to that conclusion Kerry?"

"Well you say your words all wrong. You say path when you should say paaath, and bath when you should say baaath. You think we sit on grass to rhyme with ass when you should say graaaasss."

"To rhyme with arse!" added Ciaran, unable to resist the temptation to play the rude word card in what he supposed was a legitimate call.

There was a general murmur of agreement to the basis of Kerry's proposition. Only Sue and Lorraine came to my defence. Both were the essence of sweet nature, with a thirst for knowledge and the ability to converse with adults that belied their years. Sue suggested that the difference Kerry had identified was not in the use of English – the words were the same, it was just the pronunciation that differed. Sue observed that some of the class were furrowing their brows and added, "Sir says those words differently because he comes from a different part of the country, not because he is wrong."

"Thanks for that Sue, I thought I was facing a vote of no confidence there! In fact it goes further than that. For it is I who is speaking correctly, and you southerners who are speaking in a later version of English," I added mock pompously.

"I think you will find that you're wrong there sir!" rejoined an unconvinced Kerry.

That started a debate about Saxon and Norman English and the way that words changed over time. I told them how Norman English had changed all the words for meat to reflect the fact that the Normans would be eating most of it, beef, mutton and pork, but were happy to keep the Saxon words when the animals were alive and they expected Saxons to tend to them, cow, sheep and pig.

We looked at rude words and their Saxon origins and I tried to develop an understanding that there was an appropriate time and place to use these. Kieron was keen to explore which rude words I knew and began to reel out some from his personal vocabulary. I suggested I could top his with a very rude word called "Detention" and his next rude word would represent a return of my RSVP to join me in an hour's detention after school the following night. I added that I'd be really mischievously happy to let his parents know why he would be late home through a telephone call. Kieron relented and looked for the next opportunity to get the upper hand.

I was particularly keen to test a theory that the more "hands on" learning became the more we could defeat Mr Ebbinghaus and his forgetting effect. I spent the best part of four years developing this theory of effective learning and ensuring that students had memorable activities which allowed them to absorb, store and recall information effectively using as many senses and visual clues as possible and not confining them to just the written word.

For many assignments I banned page after page of written work until the big picture could be established on what others referred to as a Mind Map. This comprised a detailed picture, with illustrations and highlights that gave the overview of a topic and the relationships between the constituent parts. For me this was an extension of the techniques I'd used so decisively in my own A levels and formed a vital foundation for effective learning.

Occasionally, at Parent Evenings, I'd had to justify this approach to sceptical parents. I kept some examples of the approach and work that there children had completed to demonstrate its efficacy. Generally they went away convinced that I had their child's interests at heart, even if my approach was considered, at best, "unconventional".

In my efforts to make learning more memorable I tried to ensure sound, motion, colour and patterns supplemented the written word in learning.

We spent a lot of time on the field, either practising Roman military tactics or recreating the Battle of Hastings. I reasoned that to have acted it out would leave a more memorable impression than reading words on a page. For the Battle of Hastings, the lack of an elevated position to recreate Senlac Hill on the Fens was a shortcoming so the Norman Knights were made to kneel when attacking to show the strength of the Saxon position on the top of the hill – a position which everyone understood they should not give up when facing a cavalry attack.

Having understood the key principles of a defensive site Lorraine, who had undoubtedly been reading ahead, added, "But they did give up the high ground so why did they do that?"

"Arrrgggghhhh!" screamed Jason, playing the role of the Norman knight on horseback and running amok across the field and into a PE lesson of astonished cricketers. "It's me horse – he's bolted and I can't control him!"

Clearly I'd have to watch Jason, it seemed his senses quickly became over stimulated.

This was so much more interesting than simply telling a narrative tale and expecting the students to remember it.

"Why indeed?" I asked and was met by a volley of theories as to the motivation of the Saxon masses.

"Harold was a trained fighter and had positioned his troops on the best ground so he wouldn't have ordered his men to abandon that position." claimed one.

"So…" I added trying to get them to extend this line of reasoning.

"Harold might have been an experienced soldier, but most of his troops were farmers – the Fyrd, so perhaps when the Norman cavalry retreated, they thought they'd won and charged after them. "

"Well done 2H, for the reasons you mentioned, that seems to be the most likely scenario for them to abandon their position on the high ground and it cost them the battle and, as we will see in the next few lessons when we explore the secondary source of the Bayeux Tapestry, written some twenty years after the event by the victors, changed the course of British history. Not to mention Kerry, your point about the way I speak. I speak like I do as I was brought up in an area which was outside the original Norman kingdom, whereas you have grown up in an area where French/Norman English influence was stronger."

I couldn't resist the temptation to be mischievous here and added, "So technically I speak a purer form of original old English than you do. You speak a fusion of English and the French that the Normans brought with the invasion."

I could see that they didn't want to leave it with me having the upper hand, but before they could marshall their thoughts, I'd moved on.

"But then again the Normans weren't originally French but descended from Viking invaders who rowed up the Seine and held the French King to ransom. So you are on dodgy ground when you are trying to say who the original English were. People, languages and countries are constantly changing, sometimes a little at a time as with the words your generation has brought into being, or quickly through an invasion or war."

At which point the words of their generation were thrown at me and we tried to understand their origins, including Joey, from Joey Deacon, a person with cerebral palsy who had become a byword for that equally unpalatable word "spastic" which I tried to challenge every time I heard it. This line of thinking went on for five minutes until the bell intervened.

I introduced my phobia of lazy language to 2H on a multicoloured, if rather hazy banda sheet which had every adjective reduced to 'nice' to demonstrate how imprecisely we spoke. Everyone badgered away to replace the word 'nice' with more appropriate words. Nice became a banned word in our room, except when making a nice distinction between two things. The rule became "Be precise when using nice!" at which all the class groaned.

There developed quite a competitive learning streak in 2H with the girls in particular going the extra mile to antiquify their versions of historical documents such as the Magna Carta and the American Declaration of Independence using a technique involving coffee and drying in an oven. Like apprentice art forgers, they presented their documents for close inspection. In some cases, it would appear that a number of historical documents had been housed in London during the Great Fire, so singed were they. A couple of lads tried to suggest that the ageing process had completely obliterated the writing and were mortally offended when I suggested that there might not have actually been any writing on the document in the first place.

"The patina of age has worn it away completely sir!" swore Jason, less than convincingly, but with commendable drama.

Three years into my teaching career I'd become increasingly frustrated by the lack of attention to the detail of learning and the fact that it was almost assumed to be the natural state of affairs that we consigned a considerable number of students to fail as learners by the time they left school.

I'd chosen Longstanton as it taught Integrated Humanities which meant that English, Geography, History and RE were all taught together in a block. This got as close as a secondary school could get to replicating the large block of time to an integrated approach to learning. I was convinced that this was the way to go in improving learning, as it allowed a proper relationship to grow between the students and their teacher and also allowed learning to take place in terms of looking for the similarities of patterns rather than stressing the differences between subjects. I hoped I was doing these advantages justice for my students.

One thing that had troubled me since my own school days was that, without prior thought it was too easy to present learners with a series of discrete pieces of information which seemingly had no relationship to any other chunk of knowledge that they had been introduced to. This was a problem in any subject, but in history, gobbets of unconnected information from various time periods were highly forgettable and gave the student little chance to put a sense of order and priority on what would otherwise be random information.

When these indigestible chunks of information were coupled to the Ebbinghaus effect, the disturbing ability of the brain to forget information (or rather to store it in a vast black hole called "unconnected bits of things") then it was no wonder that students found much learning difficult and forgettable and came to the unwarranted conclusion that they were poor learners.

I worked on the basis that all the students started with the same model of brain and that differences in performance were down not to the absolute capacity of individuals to learn but to how well or how badly they had learnt vital skills to assimilate information effectively. Some students had an advantage. If they came from a family which was highly numerate and literate then they might develop effective study skills in their home environment, but for many students this was not the case. Generally parents who had done well in the education world, would be well placed to support their children and to give them the vital confidence to attempt new learning tasks.

On the other hand, children who came from homes in which the education experiences of the parents had been unsuccessful, or who did not value education due to their own experience of it, had a doubly difficult task to achieve well at school as their own lack of confidence and the lack of practical support from home got in the way of them being successful.

To make sense of information, children needed to be shown systems for storing all the things they were expected to remember. I'd had this graphically illustrated to me by the efforts of Andrew, a wayward lad for whom learning didn't come easy.

Andrew had parents who had not enjoyed their own educational experience and there were gaps in their knowledge of writing and grammar that made them particularly prickly in their relationship with school. This antipathy had been passed on to Andrew, no doubt with advice not to let the teachers boss him about, which put Andrew on a direct line for confrontation in school.

Andrew struggled with retaining information and exhortations to "try harder" without any more specific guidance, led to him physically straining to hold onto information. His approach to learning was indistinguishable from that to constipation, a highly strained facial expression. Unfortunately, whilst this might have cleared the constipation, it had precisely no beneficial effect in retaining information, particularly where facts and figures were concerned.

Things came to a head one day in registration. I was calling the register and a rather strangulated "Here" came from Andrew. I looked over to see him stiff necked and looking skyward with a pained expression.

"Whatever is wrong Andrew?" I asked concerned. "Have you injured your neck? You can't be too careful with neck injuries, perhaps we should get you to the nurse."

"Nothing, vocabulary test in French, remembering!" came his terse reply.

He manoeuvred himself out of the class at the end of registration period, head staring upward to the ceiling and walking unsteadily with his hand outstretched down the corridor to the French room. He'd entered the room to the same concerned voice from Mrs Sloan, the Languages teacher.

"Andrew, whatever has happened, have you injured your neck? It might be best to see the school nurse, it is always serious, a neck injury!"

"Vocabulary test, get on with it!" was all she got by way of reply.

"Well, if you are sure you are all right, let's get on with the vocabulary test. Now then, just for a bit of fun, let's try the words in random order!" added Mrs Sloan to groans from the class.

"Question 1, what is the French for railway station?"

"Question 2, what is the French for a stamp?"

"Question 3, what is the name of the building in which I would buy the stamp? And yes Marie, I know you can buy the stamps in many shops, like you did on your holiday in the Dordogne, but I want the French name for the post office."

On Question 1, Andrew had tilted his head forward. He had been working on the idea that he would retain all the words for the test by staring at them for long enough, and to give the lad credit, he had spent two hours last night staring at the twenty words and a further hour this morning. The reason his head was tilted was that he was afraid that if he looked forward or down the words would simply tip out of his eyes and onto the floor, never to be remembered. As a learning style it had little to commend it, but it was in fact the passive way in which most people, without a better and more purposeful approach, would try to learn volumes of information – simply read it and hope that the brain would work like a photocopier to retain the information.

It was the failure of this technique which led a sizeable number of people to come to the conclusion, early in their learning career that either, they were not clever, or that they could not remember things.

The fact that the languages teacher had decided to re-order the words completely confounded Andrew, who saw his three hour sustained attempt to learn the twenty words fail disastrously. Andrew reacted in characteristic style when thwarted. In exasperation that the words would not come he shouted "Shit!" pushed over his desk and headed for the door.

Knowing Andrew would make his way back to my room, Mrs Sloan had the good sense not to make a disciplinary issue out of an incident that was based in frustration rather than malicious intent. Andrew arrived sheepishly at the threshold of my door a few minutes later and lingered, waiting for me to invite him in. Luckily, I had a preparation period and was hastily re-arranging the room and arranging my resources for the lesson. I bade him in and allowed him to sit quietly for a few moments to compose himself and dry the tears that had run down his face. His solution to this was to wipe his face and nose with his sleeve. Once the tears had subsided he began falteringly to tell of how he had stormed out of the Languages lesson and how he was sorry that he had sworn but he was annoyed that he had spent all that time learning the words properly and he couldn't remember any of them when the teacher had changed the order. He ended by saying that he hated being thick and that all the teachers, his friends and his parents knew he was.

I had been increasingly alarmed that in a large percentage of the disciplinary issues I was asked to intervene in as a form tutor, with Andrew and others, beneath the eruption of bad behaviour, was an underlying fear of being shown up in front of their peers. It struck me that "messing about", being asked to wait outside the room for bad behaviour and truancy might well appear as a rational strategy to students whose reading, writing and numeracy skills meant that they struggled in most lessons. The standard response to such behaviour in most schools was to press the button that brought the disciplinary system into operation. The problem with the disciplinary system was that it was a giant systematic edifice which completely failed in its primary mission, to modify behaviour.

For students like Andrew, a detention or a letter to a parent was not going to change the dynamics of school life for him, nor prevent such incidents from reoccurring. Nevertheless, records would be made, letters sent and phone calls initiated to share the displeasure of the school with the parents. In Andrew's parent's case, this would only increase the antipathy of them to the efforts of the school.

I had once checked the monthly record of a child similar to Andrew in my class. In that one month, the highly efficient pastoral system had communicated thirty seven times with the single parent through notes in the student planner, letters and telephone calls. Everyone outlined some negative aspect of behaviour – and we wondered why we couldn't get parents like Andrew's to support the efforts of the school! What was more, the Year Manager was proud to show me how efficient he had been in keeping on top of the paperwork for the case - all this valuable time spent on reinforcing failure within and beyond school.

I realised that the majority of children were like Andrew, stumbling on ways to learn effectively, rather than being taught how to go about learning. It was clear that over time these children would have the fear of failure reinforced by not having ways to store and recall information or to put it down on paper effectively. At some point in their educational careers they would default to becoming disciplinary problems as this was the most efficient way to avoid the humiliation of being shown up daily in front of their peers.

I was surprised how strong the opposition was from teachers when I discussed concentrating more clearly on study skills. Clearly for many teachers, I was blurring the black and white distinction between good students and bad ones. One told me it was all she could do to cover the content of the syllabus, without having to teach *how to learn* effectively in addition. This seemed a peculiar standpoint to me, to have no interest in the children as learners and in their life beyond school, only as receptacles for the chosen knowledge presented in the curriculum.

A science teacher, speaking loudly for effect in a crowded staff room, insisted that study skills should be presented in the context of the particular subject, rather than as a separate topic. I heartily agreed with him and watched a smug grin appear on his face as if he had won me over to his way of thinking whilst in earshot of the senior leadership. I might have been more sensitive at this point, but the smugness, and his insistence on telling the children he was a "scientist", when in fact he was a teacher of science, made me uncharacteristically intemperate.

"Can you show me where study skills are taught in your science curriculum plan then?"

There was considerable bluster and talk of "developmental stages" and "moving towards implementation".

I stopped him with a raised hand and stated, "So you don't teach Study Skills in your department then?"

"I'm probably at the leading edge of experience in Study Skills in the overall department and it is part of my developmental schedule," came a less than fluent reply.

"So you teach study skills in your department inconsistently and the quality of what is done is determined by teacher competence and not student need? I'm assuming that you teach the lower sets then to ensure that your expertise is delivered where it is most needed?"

I knew this was a conversation stopper as he was one of a handful of Heads of Department who considered the top sets to be his fiefdom as they required careful handling to "fully develop their potential". Lower science sets were always given to junior members of the department to afford them a valuable professional development opportunity and the chance to develop their class discipline skills. Seldom, apart from the SLG group foisted on me, had a series of unremittingly difficult classes been so blatantly oversold as a professional development opportunity.

Clearly I needed some clear strategies to win over the staff, let alone to help the students. My opportunity came in a school assembly I was scheduled to take in a week's time. The assembly would have the whole school present as well as all the teachers in their capacity as form tutors. The Head, being a former military man, would also be in attendance as he considered the whole school assembly, or "muster" as he called it, to be one of the highlights of the school week. If only the students had shared his enthusiasm!

It was a difficult task finding a way to present study skills which would have meaning to all the students with their differences in ages. It caused me several nights of lost sleep and pre-dawn awakenings with spectacular plans before the assembly text was prepared. At that point I lost confidence and thought it would be presumptuous of me to even attempt to broach the subject of better ways of learning. My resolve returned one early morning and I retrieved and added to the acetates which would form the text for my twenty minute talk.

It was going to be difficult to do the subject justice in twenty minutes so I needed ideas that would engage the students, particularly those who were seen as poor students quickly and keep them engaged to the point that they were convinced of the idea that they could be successful.

As always in an assembly, I stood nervously, mentally rehearsing what I was going to say as the students filed into the Hall. I thought again that I might be committing professional suicide and realised that I had not prepared a plan B. I had plan A or nothing.

The Head, in his avuncular way, read out the notices for the week before he announced me.

"I know we are all interested in hearing from Mr Hughes about different ways of learning..."

The students seemed less sure of the level of their interest. I thought he was going to add his usual, "so, without further ado, the stage is yours Mr Hughes…" but he didn't, so there was a short but discernable hiatus before I walked forward to the centre of the stage and switched on the overhead Projector. Even at this stage I could hear conflicting voices in my head. One was clearly saying, "For God's sake, don't do it!"

The other, which sounded remarkably like my mum's voice quietly declared, "Tell them and do some good."

I would have liked time to join in this debate, but the audience was growing restless and one science teacher, several maths teachers and the Head of English sat smiling with arms and legs folded waiting for me to attempt to tell them about different ways of learning and make a fool of myself in the process.

"Who is the cleverest person in the school?" I asked and left a pregnant pause into which some bolder students muttered comments of self publicism. Stuart was pointing to himself with a confidence that belied his academic performance. I let the clamour build for a while so that the students felt fully engaged.

"My guess is that it is probably the Head, Mr Felstead, as he has had more time to develop his learning techniques," I continued, allowing the room to drink it what looked like a blatant attempt to suck up to the Head.

"Let's ask a question which you should have a clearer view about. Who is the cleverest person in your class? Point now to the cleverest person in your class."

There was remarkably little hubbub as a series of class based circles formed of arms all pointing in the same direction. In 2H's class all arms pointed to Sue and she blushed with embarrassment and fluttered her eyes as she tried to regain her composure. Some classes had two people highlighted as what students were now referring to the "brainiest" person in the class. Some of the chosen few were highly pleased to be identified in this way as it reinforced what they believed of themselves.

"It's interesting the amount of agreement there seems to be. I'm afraid every one of you is wrong though."

The students looked around wondering if there is someone they had misplaced or forgotten.

"The answer is that the cleverest person in the room is you." There was a fleeting swelling of individual pride before it dawned that everyone couldn't be the cleverest person in the room.

"What I am saying is that firstly, you all have the capacity to be the cleverest person in any room. It is all down to how much you want to improve your learning and secondly it requires you to use the right techniques."

There was an air of scepticism in the room, palpable in the moving lips of Mr Studdard the "flog em' and throw away the key" timeserver from the Maths department who was mouthing "socialist bloody claptrap!"

"Furthermore I can prove it to you," I continued trying to counter the storm surge that was rising.

"I'm going to give you a simple test that involves learning twelve words in thirty seconds. This should be no problem as you all have the same model brain which has an extraordinary capacity for learning, and, in a few cases, the brain hasn't been used fully to date so there should be plenty of grey matter to store the words."

This raised a laugh and refocused the group.

"Are you ready?" and the students leaned forward in their chairs, always keen to take part in some competitive endeavour, particularly if it meant putting one over on a mate.

"Here is your list of words, you have thirty seconds to remember them...."

I placed the acetate on the projector and it lit up the projection screen with the words:

Yellow, November, Thirty Six, Seventeen, Sierra, Blue, January, Austin, December, Twelve, Red, Mini.

I stood silently for the allotted thirty seconds to elapse, watching as the students applied their current study skills to the task. Clearly there were a lot of people employing Andrew's random staring at the information method, hoping to take a photocopy of the information. It seemed that a fair number of the teachers were employing the same technique.

At the end of the thirty seconds I removed the acetate and substituted a multicoloured one stating,

"Whatever you do, do not look at this acetate. Under no circumstances look at it as it will only confuse you."

The exhortation not to look proved too much and, like moths to the flame, every student looked to the projected image anxious to find out what they should not be looking at.

"Actually, perhaps I shouldn't even put this acetate up as it will confuse you. Then again, I know I can trust you not to look at it." It was good fun being able to taunt over seven hundred students and fifty teachers in this way, and I replaced the acetate, on the sworn basis that they wouldn't look at it.

All the acetate said, in multicoloured text and fonts, some words in capitals and some in lower case was:

"dO NOT rEad tHIs aCetAte as IT wilL ONlY confuse yoU.
You are beginning to forget the words
You are beginning to forget the words
What is your faVourIte TV pROGraMme?
You arE Beginning tO forGet the woRds
It's chips for dinner today
You are beginning to forget the words
What is the greatest film ever?
I know who you fancy!
You have forgotten the words
What words?

Whilst the audience were transfixed on the words, despite my instructions, I had been overviewing the work of Mr Ebbinghaus on the way the brain learns. I'd explained that the brain liked patterns and linkages and that without them, the brain had a remarkable capacity to forget, or rather, to store information in a random way that made it difficult to retrieve.

"You think that the cleverest person in your class has a better model brain than you, but they haven't, they simply have better techniques for storing and recalling information. The good news is that, if you are prepared to put in the effort and discard the poor techniques you have used up to now you can seriously improve your performance in all areas of your life."

I detected some huffing from the Maths department who had a view of the world which segregated people into those who understood algebra and those who didn't.

I paused for effect.

"I can see you remain unconvinced. What I have just done in showing you the slide and telling you not to look at it has been to accelerate the Ebbinghaus Effect. Your brain has switched from a random series of words that has little meaning to you to some issues which are very more interesting. You can't stop your brain doing this, so you need techniques to ensure you can take in, store and recall the information you need for learning. However, it was a simple list and you only learnt it a few minutes ago so let's recall it. Can I ask Simon to stand up please."

Simon was the leader of the provisional wing of the know-alls of the school. He was arrogant and contemptuous of those he felt to be his intellectual inferiors, this included a fair proportion of the teaching staff. He also had a cruel streak of using words to belittle fellow students. He had basked in the approbation of twenty nine hands pointed in his direction as the cleverest boy in the class and considered himself the cleverest student in the school. Simon stood up disdainfully for the challenge, his every fibre showing that he considered the retention of twelve words for five minutes beneath his intellectual dignity.

"Can you give me the twelve words in the order they appeared on the screen please Simon."

Simon had remembered all twelve words but not in the order they had appeared on the screen. He had applied his own learning technique to them. He started confidently reeling off the first three, then there was a hesitation. The room gasped that Simon had faltered.

"Sierra," he continued confidently.

"Sorry, wrong, you've missed one out. Sit down please."

Had Simon had a crest, and I was pretty sure his family would have one, it would now be fallen. He slunk down into his chair, his face red with embarrassment. Somebody sitting next to him clearly said something inflammatory to him as he dug his elbow into his partner's ribs with real venom. There was a muttering in the room which sounded like "Simon got it wrong." which started as an incredulous whisper and transformed into a quiet chant as those humiliated by Simon in the past saw their chance to return an insult to the centre of Simon's ego. Simon glowered incandescent with rage. Had someone blown gently into his face, he would have burst into flames.

I repeated the process, choosing two of those selected by their peers as the cleverest in their class. The first, building on Simon's three correct answers, managed five and the second seven.

I shook my head in amazement. "So," I continued, "the people you consider the brightest and best students in the school cannot remember twelve words for five minutes! What future do you all have with attention spans and memories the size of small goldfishes! Actually there is a reason why you failed to learn when presented with information in this way – it has to do with what I said earlier about the brain liking patterns and links to things it already knows. We are going to do the same test again and this time you are all going to do well."

I placed a new acetate on the projector, this time with the twelve words sorted into four groups of three.

"Your brain works perfectly well when it is given a chance to organise the information before trying to remember it. So one way which never works when trying to remember things is to simply stare at the words because one thing your brain is not is a photocopier. It is a super computer, and like all computers, you need to process information if you want it stored and recalled efficiently."

The list read:

Colours
Blue
Red
Yellow

Numbers
Twelve
Seventeen
Thirty Six

Cars
Sierra
Austin
Ford

Months
December
January
March

"Now then, still twelve words but psychologically it looks and feels easier to remember four lists of three. Actually your brain begins to lose interest with lists that extend beyond seven items so it is always worth trying to keep things to remember to below this number by organising them."

I place two pieces of white paper on the projector in such a way that only the three colours were showing.

"I said the brain likes patterns, particularly if they link to information it already knows. Does anyone know what links the colours Blue, Red and Yellow?"

Mr Close, the Art teacher beamed gratified when a forest of hands sprouted accompanied from the Year seven's with hisses of "Sir! Sir! Sir!" indicating supreme confidence in their answer. I duly asked one of them, who told me they were the primary colours.

"That's right. So as you have that knowledge already I don't want you to think about the individual colours, leave your brain with two words: Primary Colours.

What about the numbers? Sometimes you can see when one number is out of a pattern. Which number is the odd one out?"

"Seventeen!" came the resounding answer from the body of the hall, as enthusiasm overtook the protocol of putting a hand up.

"Excellent. Can you guess which number the brain would prefer seventeen to be?"

There was a little discussion and two numbers were put forward – eighteen and twenty four.

"Your brain has done this before, but maybe you weren't listening to it! Why did you choose those numbers?"

A bold year eight girl ventured that it was because they were in patterns she already knew from the six and twelve times table. I thanked her for her insight and continued.

"So you don't need to worry about twelve and thirty six as they are in a pattern you already know. Just remember seventeen. In fact, I predict that if you make a mistake remembering this you will come up with eighteen or twenty four as the wrong answer, so strongly will your brain try to reinforce the pattern."

I looked at the Maths department who were now exchanging confused glances, which was gratifying given that the foundations of their subjects were all based on patterning.

"If I gave you a list of months of the year to remember how would you organise it?"

"January, February, March!" the whole room sang out and even some of the teachers were now joining in, particularly the Humanities and Special Needs department.

"Exactly, you'd go to the pattern you were familiar with…but there are times that you have to see beyond the pattern and use what is called lateral thinking. I don't want you to start with January. I want you to start with November and then to apply the rule…and the rule is…well, you tell me what the rule is?"

About Kings Hart Books
Kings Hart Books is a small, independent publisher, based in Oxfordshire, England.

<u>Other books by Ambrose Conway:</u>

The Reso by Ambrose Conway (also available for Kindle at Amazon)
ISBN 978-1-906154-01-1
Beyond the Reso by Ambrose Conway
ISBN 978-1-906-154-12-7

<u>Our other fiction titles:</u>

Meeting Coty by Ruth Estevez
ISBN 978-1906154-03-5
Apartment C by Ruth Learner
ISBN 978-1-906-154-06-6
The Price by Tony Macnabb
ISBN 978-1-906-154-08-0
St Anthony's Fire by Rod Sproson
ISBN 978-1-906-154-10-3
Nyabinghi by Shamarley Fontaine
ISBN 978-1-906-154-09-7
The Jewel Keepers: Albion by E J Bousfield
ISBN 978-1-906-154-14-1

Please visit our website at **<u>www.kingshart.co.uk</u>** for extracts and further information.

Available to order at all bookshops or through online retailers worldwide.